ZERO DWARFS GIVEN

ZERO DWARFS GIVEN

DWARF BOUNTY HUNTER™ BOOK FOUR

MARTHA CARR

MICHAEL ANDERLE

DISRUPTIVE IMAGINATION®

First Version, January 2021
Version 1.01, January 2021
ebook ISBN: 978-1-64971-398-8
Paperback ISBN: 978-1-64971-399-5

THE ZERO DWARFS GIVEN TEAM

Thanks to our JIT Team:

Deb Mader
Dave Hicks
Diane L. Smith
James Caplan
Debi Sateren
Dorothy Lloyd
Paul Westman
Kelly O'Donnell
Peter Manis
Jackey Hankard-Brodie
Jeff Goode
Thomas Ogden

If We've missed anyone, please let us know!

Editor
SkyHunter Editing Team

CHAPTER ONE

Federal Agent Lisa Breyer rolled over on the bed in her hotel suite outside Everglades City and thumped a fist on the mattress. *If I can't get rid of these nightmares soon, I'm gonna have serious issues. It's been two weeks already.*

She glanced at the digital clock on the nightstand and groaned. *No one should have to lie awake in bed for two hours.*

After pushing herself up, she paused and turned her head slowly toward the bedroom door, which she'd closed despite being in the hotel suite alone, simply because the air conditioning was triggered by movement. Fortunately for her in the early August heat in the Everglades, she'd moved a fair amount during the last two hours.

With a sigh, she whipped off the covers, slipped out of bed, and stepped into the small living room. She went to the desk where her laptop had been plugged in for an overnight charge. Once seated in the desk chair, she turned the device on and wrinkled her nose as it powered up. "Fine. If nightmares from that dark witch's overactive potion insist on keeping me up, I insist on tackling the other half of that trip."

The other case was Johnny Walker's fifteen-year-old murder

case. Or his daughter's, to be more precise. Which included the drug kingpin the bounty hunter couldn't get out of his mind long enough to focus on only one case at a time.

"And now I can't get the bastard out of my mind either. He's back, his drugs are stretching across the country, and—" Lisa uttered a wry, weary chuckle. "Look at me. Talking to myself in the middle of the night and I don't even have two dogs with magical collars as an excuse."

Tabling the issue of her full sanity for another time, Agent Breyer signed into her laptop and pulled the Wi-Fi hotspot device she'd received from the Department toward her. Tapping into the dark web just after midnight on a hotel's internet signal wasn't exactly the best choice, even for a federal agent. Fortunately, she didn't have to.

After setting up the hotspot and running the virtual personal network to keep her IP address and her system as safe as she knew how from whatever lurked on the dark web, she hopped onto a directory service to start her search. "We found Lemonhead on the dark web the first time. I can't imagine I won't be able to find him again."

But twenty minutes of searching for their elusive quarry gleaned only what she'd already seen—a connection between that username and the despicable auction bidding gearing up before the Monsters Ball two and a half months earlier. Beyond that were brief mentions of Lemonhead from years before. The real Lemonhead was murdered by the Red Boar without anyone knowing it and used for his black-market reputation as a "purveyor of magical commodities."

Those won't help. It's not the same guy.

With a slight frown of concentration, she tried searching for "Red Boar" but that was even less successful. She obtained the same results she'd pulled up on a public Google search in Portland and from sniffing through federal records—or at least the ones she had access to. But Johnny already had everything the

Bureau had gathered on the Red Boar in his cabin somewhere with the cases labeled *D Walker* and *Operation Deadroot*.

"Great." She stood quickly from the desk chair and headed into the suite's kitchen. Only one beer remained from the six-pack she'd bought four days before, and the sight of it sitting there by itself between the leftover salad from dinner that night and the half-empty carton of eggs made her frown. *I think I'm starting to understand why Johnny drinks so much. And I should stop.*

She closed the fridge and went to the sink instead and took a glass from the overhead cabinet to fill it. *He's convinced the Red Boar was in the comic shop that night. Off-camera. Vilguard practically gave up that much all on his own. And Dawn tried to threaten the drug-dealers by dropping Johnny's name.*

The agent paused with the glass of water raised halfway to her lips. "That's why Prentiss shot her. Isn't it? The Red Boar heard a little girl's threat and didn't want to take any chances. Seriously, what are the chances of there being more than one high-level bounty hunter dwarf with a twelve-year-old daughter? Especially fifteen years earlier when the Department was only a decade old?"

A door opened in another hotel suite out in the hall, and Lisa glanced at her entrance door. She chuckled at herself. *Jumpy much? Stop talking to yourself, Lisa. Someone's bound to think the half-Light Elf agent's finally lost her mind.*

She took her water to the desk, swallowed half of it, and set the glass down and stared at the laptop screen. *The Red Boar wouldn't have ordered that shot if he didn't know who Johnny was. And we all met face-to-face in New York.*

After typing two new words into the search, she took a deep breath and scrunched her face up. "It's not very likely, but I guess it's worth the attempt."

Her finger came down on the Enter key, and her eyes widened as hit after hit pulled up on her screen. "Holy shit."

The decision to search the dark web for Johnny Walker had

been a whim based on nothing but a hunch she and the bounty hunter now shared. If she hadn't been so exhausted from all the hours of lost sleep over the last two weeks, she probably would have written the idea off as a desperate attempt to be more useful or more productive. Why the hell would Johnny Walker have anything on him floating around on the dark web?

Lisa laughed and scrolled through the search hits. "Okay. I've now found one good thing to say about the nightmares. Jesus."

There were five pages of search results, all with Johnny's name in the title. Most of them were snippets of articles or posts painting the bounty hunter in a seriously unflattering light. And they were very old.

Bounty Hunter Had It Coming.

Retirement, or Did He Kill Himself?

Guess Who's Throwing in the Towel.

Best Bounty Hunter My Ass. Look at This.

Lisa stopped on the last one and saw a blurry image of Johnny, his finger smudging the upper-righthand corner of the frame as he scowled at whoever snagged the shot. Red-rimmed eyes, unwashed hair, and either crumbled food or lint caught in his beard created an unflattering picture.

The post was dated December 2005.

She grimaced. *Assholes. Leave it to criminals to kick a guy while he's down and mourning the murder of his daughter.*

Beneath the post title was a snippet of the post itself:

...shoved in our faces for years that the asshole dwarf bagging and tagging alleged criminals and calling it all in good fun was 'one of the best damn bounty hunters in the business.' Well, guess what? Johnny Walker's done. You'd think the best would have been able to save his daughter from catching a bullet in the back of the head. You'd think he'd take down the guy who put that bullet there in the first place. But no. We all need to take a good, long look at this dwarf right here and ask ourselves why any of us give a fuck about what he does next.

Because it looks to me like Johnny Walker's all washed up. He looks like he's about to...

The preview ended there, and she clicked on the title link to keep reading. A new webpage loaded, then a popup box appeared in the center of her screen and prompted her for a password or a second option to create an account.

Ungovernedunderground.onion, huh? She went back to scroll through the search results and found that many of the same flavor of Johnny Walker posts and articles were from the same site. *Yeah, I won't try to get a password to join a Shit on Johnny Walker forum, even if it isn't full of criminals.*

She continued to scroll and stopped when she saw an image of the dwarf in his usual all-black and dark sunglasses, one thumb stuck through his belt loop and the other hand raised to flip the middle finger at the camera. It was a surprisingly professional-looking shot, edited with impressive attention to lighting and detail. It took Lisa a few seconds to realize the photo was the thumbnail cover for a TV show.

"What the fuck?" She leaned back quickly in the chair, took another sip of water, and closed her eyes. *I'm hallucinating—not enough sleep. That's it.*

But when she opened her eyes again and peered at the image, nothing had changed.

"*Dwarf the Bounty Hunter* Season 7? Are you shitting me right now?" She laughed again and slapped the desk. "That's what everyone was talking about. Oh. My. God."

The title of the forum made the hilarity of it even that much more cringe-worthy—*Dwarf the Bounty Hunter: The Official Site—Your One-Stop Shop for All Things Johnny Walker, Bounty Hunting, and the Best Oriceran-Hosted Show on Earth.*

"No way." Lisa grimaced and turned her head slightly away from her laptop. *He would kill me if he knew I'd found this.*

She returned her focus to her screen and clicked on the site.

The forum was one of those loud, busy websites with ads

littering the sides and tops in every color imaginable—most of them ads for boxed sets of the show's seven seasons, clothes and sunglasses that mirrored Johnny's, vacation packages to Florida and specifically the Everglades, and one ad running in multiple places boasted a black leather jacket the private seller insisted was left behind during one of the dwarf's more intense fights and ensuing getaways.

Five thousand dollars for a so-called authentic Johnny Walker jacket. What the hell is wrong with these people?

Trying to navigate the site's multiple tabs and various forums for at least twelve different aspects of the show—not including each episode of all seven years—took more brainpower and focus than she had at twelve-thirty in the morning. She clicked onto the Fansite Forum tab instead and scrolled through the comments.

Wow. Fifteen years later and people are still picking this apart like they just binge-watched it on Netflix.

The topic threads were a random mash of show-related drivel.

S3 Episode 4: *Bone to Pick*. This is the best episode of the entire season. Fight me.

The real reason behind Johnny Walker's unexplained trip to Las Vegas in Season 5.

Long-time fan since childhood looking for a way to become a bounty hunter. Anyone have any tips?

She had to look away from her laptop for a moment to give her eyes a rest. "There's so much to sort through."

After a deep breath, she decided she might as well start at the top and browse methodically. The first three threads were less related to the show and more about "how profoundly Johnny Walker played a role-model role in his viewers' lives." The others were simply more hearsay, personal opinion, and a few arguments over the "deeper meanings" behind Johnny Walker phrases like, "Watch me," and "If it ain't the truth, it ain't worth tellin'."

One fan had uploaded several pictures of herself with a badly photoshopped Johnny Walker at the beach with her, at the shopping mall, and lying naked in bed.

"Oh, hell no." Lisa clicked out and shook her head. "How is this such a huge deal and I've never heard about it?"

A flashing ad on the right side of her screen screamed at her in bright neon. **Click Here for Episode Recaps and Discussions.**

She laughed, too tired to keep scrolling through thread after thread from people who wrote these posts like they'd known Johnny all their lives. *It looks like I'm getting a pop-culture review of Johnny Walker's career before retirement.*

When she clicked on the ad, it took her to a different page that didn't have its own tab on the main menu but was far more organized. The site broke discussion topics down by season and then by episode, and she opened the first review of Season 1, Episode 1: **Who is Johnny Walker?**

The discussion started intelligently enough, then very quickly took a turn toward fans bashing each other for differing opinions. Of course, a comment written in all-caps caught her attention almost immediately.

User5507: I don't see why everyone makes such a big deal about this guy. You're obviously biased against wizards if you think Hammond Farth is the real criminal in this episode. That wizard's an entrepreneur. All he was trying to do was make life a little easier for the people in his city, and what did he get for it? Tossed over the hood of his car and cuffed like he was merely another one of the dwarf's hunting trophies. Johnny Walker's the real criminal here. Who gave him the right to butt into anyone's life?

User1302: I'm very sure local authorities gave him the right, man. No one's denying the fact that Farth was experimenting with how to improve the water filtration system. But when he almost blows up a nuclear plant trying to get "ingredients," then yeah. That essentially makes him a criminal.

NoApologies42: Plus the fact that he didn't even try to sit down and have a conversation about what he was doing. The minute he saw Johnny pull up on his property, he ran. Anyone who runs is automatically guilty. Duh.

Lisa raised her eyebrows and moved on to the next few episodes. In each one, at least one "fan" left a comment trying to defend the criminal bagged and tagged during Johnny's show. They were regular people—or magicals—and were minding their own business until Dwarf the Damn Bounty Hunter arrived. No one deserved seven years in a max-security prison for trying to gather eggs from giant Oriceran slimetoads, and forget the fact that the slimetoads were under Earth's various new environmental protection acts.

Episode after episode showed some disgruntled fan unsatisfied by the treatment and sentencing of whatever bounty Johnny had taken into custody. Lisa counted at least six different usernames for these unhappy Johnny-haters, although they were all numbered generically according to the forum's system.

Yeah, no one wants to stir the pot like that without hiding behind even more anonymity.

She filtered the comments to show the most recent additions, then froze. "What? There's no way this is real."

Lemonhead: Right there with you on the unethical treatment of the disenfranchised. I wonder if anyone pays attention to the kind of physical, emotional, and mental damage incurred by being treated in this way by an icon as admired as Johnny Walker. And trust me. We're not the only ones. PM me for more details.

Her jaw dropped. Lemonhead's comment— it had to be the Red Boar's comment—was dated three weeks earlier. She scrolled through the comments and switched to a different episode chat when she didn't find anything else from the exact criminal she'd hoped to find.

Half an hour later in Season 3, Episode 9: *Shift This*, she found another comment from Lemonhead buried among the replies to a disgruntled fan's dismantling of the television idol that had been Dwarf the Bounty Hunter. It was the identical message dated six weeks before and aimed at a completely different generically numbered username.

Dammit. This will take forever.

Fortunately, after scrolling up and down and moving the bottom scroll bar left and right, she found a tiny search bar at the bottom beside the barely visible copyright information and link to the privacy policy. Lisa typed in *Lemonhead* and clicked on the search icon.

She was rewarded with the comments from Lemonhead in one nice, neat collection—fourteen in total—all of them replying to the same kind of agitated comments either trying to defend the captured criminal in each episode or downright bashing Johnny for apparently no reason. Each one said the same thing as Lemonhead posed a shared dissatisfaction with the show in general and the bounty hunter in particular. The most recent was dated only five days earlier. The first was dated the end of May, two days after Lisa and Johnny had crashed the Monsters Ball in New York.

"This is insane," she whispered and skimmed the comments to which Lemonhead had posted his replies. *He knew exactly who Johnny was in that penthouse. And he's been reaching out to a number of seriously pissed-off criminals. How many of these guys were actual bounties Johnny brought in?*

That was impossible to tell with the information she had and so many numbered usernames generated specifically for this site alone. But she could still try to get in on the action.

She retrieved her phone from beside the laptop and snapped a quick series of pictures, then scrolled down to capture every single comment with the dates and times. That done, she clicked on Lemonhead's most recent comment and was prompted with an option to create her username or use a randomly generated number. She went with the second option and created a basic account under the name Rex Coon. It made her grimace but it was the first thing that came to mind. *Better than Light Elf.*

Once she'd tagged both him and the original commenter in her reply, she typed her message.

User7495: There has to be a better way to spend our time than going through a host of old episodes and hate-posting at our desks. Right? What about *doing* something?

Her palms were sweaty when she posted the reply, so she wiped them on the thin cotton of her pajama shorts and downed the rest of her water. *Don't blow this, Breyer. There's no way anyone knows who you are. Imagine hating his guts so much that you'd troll a fan site.*

That made her laugh but the sound cut off abruptly when her laptop screen flashed with a horizontal line of white. A small black box appeared in the center of the screen and it looked way too much like a command prompt.

"Uh-oh."

White letters scrolled across the box after the blinking cursor and paused, waiting for her reply.

8/14 11:00 p.m. Baltimore, MD. If you want in on this, you'll have to prove your vision aligns with the rest of us. Background check. The kind you wouldn't want your mama to see. Full-color photo. Any possibly useful skills. Send it all to this link in the next five days or you can fuck off. Write it down. This isn't a chat.

Below that was a hyperlink of incomprehensible numbers and letters that didn't say what the hell it was for. Lisa fumbled with her phone and managed to take a picture of the command prompt box a second before the screen flashed again and the box disappeared.

She checked to make sure she'd obtained a clear image and breathed a sigh of relief. *Something tells me asking nicely for a do-over isn't an option.*

In the next moment, the pieces of the puzzle all clicked together in her head.

"Wait a minute—" She leapt up and practically ran into the bedroom to retrieve her tablet. It took her two attempts to unlock it and she pulled up the digital file for the next case Agent Nelson had sent her the day before with a request to pass it on to Johnny. She swiped through the first page detailing all the various internal accounts to which the file itself had been sent, then stopped at the front of the case report. "Baltimore. Ha!"

Lisa scratched the back of her head absently and mussed her sleepless bedhead even more as she stared at the case file. She returned to the desk in the living room for her phone. *Tommy doesn't want him to lose his shit over this. No one does. And no one cares how Johnny's handled with these cases as long as he's handled. It's not like Tommy's completely in the dark.*

"Screw it." She pulled up Agent Nelson's personal cell number and made the call. When the line rang four times, she almost hung up but fortunately stopped when a loud click and rustle came through from the other end.

"Fuck," the man grumbled.

"Oh, hi, Tommy." She lowered herself slowly onto the hard cushions of her hotel couch and rolled her eyes. "I'm good. Thanks for asking."

"What the hell, Breyer." Tommy inhaled deeply and grumbled a little more, accompanied by the rustling of bedsheets. "It's almost two in the morning."

"Shit. Right."

"If this isn't an emergency—"

"Well, it might be—but the good kind."

"Dammit. Give me a sec."

It sounded like he dropped the phone onto the bed, but instead of the sound of lights clicking on or footsteps across the floor, she heard three swift, sharp smacks of flesh on flesh. She pulled the phone away from her ear and glanced wearily at it.

"All right. Shit." He groaned. "I'm up. What's the...good emergency?"

"I found Lemonhead."

"What?"

"I mean the Red Boar. He took over all Lemonhead's—you know what? It's not important." Lisa shook her head and took a deep breath. *Keep it together and stick to the facts.* "Did you know there was a *Dwarf the Bounty Hunter* fan site on the dark web?"

"What the fuck?" Tommy cleared his throat. "First, I have to deal with Johnny slipping back into his old drinking habits and now, you're...what? Tweaking in the middle of the damn night and calling me about that stupid fucking show?"

"Huh. Well, first of all, I'm not on drugs, Tommy, but you might be if you'd seen what I saw in Portland—"

"Yeah, I heard it sucked. Are you okay?"

"I'm fine, merely putting in overtime because I haven't quite caught up on lost sleep. Please hear me out and pretend like everything I tell you makes sense, all right?"

"Lisa..."

"I was looking for the Red Boar. If the guy was there the night Dawn was murdered, he would have guessed she was Johnny's daughter and he would've confirmed that again when we crossed paths in New York." She glanced at the tablet in her lap and tried to gather her thoughts. "But what I found, Tommy, was a fan site of people freaking out over Johnny's old show."

"It's been off the air for fifteen years."

"I know. But the site's still active and Lemonhead's posting on it."

"Who the hell is—"

"The Red Boar. Deadroot. Whatever the hell his name is. I think he's recruiting some of Johnny's old bounties to form some kind of...team. Most likely to target Johnny."

Tommy groaned. "Payback's a bitch. Look, if those idiots want to slog through the muck to find that dwarf and get their heads blown off for their troubles, that's their choice."

"Not if we find them first. They're meeting in Baltimore on Thursday."

"Wait. That's where—"

"Yeah. The Hugh case." Lisa sat up straight on the couch and scanned the walls of her hotel suite. *Come on, Tommy. Wake up and use your brain.*

"And you want to crash this meeting and go after the Red Boar instead?"

"Not exactly. But I do want to run something by you right now before I take it all to Johnny tomorrow. And if this works, we might bring back a hell of a lot more than one Kilomea with a blackmailing problem."

"Huh." He sniffed. "What exactly did you have in mind?"

She grinned and leaned back against the couch cushions.

CHAPTER TWO

"There's more than one use for everything." Johnny hauled the stiff, wobbling folds of thick chicken wire across the dry grass of his back yard.

Luther yelped and skittered away from the clattering pile of metal mesh. "Hey! Watch where you're throwing things, Johnny. Come on."

The dwarf pointed at his smaller black-and-tan coonhound and frowned. "You watch where you're sniffin' while I'm workin'. It's as simple as that."

"You could've taken my head off with that," the hound muttered as he skulked away.

Rex left the six-inch hole he'd been digging in the dirt and turned to face his brother. "You have no idea how gravity works, do you?"

"Huh?"

"It's all about the size, bro." He stuck his snout back into the hole and snorted. "It's not big enough to cut your head off."

Johnny grunted and stalked toward the storage shed for his power tools he'd left charging overnight. *I ain't fixin' to sit down and explain physics to a couple of boneheaded coonhounds.*

"Hey, where ya goin', Johnny?" Luther trotted after his master, his alleged close call with death completely forgotten.

"Tools."

"Tools for what?"

Rex whipped his head out of the hole and stared at the dwarf. "Huntin' tools?"

"Ooh! You make something new, Johnny? Something new and super-cool?"

Johnny spun in front of the shed's open front door and gestured sharply toward the wooden structure in the middle of his yard. "Tools for that. For building? The project we started yesterday? Is it ringin' any bells?"

Luther sat and his mouth popped open as he panted quick, heavy breaths and stared at his master. "Nope."

The dwarf scowled and uttered a low growl of restrained frustration before he turned and stepped into the shed.

"Well?" Luther called behind him. "Come on, Johnny. Spill it!"

The bounty hunter ejected the two thick batteries from their chargers and inserted one onto the base of his impact driver. "I ain't gonna waste my breath tellin' you somethin' you're gonna let slip out your mind two minutes later. Again."

"Yeah, yeah, okay." Luther trotted away from the shed and stopped when he saw the half-erected wooden structure sitting in the yard. "What is that?"

Rex stared at his brother. "You need help."

"Aw, you're jealous. We both know I got the best—hey!" Luther barked. "Johnny! It's a—" Without finishing the thought, he uttered an earsplitting bay and raced across the yard toward the side of the house.

The dwarf straightened to turn toward the shed door and bumped his head against the bottom of the shelf over the worktable. "Dammit!"

"Johnny, someone's here!" Rex called. "Someone's coming!"

"In the road!"

"Moving fast! A big ol'—oh." The hounds skidded to a stop in the gravel drive out front as the crunch of pebbles beneath slowing tires filled the air.

With his impact driver and nail gun in hand, Johnny stepped slowly out of the shed and frowned at the sudden silence. A car door opened and shut. "Boys?"

"Hey, lady."

"Ooh! Ooh! Is that for us?"

"What did you bring us, huh? I hope it's treats."

"Or trash."

"Or a stick."

Lisa's laughter carried past the house. "Okay, boys. Chill out. You know I'm—*Luther*!"

"Ha-ha, no, you're not."

"You already know what I smell like, dogs. Back up."

The hounds' tittering laughter filled Johnny's head and he snorted. *The hounds are gettin' more friendly with her than I am.*

"Can't help it, lady," Luther said. "You smell like food. And two-legs. And two-legs food."

"Lemme guess," Rex added. "You had eggs for breakfast."

"Wait, eggs? Eggs...something about that sounds important."

When the door of the screened-in porch creaked open, Johnny called, "Out back, darlin'."

"Oh." The door clicked shut again and Lisa moved down the side of the house. Both hounds trotted beside her.

"Johnny. Hey, Johnny. It's your lady friend."

"Yeah, I thought she'd bailed but she didn't forget about you, Johnny."

"Hard to believe. How long's she been gone, Johnny? Two years? Three?"

Rex snorted. "Feels more like five."

Lisa rounded the corner and stopped when she saw Johnny scowling at the small wooden hut with a power tool clutched in each hand. "Wow. I didn't know it was project day."

He glanced briefly at her and sniffed. "Ever since yesterday."

"What are you building?" She stepped around the structure and scrutinized it with a raised eyebrow.

"A goddamn chicken coop."

She burst out laughing.

"How's that funny?"

"Only the…" She waved him away and shook her head. "It's the thought of you raising chickens."

"Uh-huh." He stared at her and finally rolled his eyes when the laughter didn't stop. "And I ain't raisin' 'em, anyhow. That's already been done."

With a deep breath to calm herself, she wiped a tear from the corner of her eye. "Grown chickens, huh? So you decided to… you know, I don't even know what to call it. Does one buy chickens or adopt them?"

"Neither." Johnny set the nail gun in the grass, picked up the long plywood boards he'd secured together at a thirty-five-degree angle, and set the whole thing on top of the structure to form the roof. "This here's only temporary."

"It is? That's considerable work for a temporary chicken coop."

"Well, Cal Hendry a couple of miles down the road ran into some kinda…I don't know. Family squabble. He's goin' outta town in a few days to deal with it and needs a place to keep the hens so I offered to put 'em up here."

Luther licked his muzzle and sat. "Chicken."

The dwarf shook his head and took two corner braces and a handful of screws from his back pocket. "So now I gotta make this damn thing gator-, fox-, snake-, and hound-proof."

Lisa waited for the impact driver's loud growl to die down before she took her tablet out from under her arm.

Johnny pulled his head from beneath the roof and looked expectantly at her. "What?"

"I hope Cal Henry a couple of miles down the road isn't counting on you to specifically be here over the next few days."

He glanced at the tablet in her hands and sniffed. "Is that another case?"

"Yep."

"Dammit!"

She frowned teasingly at him. "Well, try not to get too excited about it."

"Oh, I ain't."

"Johnny..."

"A dwarf can't get a little peace and quiet around his own home? Nelson with his cases. Come on. I ain't been back long enough to put my feet up and soak in the good things in life I spent a helluva lotta time diggin' up."

Lisa raised an eyebrow. "Portland was two weeks ago."

He returned to the pile of partially completed chicken coop pieces and selected the long ramp with the thin strips of elevated wood running up the length like steps and rested it against the open side of the coop. "That ain't nearly long enough, darlin'."

"Okay, well, you're officially out of retirement at this point." She winced when the nail gun hissed and thumped into the wood. "So the cases will most likely keep rolling in—which I know you expected."

"It doesn't mean I gotta be happy about it." The nail gun hissed and thumped again.

With a sigh, Lisa approached him and unlocked the screen of her tablet. "Take a look at this one with me, will you?"

Johnny peered at her tablet and frowned. "No paper copy?"

"No." Her knowing smile made him scowl. "There are a few pieces to this next case that aren't exactly...uh, in hard copy anywhere. Or even digital."

The nail gun dropped into the grass, and the dwarf straightened to fold his arms. "I don't know what the hell that means but I have a feelin' it ain't somethin' I wanna hear."

"Why don't you listen to everything first before you make that call, okay?" She swiped through the case file, then turned her tablet toward Johnny. He stared at her with a frown and didn't bother to look at the screen. "Right. This one's fairly simple as far as your cases go. A Kilomea in Baltimore's been blackmailing Senator Richard Hugh—"

"Damn. Nelson's getting' desperate, ain't he?"

"What?"

"Tell him to get someone else. I'm sure he has a dozen other bounty hunters who could round up one Kilomea idiot tryin' to pick a senator's pockets for fun, as dirty as they are."

"It's a sensitive situation with this specific senator," Lisa explained. "He has friends in the Bureau—particularly Director Vance."

Johnny wrinkled his nose. "Who?"

"Seriously?"

"I never met the guy."

She tried to hide a patient, knowing smile. "Well, that would be because you've only been back in the game a few months and haven't been to HQ."

He cleared his throat. "I never got an invitation, either."

"Oh, so if you were invited, you'd make the trip?"

"Probably not."

Lisa shook her head and glanced at the file open on her tablet. "Senator Hugh also has friends in Washington, which means the Department wants this done cleanly and efficiently. So no, I don't think they have another dozen bounty hunters who can take care of this the way they want it taken care of."

The dwarf rubbed his mouth and the top of his beard. "They want me."

"Yes, they do." She grinned. "And now, I'll be completely transparent with you—"

"I still ain't takin' the job."

"This is way less about the department and much more about why *you* need to take *this* case."

The hounds splashed through the swamp on the other side of the yard, sniffing at soggy reeds and fortunately too focused on exploring to say anything. Johnny narrowed his eyes at her. "What are you gettin' at?"

"Something big, Johnny." She closed out of the case file and pulled up a series of photos, handed him the tablet, and nodded. "Something you don't want to miss out on. Quite frankly, neither do I."

With a grunt, he took the device in both hands and looked down. "Goddammit. Why are you bringing this to me?"

"You have a fan site, Johnny."

"Yeah, I can damn well see that." He swiped to the next photo. "Fuck. Uh-uh."

Forcing back a laugh, Lisa folded her arms and didn't let him shove the tablet into her hands.

"Take it."

"Not until you go through all those photos, Johnny."

"I ain't goin' through photos and I ain't walkin' down memory lane on your fancy whatever-the-pad, all right?" The dwarf gritted his teeth, glanced at the screenshots of *Dwarf the Bounty Hunter: The Official Site*, then snarled and jerked his head away. "This is a breach of privacy, you know that?"

"Not really. It was all over the dark web—"

"That's what I'm sayin'! Look at this shit. Pictures of my mug on every damn page. What is this? Some asshole tryin' to sell one of my jackets? Shit, Lisa. I don't even give out my phone number or take selfstagrams or whatever the hell it's called, and I did not sign off on having all this bullshit floatin' around the dark web. Take it down."

She shook her head and leaned forward to catch his gaze. "That's not how it works. And besides, you don't want me to take it down."

"The hell I don't."

"Johnny."

He gritted his teeth and exhaled a long, growled sigh as he glared at her.

"Go through the rest of the photos."

"What the hell does any of this shit have to do with the case, huh?"

"So far? Only Baltimore. But we're about to change that." Lisa turned to step beside him and her bare arm brushed against the rolled sleeve of his black button-up. He glanced briefly at the contact and sniffed. She swiped her finger across the tablet in his hands and leaned toward him to point. "Look at this."

Johnny snorted. "Some asshole's tryin' to defend a damn criminal bounty. Big whoop."

She swiped again. "And the comment?"

His eyes widened when he saw Lemonhead's username beneath the disgruntled poster's comment. "Motherfucker."

"There you go." Stifling a laugh, Lisa moved on to the next photos. "He replied as Lemonhead to every single one of these 'defend the criminal' comments. There are fourteen in all. I ran a search through the site and this is the only thing he's commented. All of them are the same. The last was only a few days ago and the first—"

"Right after New York." Johnny snarled. "I shoulda put a bullet in that burned fucker's head when I had the chance."

The agent turned toward him and studied his scowling profile. "And if you had, Amanda would be somewhere unfathomably worse than where she is right now. So look at this and then we're done with photos."

She swiped to the final shot of the private command-box message she'd received from this anonymous organizer. Johnny sighed. "Baltimore."

"Baltimore."

"Shit." He sniffed and read the private message over and over.

"The Red Boar's been doin' his research too. I assume he knows exactly who I am at this point."

"Well, we didn't count on the Bulldog alias to last longer than the Monsters Ball."

"Uh-huh. Do you think he's the bastard who sent this to you?"

"Maybe." She shrugged. "There's no way to tell for sure—or at least no way for me to tell. I know enough about the dark web to get in, keep quiet, and get out again, but I'm not what anyone would call a computer whiz."

Johnny tapped the edge of the tablet. "This ain't a computer, darlin'."

"Correct." She smirked and shook her head. "I uploaded these images from my phone."

"You went through the dark web on your phone?"

"No, Johnny. Can we get back to the important part of the conversation now?"

He grunted.

"So obviously, the Red Boar's been looking for other people and magicals who want to see you eliminated as much as he does—"

"And he's puttin' together a 'take out Johnny Walker' powwow in Baltimore with a group of my ex-bounties." The dwarf grinned and stared intently at the tablet. "Then fuck yeah, darlin'. I'll take the case."

"That's good to hear." Lisa turned the tablet off and slid it under her arm. "Because now—"

"So when do we leave, huh?" He dropped to one knee to retrieve the nail gun and aimed it at the other side of the ramp.

"Slow down for a second. There's a whole—"

The gun hissed and thumped. Johnny tested the ramp, nodded, and stood. "'Cause I can load up and head on out tonight if we have to. Tomorrow mornin' at the latest. As long as Nelson gets everythin' put together the way he knows it needs to be done—"

"Johnny, stop."

He turned toward her with wide eyes and a crooked smile. "You got me to take the case, darlin'. Good work. How is that not enough?"

"Because there's more."

"Go on, then."

Lisa pursed her lips and tried to go as easy on him as possible with the next part of her plan. "I don't think the Red Boar will risk showing his face at this meeting. The chances of that are slim to none, and I'm banking on none. I talked to Tommy last night and he agrees with me."

"Why ain't he here to tell me that himself?"

She wrinkled her nose. "After last time, it's probably best for both of you to have a little space from each other, don't you think?"

The dwarf sniffed. "Don't matter. We can still roll in, take out a few conspirators, and squeeze that ugly bastard's location outta them."

"Yeah. And that'd be painting a huge neon sign for the Red Boar that we're in Baltimore, we know he's there, and we're coming."

"Hmm." He stroked his beard and pointed at her. "I'd call it more of a huge bloody sign. It feels more accurate."

"Johnny, he managed to slip away from the Bureau fifteen years ago before what was probably one of their biggest operations and he's been underground this whole time. I don't think that kind of message will make him easier to find or deal with."

"But you have a different message."

"I do." Lisa took a deep breath. *Here comes the final bomb drop.* "Even though he most likely won't make it to this ex-bounty meeting, he'll probably still be in Baltimore to oversee the whole thing and make sure the thugs he's bringing together are on the right track. He'll stake the meeting out and vet his potential…uh, partners before any of them see his face. Which, fortunately for us, we've already seen."

"Uh-huh."

"What we need to do is draw him out, Johnny. Into the open. Give him a reason to attack you first and then we can close in. Because we'll be expecting him but we need to make the Red Boar think we have no idea what's coming."

The dwarf regarded her speculatively and drew a sharp breath. "Or we could find where this fucker's stayin' in the city and bash his damn door in."

"Or we can set a trap he won't be able to resist."

"Well. I like traps." He nodded cautiously. "What are you thinkin'?"

"Hear me out, okay?" Lisa glanced at the chicken coop and pretended to study it with marginal interest. "I have the whole thing mapped out, so whatever potential loopholes you might immediately shout at me, I'm very sure I've already covered them."

"Uh-huh." Johnny waved his fingers at her in a gesture to continue.

"And I've already gotten the go-ahead from Tommy and the Department to get this rolling."

"Come on, darlin'. You're settin' up for a big reveal. I get it. Quit beatin' around the bush."

She raised her eyebrows and drew a breath. "We're bringing *Dwarf the Bounty Hunter* back for a final season."

He sniggered. When she looked at him and smiled, he stepped away from her, completely expressionless. "What. The. Fuck."

"Johnny, listen—"

"No. No, no, no." He dropped the nail gun and made her jump away in case it decided to fire on its own, and stormed across the yard toward the shed. "I ain't doin' it."

"It's already been done." Lisa followed him and stopped when the dwarf disappeared inside the shed. "We've already sent a press release out to multiple networks and media outlets. The crew's been hired and they are coming with us to Baltimore. And Tommy bought the tickets."

The sound of rummaging through tools and pieces of wood and metal rose from inside the shed. Johnny thumped a fist on the wooden workbench beneath the shelves, then poked his head through the open doorway. "Are you tellin' me that balding fuck has legit authorization from the Department to fund a goddamn reality show?"

"Probably not."

He disappeared inside the shed again.

"But he's the only liaison who can bear to put up with you, Johnny. I'm very sure they simply give him a budget for your cases and don't ask any questions beyond that. They don't need to know how it's spent or what we do with the funds as long as you take the case and close it exactly like you always do."

The shed was intensely silent for a long moment before Johnny exhaled a long, heavy sigh that sounded like compressed gas escaping from a release valve. His boots clomped across the floor and he stepped onto the grass and slammed the door shut behind him. "The Red Boar knows I did the show before. He'll see this."

"That's the plan."

"The plan?" The dwarf rubbed his mouth vigorously, then folded his arms across his chest somewhat belligerently. "Our plan is to go to Baltimore with a whole filming crew under the ruse of one more season of the damn *Bounty Hunter*. Is that about right?"

"Mostly." Lisa stepped away to let him pass as he stormed across the back yard again. "Except it's not exactly a ruse."

"Either it is or it ain't, darlin'. Which one?"

"Well, we're not doing this for the sole purpose of how much fun it would be to bring Dwarf the Bounty Hunter back and follow him around Baltimore."

Johnny scoffed. "Careful."

"But we will be filming, Johnny. The whole time."

He whirled to stare at her. "Say again?"

The agent nodded. "And they'll be live-streaming parts of it—obviously not while we're talking about this Kilomea or Senator Hugh or the actual case and definitely not while we're working on setting things up to draw out the Red Boar. But the crew has permission to reach out to multiple network audiences and draw in more live viewers that way, plus a few clips posted to the YouTube channel—edited if they have to be, of course. And yes, there will be a full episode airing after we close the case and the Red Boar gets what he deserves."

His nose wrinkled and his mustache twitched from side to side beneath a constantly shifting grimace. "Fine," he said after a long moment

"Good."

He pointed at her. "I have one question."

"Go for it."

"What the hell is live-streaming?"

CHAPTER THREE

The next morning, Johnny stood at his stove with a pair of tongs in his hand. Half a pound of thick-cut bacon hissed and sizzled on the back burner in the massive frying pan, and the eggs he'd cracked onto the other pan in the front had almost heated enough to start scrambling.

"Johnny." Luther's tail beat urgently against the end of the cabinets beneath the kitchen counter. "Johnny, is it done yet?"

"No."

"Smells done to me." Rex uttered a low whine, licked his muzzle, and stood to prance from side to side before he sat again. "Very done."

"Yeah, you don't wanna ruin it."

"We'd eat it raw, Johnny."

"We'll eat it like it is right now."

"Y'all need to get on out the kitchen." Johnny flipped the bacon strips one by one. Grease spat over the sides and landed on the floor. Both hounds turned their attention to the fatty splatter and licked in wide circles far beyond the treat they were cleaning up.

"We got it, Johnny."

"Yeah, you drop anything, spill anything, pour anything over here, don't even worry about a mop."

"We're the mop."

"Get on." The dwarf shooed them away, then set the tongs down to turn his attention to the cheese grater and the block of sharp white cheddar out on the cutting board.

"But the bacon, Johnny." Luther whined.

"Which you ain't gettin' unless you do what you're told."

"Yep." Rex spun and trotted obediently through the back of the house toward the living room.

Johnny shot a sidelong glance at Luther as he grated a heaping pile of cheese into the egg pan. "Don't tell me you ain't listenin'."

"What?"

"You want any of this kinda breakfast, boy, you'd best get on out."

"But Johnny, I—"

A massive bubble burst in the bacon pan and flecks of grease spat onto the side of the hound's face. "Ow!" He yelped, scrambled away from the stove, and raced through the workshop and into the living room. His claws scrabbled across the wooden floor, then stopped when he reached the thick area rug. "How can something that tastes so good hurt so much?"

Rex padded toward his brother and sniffed. "Wait, come here."

"I'm fine, thanks for asking."

"Yeah, but you smell like—"

"Stop. Hey, leave me alone, Rex. I don't know where your tongue's been."

"Same places yours has been. And none of the weird ones, either."

"Stop, stop, stop, stop— Hey!"

Both hounds barked and spun toward the front door. "Johnny!"

"Someone's coming!"

"If it's that salty two-legs again, we'll eat him."

"Yeah, appetizer for that bacon."

They bayed madly, raced to the back of the house, and yipped at each other when they both tried to scramble through the dog door at the same time. The barking and shouted threats aimed at Agent Nelson continued around the side of the house.

Johnny shook his head and picked the spatula up to start scrambling the eggs. *I doubt it's Nelson rollin' up to visit us today. Not if he needs some so-called space.*

"Whoa, Johnny!" Rex called from the front. "Holy shit."

"Lots of people coming up the drive, Johnny."

"Big van. Two big vans."

"And the lady's car."

"What?" He tossed the spatula onto the counter and turned, then remembered his breakfast. "Whoever the hell it is, boys, hold 'em there a minute. I ain't leavin' these eggs."

"Or the bacon." Luther barked wildly.

"We got it, Johnny."

The dwarf turned the heat up beneath the egg pan and scrambled them furiously until they resembled what he wanted. He extinguished both burners, ripped off two sheets of paper towels, and covered the pans. *Fuckin' vans comin' down my drive in the mornin' and interruptin' my meal. Shit.*

He wiped his hands on his jeans and strode toward the front door as the sound of multiple heavy tires on the gravel drive crunched to a halt. Johnny threw the door open and stormed across the porch. The screen door lurched open with a bang before he hurried down the stairs and gestured widely at the arrivals. "What the hell is all this?"

Lisa shut the door of her car and headed toward him with a grin. "It's the film crew."

"Yeah, I can see that, darlin'. What are they doin' on my property?"

"It's good to see you too, Johnny. I'm having a great morning, thanks."

31

"Look, this ain't somethin' I agreed to—"

"I told you they'd be filming the whole thing." She fought a smile and turned to gesture toward the two large, white vans parked beside each other on the gravel. "So they came out here to start."

"Naw, the case starts when we leave the ground in a damn plane."

The sliding doors of both vans opened, and four crewmembers emerged from each vehicle, dragging out equipment and gear with them and talking excitedly about their plans.

"They're harmless, Johnny." Lisa nudged him with her elbow. "Act like they aren't here unless we're sitting down for some of those Q&A shots."

"I hate those."

She shook her head with a tiny smile. "Stop."

A man with thin, fuzzy brown hair sticking up in all directions approached them and extended a hand toward Johnny. "Phil Ploster. I'll be directing this. Nice to meet you, Mr. Walker."

"Just Johnny." The dwarf sniffed and looked away from the man without shaking his hand. "I don't need all this out here at my home, man. This ain't goin' out on TV."

"Oh, sure. No, we won't film the outside or anything. We can crop the shots, no problem. Listen, I want to tell you personally how excited the crew is about getting to do this with you. You know, I spent hours as a kid watching you back when you were doing this full-time."

"Uh-huh." He darted Lisa a contemptuous glance as the director blathered on.

"I've seen all seven seasons—multiple times, in fact. Hey, I know it's kind of weird to ask, but would you mind—"

"All right. That's his house, yeah?" Another man with closely shaved hair and wearing bright-yellow shorts at a barely acceptable length on a man's legs pointed at the front porch. "We want the best lighting. Go check it out."

Johnny turned after him as the crew ran toward the front porch. "What the hell? Hey!"

Lisa reached for his arm but he shrugged away from her and jogged after the crew.

"Hey! That's my house!"

The agent smiled apologetically at Phil and shrugged. "We're good."

"Great."

The screen door slammed behind the last of the crewmembers hurrying inside. Johnny snarled and threw it open again. "Boys!"

Rex whipped his head up from where he'd been sniffing one of the vans' tires. Luther finished lifting a leg against the other van's tire. "On it!"

"We're coming, Johnny. But—hey." Rex stopped when the screen door slammed shut again and blocked their entry.

"Dog door, bro." Luther raced past his brother toward the back of the house.

"Oh, yeah!"

Johnny fumed as seven crewmembers swarmed through his cabin, opening doors and peering into rooms and closets and cabinets. "Y'all need to—"

"Okay, the living room in the back looks like our only option right now."

"Devon, there aren't any windows. Look at that. It's like a cave."

"Fine. Natural lighting, then?"

"There isn't much of that in here, honestly."

A woman with a bandana tied around her head and a perpetual scowl that rivaled Johnny's slipped past him to enter the workshop.

"No!" He whirled toward her. "That room's off-limits. The whole damn house is off limits!"

She moved directly to the window and pulled the curtain

aside before she turned to raise an eyebrow at him. "Is this the only window you have in the front?"

"We're not doin' this—"

"Hey, this room looks good." Someone had opened the door to Amanda's room and peered inside. "Nice light. But we'll have to clean up a little. Did anyone know this guy has a kid?"

"Well, he did."

"I mean right now."

Johnny growled and stalked toward the shelf in his workshop. He snatched a huge old cannon of a shotgun from behind the more regularly used weapons in his collection, completely unnoticed by the crew buzzing around in his belongings. But the loud and unmistakably decisive double-click of the shotgun's slide brought the incessant conversation to an instant stop.

The woman turned away from the window and saw the weapon in the dwarf's hands and realized that his face had turned a dark shade of red beneath the brighter red beard. "Holy shit."

"Everyone out!" Johnny roared.

"Hey, Cody. Are we rolling?"

"Uh-huh…"

He swung the shotgun toward the front door and the woman nodded before she slipped past him and headed outside. As he marched out of the workshop toward the hallway, the edge of a filming camera appeared from around the corner of the doorway. He released his weapon with one hand and thumped his palm against the camera lens. Cody uttered a yelp of surprise, then backed away from his equipment when the dwarf scowled balefully at him. "You ain't filmin' now. Not in my house."

The skinny man gulped and nodded. "Got it."

"Now get the fuck out. All y'all."

The woman with the bandanna had left the front door wide open, and the crewmembers hurried outside. The screen door creaked repeatedly as each person pushed it open again behind the next.

The hounds trotted down the hallway from the back and their nails clicked loudly in the sudden silence. "Damn, Johnny. That's officially the most two-legs we've had in the house."

"You throw a party and didn't tell us about it?"

He turned toward them and pointed at the open door. "Out."

"Aw, come on, Johnny." Luther's ears flopped against his head when he turned sharply to face the kitchen. "We haven't had any of that bacon—"

"Now!"

Both hounds shied away from him before they trotted obediently through the open door. "Jeez. We live here in case you forgot."

"And we earned our treats. Can't say we didn't after this, Johnny."

The dwarf watched his hounds pad across the front porch. Rex nudged the screen door open with his snout and Luther scurried through after him.

Earned them, huh? This was a home invasion and the damn hounds didn't do shit.

Johnny held the shotgun in one hand and pulled the front door shut behind him to slam it loudly. Then, he threw the screen door open and marched down the steps again to stop at the foot of the stairs. The screen door banged shut, and he lifted the shotgun to return it to both hands. "If I see any of y'all so much as look like you're tryin' to get inside, I ain't got reservations 'bout firin' this. Understand?"

The crewmembers stopped their muttered conversations and turned toward him.

"Is that even loaded?" someone muttered.

In answer, he spun and fired a round into the reeds of the swamp beside his house. The deafening crack echoed across his yard and a thick spray of swamp water and reeds exploded high into the air.

The crew ducked, clamped their hands over their ears, and backed toward the vans.

"Any other dumbass questions?" The bounty hunter sniffed and scanned their wary faces.

"Okay." Phil clapped briskly and plastered a wide grin on his face. "Change of plans! We'll do the first intros out here in the yard. Mr. Walker, do you—"

"Johnny." The dwarf didn't move.

"Right. Johnny. Can we, uh… Can we use those Adirondack chairs for this first part?" Phil pointed to the side of the lawn that hadn't been obliterated with a shotgun and spread his hands out in front of him in a mock panorama. "'Cause I see this perfectly now that we're here. It sets a great mood for the whole thing. Swamp. Got that big old Live Oak right there in the corner. A few cattails…"

Tuning out the guy's blathering, Johnny met Lisa's gaze as she walked calmly toward him. "What the hell's he talkin' 'bout?"

"Setting up for the first shoot." She pointed to the other side of the yard where Phil had now directed the crew to move Johnny's Adirondack chairs and attend to whatever he thought needed to be cleaned off the grass. "Like I said, they're with us the whole time. Beginning to end."

"We don't need this shit."

"But your viewers do, Johnny. And your fans." She grinned and placed a hand on his shoulder. "You want this to look real, don't you?"

He growled and glared at the crewmembers buzzing around his yard.

"Which means we have to do this the way you did it back in Dwarf the Bounty Hunter's prime."

"I ain't stepped outta my prime, darlin'."

She pressed her lips together to hide a smile and removed her hand. "I meant the show. And after seven seasons and sixty-eight episodes, I assume you still have a good idea what this first part is about."

Johnny grumbled and scratched the side of his face. "Damn Q&A."

"Okay, so let's go answer some questions. Oh. But first..." She closed her eyes, took a deep breath, and began to glow within a haze of golden light.

He stepped away from her with a scowl and scrutinized her warily. "What are you doin'?"

The magical light faded and when she opened her eyes, they'd gone from a soft brown-hazel to an intensely bright green. Strawberry-blonde hair had replaced the long dark chestnut, and it was cut shorter to tumble in loose curls around her shoulders. Freckles dotted her much paler skin, and the completely wrong shape of lips parted when she grinned at him.

Why the hell am I thinkin' about her lips? Cut it out, Johnny. He grimaced. "Why?"

Lisa gestured toward the film crew getting ready for their first shot. "Some parts of this will be live. The rest will be all over the Internet, most likely before we set foot in Baltimore. And I'm a federal agent."

"You don't gotta say that on camera."

"No, but the Red Boar saw my face in that penthouse too. If he sees Agent Lisa Breyer on a reality TV show with Johnny Walker, do you think he'll ignore how suspicious that is?"

Johnny grunted.

"Does that answer your question?"

"Naw. I meant why you gotta do yourself up as a redhead. Now we got two on this damn show. Ain't no one will watch it."

She choked back a laugh. "That's what bothers you?"

"All right," Phil called and gestured for them to join him. "Johnny and..."

"Stephanie," Lisa called with a nod. "If you forget everything else, don't forget that's my name now."

"Got it. Johnny and Stephanie. Let's get rolling!"

The dwarf grunted, gave her another slow scrutiny, then stalked away toward the makeshift studio on the side of his lawn.

"Hey," Lisa called after him, "do you want to put that shotgun down—"

"No."

CHAPTER FOUR

"Okay, Johnny." Phil stood off to the side as the crew rolled cameras and zeroed in on the bounty hunter's scowl. "We'll simply ask a few questions about the case and going to Baltimore. Don't give us too many specifics. Parts of this will get to the east coast before you do."

The man sniggered and Johnny rolled his eyes. Beside him, Lisa in her Stephanie disguise crossed one leg over the other and leaned back in the Adirondack chair, her arms resting casually on the wide armrests.

"So answer honestly. That was the best part of the show back in the day. You didn't hold back so feel free to let it all fly now, okay?"

"Uh-huh."

The woman with the bandanna approached Johnny with a makeup pallet and a sponge in hand. "I need to—"

"No, you don't." He glared at her from his chair.

She returned his scowl, glanced at Phil, then snapped the compact shut and stepped away.

"Here we go." The director stepped back and spun a finger in the air.

A man with a thin line of a beard and mustache trimmed around his mouth and jaw stepped forward and lowered the boom mic over Johnny's head. The dwarf jerked his head away from the equipment and growled. "Man, get that fuckin' thing and your douchebag beard outta my face."

At a nod from the director, the man stepped back two paces.

Phil nodded. "So tell us about this new—"

"Hold up." Johnny stood with a grunt and took the shotgun with him as he strode down the side of the house.

"Wait. Where are you going?"

"We're missin' somethin'."

The director frowned at Lisa. "Will it be like this the whole time?"

She smiled and nodded slowly. "Probably. But you guys are the professionals. I'd say roll with it."

"Yeah, we're flexible." The man scratched his head and focused on the side of the house where Johnny had disappeared.

When the dwarf returned, he'd lowered the shotgun at his side in one hand and now had a neon-pink plastic yard flamingo cradled under the other arm. Lisa snorted.

The hounds trotted behind him and sniffed at the long plastic feet and the stake at the end of the flamingo. "What is this?"

"Looks like a bird, Johnny."

"Smells like dirt."

"Hush." He returned to the interview setup, drove the flamingo stake into the soil beneath the grass, and gave it a good hard push to be sure it stayed in place. That done, he sat beside Lisa again and settled the shotgun across his lap.

Cody looked up from behind the camera with wide eyes and shook his head at Phil.

"Let me see." The director headed toward the camera to check the shot and grimaced. "That's too close. Johnny, we need to move this somewhere—"

"It ain't movin'."

Phil glanced at the shotgun in the dwarf's lap. "It's taking up a quarter of the frame here."

"You can land in Baltimore with or without your leg blown off at the groin, pal. Your choice."

Clearing his throat, the director clapped a hand on Cody's shoulder and nodded. "Roll with it."

"Okay..."

Lisa looked at the dwarf in exasperation. "What are you doing?"

"Makin' it my own." He shifted in the chair. "And if Ronnie gets wind of this damn show filmin' here in the Glades, I ain't never gonna hear the end of how that flamingo didn't get its time in the spotlight."

"Huh. That's an odd promise to make someone before you even knew this was happening."

"It's unspoken code down here, darlin'. I don't expect you to understand."

With a wry chuckle, she tossed the curls of her illusioned strawberry-blonde hair over her shoulder and nodded at the camera. "We're ready."

Rex and Luther sniffed around the chairs and moved between them and the film crew. "Hey, Rex. How come we never noticed all this out here in the yard before?"

"What?"

"Chairs. Cameras. All these shoes." Luther's snout bumped against a woman's shoe and he snorted as she stepped away. "It's like it showed up outta nowhere."

"Boys." Johnny snapped his fingers. "That's enough."

"Oh, hey. Yeah." Phil grinned. "Let's get the dogs in the shot too. That'll be great."

"Yes!" Luther barked and trotted to his master's side. "You hear that, Johnny? He wants us in the shot. We're in the shot!"

"We're gonna be on TV!" Rex spun in a tight circle, then raced toward his master and skidded to a halt in front of the chairs. Lisa laughed as the larger hound spun and sat, panting.

Luther sat but looked at Johnny instead. "This is the coolest thing I've done all day, Johnny." His tail swept across the ground, scattering dry grass and twigs and dirt.

The dwarf sniffed and gestured to the crew. "The camera's that way."

"What? Oh!" Luther spun to face the right way and sat again. "Awesome."

"Okay, here we go." Phil twirled his finger in the air again. "Johnny, you're heading out to Baltimore for a new bounty. Tell us about it."

Johnny glowered at the center of the large camera lens and cleared his throat. "Well, some asshole's blackmailin' a...person of interest. It sounds like he's makin' a mess of his target's life, so I aim to clean up and throw the bastard out with the trash."

Phil pumped a fist in the air and grinned. "Is it a human bounty or magical this time?"

Lisa—as almost-redheaded Stephanie—leaned forward toward the camera. "Johnny doesn't discriminate when it comes to doing his job."

Luther sniggered. "Or ladies."

Johnny snapped his fingers. "That's right. If a criminal's doin' enough to get my attention, I don't give a shit who they are, what they are, or how smart they think they are. I take 'em down and turn 'em in."

"Excellent. And what's the price on this bounty in Baltimore?"

The dwarf glanced briefly at Lisa and she shrugged. "Naw, I ain't talkin' 'bout money."

"Okay. Is it more or less than your usual bounties? I mean back in the day, of course."

"It's enough, okay?" He scowled at Phil and not at the camera now. "Move on."

"Sure. How do you feel about going into this one, Johnny?

From what you know, would you say this will be an easy retrieval, or will you have to work a little harder—"

"Who wrote these questions?"

The director looked startled. "I'm sorry?"

"They're shit. Look, I ain't takin' cases 'cause they're easy or hard. I take 'em 'cause somethin' needs doin' and I'm the one to do it."

Beside him, Lisa lifted her chin toward the camera and smiled sweetly.

Luther lowered himself onto his belly and stared at the device. "TV's so boring."

"All right. We'll move on." Phil cleared his throat. "You've spent fifteen years in retirement after suffering a family tragedy."

"Are you for real?"

"You stopped the show and holed up here down south," the director continued, "leaving your bounty hunter days behind you. How do you feel about getting back into the business after all this time?"

Johnny turned to scowl at Lisa and pointed at the man as he muttered, "Is this guy for real?"

"Johnny?"

"Phil."

"Do you have any concerns about your ability to find and apprehend this next bounty, given your previous record as a bounty hunter and your rather long hiatus?"

His disbelieving snort matched his disdainful expression. "I'm a dwarf, asshole. I coulda stayed outta the game for thirty years and still known exactly what I'm doin'. This is bullshit."

He started to stand and Luther leapt to his feet and blocked his master momentarily before he padded across the grass toward the yard flamingo.

"You were a household name by the time the seventh season of *Dwarf the Bounty Hunter* ended so abruptly. Is there anything you want to say to your viewers and fans around the world who are watching this now?"

Johnny stared at Phil and his lip curled at the corner of his mouth in a half-snarl. *The plan's off if this asshole keeps pryin' where he don't belong.* Before he could say anything, the steady, hollow patter of Luther relieving himself against the plastic flamingo filled the silence.

The dwarf gestured toward his hound. "That about sums it up. We're done."

This time, he didn't have a hound to prevent him from standing and he walked away with his shotgun cradled in one arm.

"Johnny," Phil called. "Johnny, I still have a few more questions—"

"No, you don't. Lisa, when's our flight?"

"One o'clock." She stood from her chair and pointed at Cody behind the camera. "Stop filming. And do not put him saying my name in anything you use, got it?"

"Yep."

"It looks like it's time to pack up and get moving." She gestured toward the scattered crewmembers. "We'll resume filming later."

The crew made no protest as Johnny and Agent Breyer disappeared inside the cabin. Rex and Luther trotted behind the house to enter through the dog door. "Man, if that's what being on TV's like, it sucks."

"Johnny did this? For years?"

"No wonder he's so grumpy."

Phil sighed in exasperation and gestured for his team to return all their equipment to the vans. "This is only the beginning, people. We'll get our gold in the next few days."

Inside the house, the bounty hunter stormed into the kitchen, whisked the paper towels off his cold breakfast, and tossed them into the trash. Lisa shut the front door behind her, removed her alias illusion, and found Johnny hunched over the stove. "Are you okay?"

"It's a loaded question, ain't it?" he asked through crunching a mouthful of bacon.

"That doesn't make it any less worth asking."

He turned away from the stove and grimaced as he sucked bacon out of his teeth. "You know how I feel 'bout cameras and attention and questions."

"Yep."

"All right. That bein' said, I gotta hand it to ya, darlin'. It's a brilliant fuckin' idea."

She grinned and turned as he strode past her and out of the kitchen toward the hallway. "I'm glad you think so."

"Oh, I do. The Red Boar and I have a beef to settle, and if he thinks he's smart enough to cut to the chase first, this is a perfect distraction. For him." Johnny disappeared into his room and she stood and listened to the sound of clothes being jerked off hangers and shoved into his duffle bag.

"Will it be too much of a distraction for you?"

A drawer shut sharply and he poked his head through the open doorway. "Naw. I handled it for seven years and I can handle it again." *The only difference is fifteen years of uninterrupted privacy and an idiot callin' himself a director.* He hauled his black duffel with him out of the room and headed to the workshop. "And that Phil fella... Hell. He knows exactly the right buttons to push, don't he?"

"I can talk to him about that if you want."

"Naw, don't bother. If I ain't lookin' pissed off and ready to bash in a few heads on camera, the Red Boar's gonna think I ain't genuine about the whole thing. It sucks but it's perfect." He rifled through his explosive gear, firearms, ammunition, and random tech stacked on the shelves of his workshop to carefully choose the best for the trip. "You said a Kilomea, right?"

"That's right." Lisa leaned against the workshop doorway and folded her arms, intrigued by the focused way he worked through his options.

"Okay." A huge metal box slid out from beneath the bottom shelf. Johnny felt inside it for a moment before he retrieved what looked like a bright silver handgun with the tops of the chamber and the barrel sawed off. They'd been replaced instead with a thick glass tube. He snatched a small canvas bag from the metal box, returned the stash with the toe of his boot, and packed it all in the duffel bag with everything else.

"What was that?"

"The little silver guy?" The bounty hunter sniggered. "That's old school, darlin'. It still works like a charm for those hairy bastards, though."

"That still didn't answer my question."

"Huh. Sleep juice."

"From a pistol?"

"Sure. What used to be a pistol, anyhow. Now it's exactly what I want it to be." He grinned at her and slung the strap of the duffel bag over his shoulder.

When he reached the kitchen, Rex and Luther sat perfectly still in front of the oven and stared up at the pans of cold breakfast on the stove. Rex's ears perked up at the sound of his master's footsteps but he didn't move. "Johnny."

"Yeah, Johnny. Come on."

"You forgot the most important part."

"Uh-huh." With a heavy sigh, the dwarf gave the hounds three slices of bacon each, which disappeared before he had time to take the remainder of the cold, crunchy meat for himself.

Luther licked the crumbs on the floor. "Bacon!"

"No one makes it like you do, Johnny."

"Yeah, yeah. Hey. You think if we caught a pig, sliced it up, and did whatever you just did to this bacon, it'd taste as good?"

Johnny and Rex both stared at him.

"What?"

"Sure." He turned toward the stove and the egg pan with a snort. "I suppose I might try it out on coonhound too."

Luther gasped. "You wouldn't."

Rex sniffed the floor behind Johnny's feet. "Dude, at this point, I'm right there with him."

"Oh, okay." Luther whipped his head up toward his master and panted, and his tail thumped against the side of the fridge. "Well, when you do try it, Johnny, don't forget about me. I've never tried hound bacon before."

"Jesus."

"What's wrong?" Lisa asked with a curious smile.

"Damn hounds." He tossed a handful of cold scrambled eggs toward Luther as a distraction, then turned toward Lisa and pointed at the smaller dog. "He makes me wonder sometimes what the hell I was thinkin' when I made those collars."

"You were thinking about us, Johnny." Rex scuttled to his master's other side. "And about how much you wanna give me some of those eggs too right now."

A glob of cold eggs landed with a splat in front of the larger hound and vanished instantly.

"And about how much you love hearing us tell you how awesome you are?"

"Well, that's a given, Johnny."

"We'll never stop."

"As long as you never stop with the treats."

Shaking his head, he scooped the last of the eggs and crammed them into his mouth. He turned toward Lisa with flecks of egg and cold cheese caught in his beard and nodded. "Ehs oh."

She laughed. "Sure. If I could understand you. You have a little something right here too…"

He swiped at his mouth and beard, then swallowed. "Let's go."

"Aw, man. That's it?" Luther sniffed the side of the oven and tried to poke his head up over the stove. "Johnny, what about all this smelly sludge up here, huh? That has to taste good."

"Shit." The dwarf snatched both pans up and headed to the back door to set them quickly out on the porch. When he closed the door again, both hounds stood in front of him.

"Go ahead, Johnny."

"Yeah, step aside. We'll handle it."

"We're headin' out front." He slid the plastic dog-door cover down in its slats with a clack. "Y'all had enough."

"So who's gonna eat it?"

"Johnny... You're leavin' bacon sludge out for the squirrels?"

"No way, Rex. It's the rabbits and birds we have to worry about."

The dwarf whistled and headed toward Lisa. "Let's go, boys."

"Dangit."

They trotted after him and Luther cast longing glances over his shoulder every few feet.

"I'm ready when you are, darlin'."

"Excellent." Lisa grinned at him and gestured toward the door. "This'll be fun."

"Hold off on that assessment for now, huh? Just 'cause I ain't got expectations don't mean it can't get any worse."

"Seriously? I would have thought you had fairly high expectations of finally apprehending the Red Boar or killing him, even in Baltimore."

He opened the front door and snorted. "I meant the damn show."

CHAPTER FIVE

Phil wanted to put one of his team in the car with Johnny on their way to Miami International but of course, the bounty hunter refused. "There ain't enough room in the truck anyhow."

"Well, what about that Jeep?"

He glanced at Sheila parked in her usual place at the edge of the large gravel lot in front of his house and chuckled. "You've lost your damn mind."

The director persisted in his mission to fully capture Dwarf the Bounty Hunter on their drive to the airport. Every time Johnny glanced in the rearview mirror, one of the white vans was gaining on him from behind. Whoever sat up front in the vehicle with Phil held a smartphone up to the window, filming, and the dwarf stepped on the gas again. "Determined bastard, ain't he?"

Lisa lurched forward when the white truck increased speed down the freeway. "He's only doing his job."

"Well, I ain't payin' him."

The one time the crew's other driver tried to pull into the right lane on the highway to get a good shot of him driving the truck was the only time. Lisa grabbed the oh-shit handle above the passenger door when he made quick work of blocking the van's attempts to drive next to his truck. He cackled the whole time. The hounds bobbed and swayed in the back seat of the cab, panted, and cheered their master on.

By the time they reached Miami International, the dwarf felt damn good about things. They unloaded their luggage—and the hounds—as the film crew set up their gear to start the camera rolling again. Checking in with their tickets was a cinch, mostly because Lisa handled all of it, but they were intercepted by airport security.

"Agent Breyer? Mr. Walker?" The huge man in uniform glanced at the hounds. "Come with me, please."

Johnny leaned toward Lisa and muttered, "What did you do?"

She darted him an insulted glance. "Don't assume it was me."

Grumbling, he followed the security guard with Rex and Luther on his heels.

Lisa waved for the crew to follow and waited for Phil to catch up. "I want to reiterate this yet again. Nothing that reveals my real identity gets broadcast anywhere. Not my name and not my face. At least, not looking the way it is right now."

"Only the redhead. Got it." He winked at her. "We'll save the live streams for the 'paint the town' shots."

"The what?"

"We have it covered, Agent Breyer. Don't you worry."

She glanced at the crew. Cody led the way with slow, careful steps to keep his hand camera steady as he closed in on Johnny from behind. "Okay…"

They were taken through a private security screening and led not to the main terminal gates for a commercial airline flight but out to the tarmac reserved specifically for private aircraft. A warm, muggy breeze blew across the expanse of black asphalt that shimmered in the August heat. It ruffled Johnny's hair and beard and made his hounds' fur stand on end.

Lisa adopted her green-eyed, redheaded Stephanie illusion as they approached the Gulfstream 450 waiting for them and nodded at Phil.

"All right, people," the man called and clapped before he pointed skyward. "We're takin' it to the skies."

The security guard nodded and returned to the building and a flight attendant stepped down the wheeled staircase pushed up against the jet and waved. "Are y'all ready to get this bird up in the air?"

The woman was tall, blonde, thin, and with bright-red lipstick that stood out harshly against her pale skin and the white exterior of the aircraft. Phil giggled nervously and stared at her and his mouth hung open slightly.

The bounty hunter snorted. "Oh, look. Dimples."

Lisa frowned mockingly. "That's what does it for you, huh?"

"I don't mind one way or the other, darlin'." He gestured toward Phil with his thumb. "But Mr. Nosy-Ass Director over there might have a thing or two to say about 'em if he could talk."

Rex looked at the man and sniggered. "Shut your mouth, two-leg. You're gonna slobber all over her."

"Yeah," Luther added and spun in a tight circle as he sniffed the tarmac, his tail pointing straight up. "That's our job."

"The captain's almost ready," the flight attendant crooned, "so you're welcome to board anytime you like."

"We, uh…I mean, we'll… That's…" Phil's mouth opened and closed.

"Thank you," Lisa said for him.

"Uh-huh." The woman smiled briefly at Agent Breyer, then scrutinized Johnny with almost avid curiosity before she turned to walk up the stairs. "We're happy to have you aboard."

"Oh, boy…" Nudging Johnny's arm with the back of a hand, the agent nodded at the jet. "This is gonna be a fun one, huh?"

"Well…maybe." He rubbed his mouth and frowned at the small aircraft. "What the hell is Nelson up to?"

"He booked us a private flight. Why are you complaining?"

"Naw. See, that's where all this smells too fishy." He wagged a finger at her and narrowed his eyes at the jet. "For about ten years straight I worked with that stuck-up Yankee and he ain't never sprung for a private flight, even when he flew with me. Are you sure there ain't something special about this case you're still keepin' on the down-low?"

She raised an eyebrow. "Johnny, I just told you there's a super-fan *Dwarf the Bounty Hunter* site on the dark web and convinced you to start filming another season so we can deal with two magical criminals with one case. Why would I keep anything else from you?"

"Good point. All right, boys. I guess it's time to—what the fuck?" He turned to Cody who held the camera in his face while Dave, the boom dude, dangled the stupid microphone over his head. "Back the hell up, son. What do you think you're doin'?"

Cody stepped away but kept his camera rolling slowly and steadily.

"Put that away, man."

"Come on, Johnny," Phil said, fully recovered now that the flight attendant had disappeared into the jet. "This is a very good time to get a few more shots in. Right before you take off from your home in Florida, you know?"

He wrinkled his nose. "Why the hell does that matter?"

"Okay, look. As far as our viewers—*your* viewers—are concerned, you haven't left the state since you moved out here fifteen years ago. No one knows you've taken other cases with... clients." He nodded at Lisa like they were the only ones in on her alias secret. "So for them, this is like a new chapter for Johnny Walker, right? A rebirth, if you will—"

"Jesus, what kinda hole did Nelson dig you out of?"

"What was that?"

"Look, I ain't panderin' to a horde of crazies I don't know simply to make 'em feel some kinda resolution fifteen years after the fact. And I sure as shit don't give a damn about network ratings. So you can move along with this whole 'create a story' nonsense and let me do my job."

Insulted, the director stepped away and glowered furiously. "Well, for this to work, Mr. Walker, you need to let me do my job."

The dwarf growled and thrust a finger in the man's face. "Don't tell me what I need to do."

"Don't you dare threaten me." Phil puffed his chest up. "I'm the director!"

"You're a nut."

The hounds tittered. "Good one."

"Yeah, bet he's as salty as one too."

"As salty as the other two-legs you hate but keep letting into the house, Johnny."

The dwarf spun away and almost stepped onto Dave's foot. "Goddammit. And get that"—he slapped at Cody and the camera narrowing in on him—"fuckin' camera outta my face."

Phil snapped and turned around to wave at another crew member with a second camera. "Get over here."

"Nuh-uh." Johnny pointed at the second cameraman. "I ain't doin' it like this. You stay right where you are."

Lisa stepped toward him. "Johnny, this is all part of the plan, okay?"

"Nope. It's not okay at all. Nelson thought he could recreate some goddamn nostalgia and instead, he gives me this."

"A private jet?"

"A film crew with extra balls and no brains—I said back up!"

Cody jolted at the dwarf's sudden outburst in his direction, then sighed heavily and lowered the camera. "Well, that shot's ruined. Thanks."

Johnny folded his arms. "I want Travis."

Lisa shook her head. "Who?"

"Howie Travis. The guy who handled the filming for me the last time I did a *real show*."

Phil scoffed. "This is real—"

"I ain't talkin' to you. Zip it."

The flight attendant poked her head out of the open jet door and grinned at them. "Y'all can come on up now. The captain says we're clear to go."

Lisa gestured toward the jet. "Everything's ready. Let's go. It's only a few days."

He stared at her with a deadpan expression. "Darlin', I ain't gettin' on this flight unless Howie Travis gets on it with me."

She glanced at the waiting crew and frowned. "You want the director of your bounty hunter show from fifteen years ago?"

"That's what I said. Travis knows what the hell he's doin' and he learned way more of it over seven years with me than what these bozos are tryin' to pretend they know."

"Wow. Okay. Fine." She pulled her phone out. "I'll make the call. Can someone tell the captain or flight attendant or whoever that we're...uh, running a little behind?"

The woman with the bandana—Alicia—rolled her eyes and trudged toward the rolling staircase. Lisa stepped away from the group and the idling private jet to call Agent Nelson so they could play Find The Director.

Johnny glanced at his hounds. Rex sat perfectly still beside his master, and Luther had sprawled on the tarmac to soak in the heat from above and below.

Phil cleared his throat. "You can't fire me from this project, Mr. Walker. You're not the one who hired me."

"I ain't fixin' to fire you. Stay on or go home. It makes no difference to me." He regarded the man disdainfully, then turned his head slowly toward the plane. "But if you don't hand the reins over to Travis when he gets here, I'll send you packin' myself."

"You can't force me to get on a plane."

"Honestly, it's fairly easy if you're in a body bag."

CHAPTER SIX

Almost forty minutes later, another security guard emerged from the building and approached Johnny, Lisa, the hounds, and the entire film crew, who were either seated or standing against the wall of the airport building to get out of the sun. A hunched old man with a long gray ponytail tied loosely behind his head stepped out slowly behind the guard. He held a walking cane in one hand and it tapped on the tarmac while he dragged a small, battered roller suitcase behind him with the other.

"Finally." Lisa stood and smiled at the men. "Howie?"

The old man squinted at her and looked bewildered. "Who the hell are you?"

"I'm—"

"Now that's more like it." Johnny approached the old man and grinned in welcome. "It's been a while, you wrinkled bastard."

"What the—" Howie stared at him, then croaked a laugh. "Well, hot damn, Johnny. Look at you. You look exactly the same. Maybe a little rounder at the middle."

The man slapped his own belly and chuckled.

"And you look..." The bounty hunter snorted. "Shit. You look like someone who knows what he's doin'. Come on. I have a private jet waitin' to take us to Baltimore. Have you ever been there?"

"Not yet." Howie nodded his thanks as Johnny took the handle of his suitcase and wheeled it across the tarmac toward the aircraft.

The hounds trotted wearily after him, too hot to comment on anything.

Lisa stared at the hunched old man and the grinning, chattering bounty hunter. *Okay. Now I've officially seen the impossible. And Tommy booked a private jet to avoid Johnny making this kind of scene in public. We're already off to a good start.*

"Let's go, then."

The crew grumbled and pulled their gear and suitcases together to head toward the aircraft. Phil didn't so much as look at her.

Thirty minutes into the flight, Johnny and Howie were well into their second glasses of Johnny Walker Black, which had been stocked in the jet's cabinets specifically for these passengers. They sat beside each other in the wide, plush chairs, clinked glasses, and roared with laughter as they relived the old days of *Dwarf the Bounty Hunter.*

"Oh, man, Johnny." The old man wiped tears away from his wrinkled eyes and caught his breath. "You almost had him eating through a tube after that."

"Naw. The bastard sucked it up. Our guys weren't too happy with me either, though. I had to buy a whole new set of lenses for…shit. What was his name?"

"Julio?"

"Naw, the other one. With the Mom tattoo."

Howie laughed. "Jackson."

"Jackson!" The bounty hunter wagged a finger at his old friend. "He was a good kid, man. A real good kid and could have gone places if it weren't for that dumbass ink he was so damn proud of."

"Well, I don't know about the ink, but that's what the rest of him did."

"Did what?"

The aged director raised his almost empty glass and nodded. "The kid went places. Now, he's out filmin' for HBO."

"No shit."

"Living the dream."

Johnny chuckled. "Ain't that the truth. To Jackson…whatever his last name was."

"Jackson Pullard."

"Yeah." They clinked glasses and the dwarf leaned toward the table in front of their chairs. "Shit. You're empty. Do you want another?"

"I'm seventy-years old, Johnny. Why the hell would I stop now?"

"That's the ticket." With a grin, he popped the lid off the whiskey bottle and filled the man's glass. "Li—" He cleared his throat. "Stephanie! Do you want one?"

Seated in a chair on the other side of the aisle with her chin propped on a fist, Lisa shook her head slowly. "I'm good for now. But you keep doing what you're doing."

"We're reminiscin', darlin'."

Howie drank more whiskey and uttered a long sigh. "I think you mean commiserating."

"It's the same thing, ain't it?" Johnny chuckled. "And we're havin' us a time."

The agent grinned. "I can tell."

"What? What are you lookin' at me like that for?"

"I merely haven't seen this full side of you before. It's…fun."

"Huh. Well, it ain't a regular thing so don't go gettin' any ideas."

"Oh, I know." She turned in her seat to where Cody knelt on the chair in front of her and aimed his camera across the aisle at the dwarf and his old friend. Leaning forward, she whispered, "Have you been on the whole time?"

Without moving the camera resting on the back of the chair, he gave her a slow thumbs-up.

"On what?" Where he lay sprawled in the center of the aisle, Luther whipped his head up and turned to look first at Lisa, then at the camera guy. "Oh. Hey, Johnny."

The dwarf sniffed and raised his whiskey glass with a crooked smile.

"That's it," Rex added and stared at the back of Cody's head from where he lay on his side toward the front of the plane. "You're supposed to smile when you're on camera. I heard that's a thing, Johnny. Right?"

Johnny almost choked on his drink as he scanned the crewmembers in their seats. Finally, he noticed Cody. "Aw, don't — Come on, man. Turn that shit off, will ya?"

"What's that?" Howie looked at the bounty hunter with a glazed smile, saw his scowl, and instantly found the camera centered on them. "Hey, that's fine."

"No, it ain't. Private jet. Private conversation." He stood and bumped his head against the boom mic dangling above him over the back of his seat. "Goddammit! You folks got some kinda deathwish or what?"

"Sit down." Howie chuckled and took another sip. "Let 'em do what they came to do."

"They ain't here to document our drinkin', Howie."

"Sure. But it'll go nicely with this new season of yours, won't it?" The man's lips parted in a wrinkled grin. "The bounty hunter who seemingly doesn't age a day and the crooked old man who followed him around the States for seven years merely to get a good shot. It gives the people something to sink their teeth into."

"They can sink their teeth in my ass. How about that?"

The old director roared with laughter.

Rex snorted and busied himself with a thorough licking of his front paw. "They're not gonna like it, Johnny. Trust me. It's not nearly as fun as it sounds."

A deep, rolling chuckle emerged from the dwarf's open mouth and grew until it filled the jet. Howie continued to laugh with him, and they clinked their glasses together again before each took a long drink.

Lisa smirked and faced forward in her seat to open the newest book on her tablet.

Cody slid slowly out of his seat and practically floated down the aisle as he moved with the camera, closing in on Johnny and his old Bounty Hunter director. The dwarf stopped laughing when he saw the guy inching toward them. He grabbed a package of fancy in-flight cookies and lobbed it at the camera. "Man, turn that off."

By the time they landed and picked up their three rental cars waiting for them at Baltimore/Washington International, Johnny was sober enough to convince Lisa he could get behind the wheel. Howie was more than happy to climb in the back with the hounds so Lisa could take the front seat, but the bounty hunter once again denied Phil and his crew any opportunity to join them in the vehicle.

The drive to the Sagamore Pendry Baltimore hotel in Fells Point was uneventful, but the second Johnny and his hounds stepped out of the rental and handed the keys to the valet, things became unexpectedly weird.

"Oh, my God. No way." A woman wearing a long jacket with a leather portfolio tucked under her arm stopped to stare at the dwarf and ignored the filming crew completely. "You're Dwarf the Bounty Hunter."

He grunted and hauled his duffel bag over his shoulder.

"Hey, look there!" A guy down the sidewalk held his baggy pants up with one hand and pointed at Johnny with the other. "That's the guy. Dude, what'd I tell ya, huh? This is for real."

The bounty hunter rolled his eyes and strode through the

front doors of the hotel with the hounds trotting beside him. Howie kept up fairly well despite his cane, and one of the other crew members had taken his suitcase with all their luggage.

Lisa swerved around Cody—who stalked after Johnny with his ever-rolling camera—to join the dwarf and his old friend. "Exactly like any other regular day, Johnny."

"No, it ain't." He shied away from a group of giggling, staring women in their mid-twenties who pointed at him and whispered about the show and the dwarf and the fact that this was real. "How the hell do all these folks already know what's goin' on?"

"We posted the first video to YouTube before the jet took off," Phil interjected when he joined them at the check-in counter.

"Say what?"

The man shrugged and raised a petulant eyebrow. "Well, you did give us an extra forty minutes to get a head start."

"Dammit." Johnny turned slowly to study the avid fans and spectators over his shoulder. "This ain't gonna work."

"This was the plan," Lisa reminded him.

"Not this part. These folks follow us to our rooms, we ain't gonna sleep the whole time we're here."

"Camera!" Howie shouted and thumped the end of his cane lightly against Cody's leg. "Take a wide shot from across the lobby, yeah? Get the whole thing—hounds, Johnny, fans, and the mic too. Better yet, turn the damn thing off."

Dave glanced at his mic, then stared at him in confusion. "But then we don't have any audio."

"Put it in a montage, okay?" He waved them both off. "And the rest of the team stays out of the shot. Unless one of you new up-and-comers have some bounty-hunter experience in you too."

The crew backed away from Johnny and Lisa and hefted their gear as they muttered to each other.

The old man turned toward Phil and raised an eyebrow. "Do you have a better idea?"

The displaced director glanced at Johnny, then exhaled a disgruntled sigh and hurried after his team.

"There." Howie slapped a hand on Johnny's shoulder. "Taken care of."

"It's a damn good thing I got you on this trip, brother."

"Ha. Well, I was practically kidnapped, but that's water under the bridge. It's time to check in."

CHAPTER SEVEN

Johnny and Lisa's rooms had been booked across the hall from each other, although with such late notice on Howie joining them right before the flight, the ex-director's room was on the third floor with the film crew instead of the fourth with his friend. "Don't you worry about me, Johnny. Something tells me I'll know exactly when you head out and need an extra pair of eyes."

The old man winked and hobbled through his door. The film crew disbursed to their reserved rooms down the hall, and Johnny, Lisa, and the hounds took the elevator to the fourth floor.

After they each settled into their rooms, Lisa took her usual next step and knocked on the dwarf's door with a perfunctory, "It's me."

Johnny let her in with a nod and a grunt before he trudged down the short hall.

"Oh, wow." She stepped slowly through the room and removed her Stephanie illusion as she viewed the large, fully equipped kitchen on the left. Suitably impressed, she turned the corner on the right toward the large living area in his suite. "It looks like someone had an upgrade."

He shrugged. "I'm sure yours is equally as nice."

"Nice? Sure, but about a third the size of this." She flopped on the luxuriously soft cushions of the couch facing the north-facing windows and sighed as she placed her tablet beside her. "He went all out."

"I don't see why." The dwarf filled a large mixing bowl with water from the sink and set it on the kitchen floor for the hounds. "I ain't exactly the type to need a big ol' fancy suite like this one. And before you ask, no. I didn't ask for an upgrade, either."

"I was talking about Tommy," Lisa replied with a smirk. "Not the concierge."

"Oh." He scrunched his nose. "Then it makes even less sense."

"How's that?"

"Private film crew, private jet, bigass suite with only me and two hounds to fill it. Looks to me like Nelson's tryin' to compensate for somethin'." As the sound of Rex and Luther lapping water rose from the kitchen, Johnny joined her in the living area and took the large armchair with its back to the north windows. "Like he all of a sudden thinks he needs to start impressin' me. Which he ain't."

"Um…well, I think all this is for the fans."

"Say what now?"

She smirked at him. "All this with the show, Johnny. It'll only work if everything looks and sounds and feels legit, right? That includes what your old fans think of *Dwarf the Bounty Hunter's* unexpected return."

He blinked and pressed his lips together. "Did you watch any of it?"

"Not yet."

"I think Nelson ain't watched a goddamn minute of it either 'cause I didn't put myself up like this back then."

"No private jet?"

Johnny snorted. "Hell no. We had a tour van."

Lisa tried to fight back a laugh and failed. "Are you serious?"

"Yep." Shifting in the chair, he looked away from her and mumbled, "It had my face on it and everythin'."

"So you drove your own bus for your own show to apprehend bounties for seven years?"

The corner of his mouth twitched in the hint of a smile, and his mustache wiggled with it. "Only for the first year—long enough for me to get a good read on the guy who ended up drivin' for us after that. I tell you what, darlin'. Roger handled that bus like it was a damn racecar."

The agent folded her arms with a curious frown. "You hired a racecar driver to drive your tour bus."

"What? No. He was a gnome."

"Johnny!" Luther trotted toward the slightly open door into the king-sized bedroom suite and nudged it open the rest of the way with his nose. The door creaked gently. "Got any treats in here?"

"Luther, we were in the kitchen," Rex called after him as he lapped the rest of the water. "Unless there's a fridge in there, you're barking up the wrong—"

Luther barked sharply, spun, and bumped his head against the door before he finally made his way out again. "The fridge! Johnny, people in Baltimore love you, right?"

"And hounds."

"Yeah, of course. So they'd put treats in that fridge, right?"

"Johnny, can you check?"

Luther raced past his brother and skidded to a stop in front of the fridge to drag his tongue across the black appliance in a long line. "Ooh, yeah. I can smell it, Johnny. They put bacon in there."

Rex nipped at the smaller hound's neck, then licked his brother's face. "Nope. That's still you."

"Leave it, boys," the dwarf grumbled.

Lisa turned on the couch to peer into the kitchen on the other side of the suite's entrance hall. "What are they up to?"

"Same thing every time." The dwarf dragged a hand down his cheek and snorted. "It's endless."

"Wouldn't be endless if you gave us treats, Johnny."

"Yeah, we don't talk with our mouths full. That's rude."

He shook his head and slumped in the armchair.

"What?" Lisa grinned at him.

"I have too much on my mind." He cast a frustrated glance toward the kitchen. "Too many voices, rather."

"Don't tell me you're starting to regret your greatest invention."

The dwarf scoffed, crossed one leg over the other, and lifted his arms almost to shoulder height to prop them on the armrests. "Collars ain't my best, darlin'."

"What?" Rex called.

Luther snorted. "Now you're being rude."

"Oh, really?" Lisa raised an eyebrow. "As far as I know, there aren't any other talking-dog collars out there. You could make a fortune on a patent with that."

"And throw the world of hound and master off balance with no return?" He shook his head. "I'm all for makin' an impact, darlin', but that's one dangerous road. And patents are a waste of time."

"Well, it can't be—"

A brisk knock at the front door interrupted her. "Mr. Walker?"

Johnny frowned at the entrance hall. "If that's room service before I even called, then I'll be impressed."

Lisa pulled up her Stephanie illusion as he stood and followed him out of the living area.

The bounty hunter reached the door and pulled it open. "If you're gonna be shoutin' my name from the other side of the door, I'm only gonna say this once. It's—aw, hell."

"Hello." Phil grinned in the hallway, surrounded by four of his team. Cody stood slightly behind him and to the side, his camera rolling. Dave dangled the mic over the director's head and tried to stretch it over Johnny's too. "Can we come in?"

"No."

"Johnny, this is all part of the process." Phil peered around the dwarf and saw Lisa-Stephanie in the hall, a hound on either side of her. "And since it looks like we're all here, we might as well pick up where we left off." He tapped Cody's shoulder lightly and muttered, "Get her and the dogs in there too. That's great."

Cody stepped forward with the camera, and Johnny pointed at him. "Come any closer, and that camera's mine."

"Only a few minutes, Johnny," the director pleaded. "Let us inside and we'll make it quick. The lighting in here is—"

"Y'all ain't steppin' inside my room. Get your shots in public like everyone else." He started to close the door but the director thumped his hand against it and managed to keep it open briefly.

"For the show, Johnny. For the fans."

"Boys."

"Yeah, Johnny?"

"We're on it."

The hounds stalked past Lisa and moved slowly toward the open door as they growled and bared their teeth.

Phil chuckled nervously. "How are we supposed to get more material if you won't let us in—"

"When I leave the room. And that ain't happenin' again tonight."

"Want us to chase 'em off, Johnny?"

"That nervous-sweaty two-legs looks like he's still learning how to run. We can teach him for you."

Hearing only the hounds' snarling and Luther's jaws snapping shut as they reached the door, Phil stepped back and swallowed. "We were contracted to—"

"Mind your business unless I say otherwise. And I wouldn't come back here without Howie if I were you." He slammed the door shut.

Luther sat and uttered a warbled howl. "And stay out."

"Johnny," the director called from the other side of the door. "We've already got some great stuff but not nearly enough for the first day."

Rex growled and sniffed the bottom of the door, snorting and pawing. "Man, this guy's dumb."

"Johnny?"

The bounty hunter ignored the desperate director and marched down the hall. "He'll get it eventually."

Lisa darted a sympathetic frown at the closed door. "Do you want me to talk to him?"

"Naw. That's settin' yourself up to have whatever you say twisted and stuck on YouBoob."

She barked out a laugh. "I'm sorry?"

"The thing with the videos."

"YouTube, Johnny."

"Sure." He went to the kitchen and opened cabinet after cabinet, searching for the one thing he wanted. *Private jet and swanky digs. If Nelson ain't givin' up all the goods, none of that's gonna save him from—* Johnny stopped at the last open cabinet and grinned. "There you are."

He took the unopened bottle of Johnny Walker Black and two glasses and turned toward his companion. "Care to join me, darlin'?"

She raised her chin and looked at him with a smile. "I'm not sure I'm a whiskey girl."

"Well, why don't you take the redhead mask off and give it a try. We'll find out together."

"Okay." She removed the illusion and glanced at the fridge. "Are there any mixers in that fridge?"

Johnny snorted. "You're lucky I like you. That there's blasphemy."

"Wow. So this is like a religion for you."

This time, he took a seat on the couch beside her and poured two fingers of whiskey for Lisa and a full four for himself. "I ain't the religious type, darlin'. But I believe in a fair number of things —the truth, my privacy, a fair exchange, a good hunt, and this."

He raised his glass toward her and winked.

"So we'll add sharing your favorites to the list." Lisa clinked her glass against his and chuckled.

"Sure." The dwarf sniffed and sipped his drink. "Right up there with justice."

"Of course. And we're closer now than you were before you had a partner to help you track him."

He looked thoughtfully at her. "I suppose we are."

Lisa sniffed the whiskey tentatively, followed by a small sip. Her eyes widened and she swallowed and wheezed a cough. "Wow."

"It gets better the closer you get to empty."

She set her glass on the round marble coffee table and nodded. "I'll take your word for it."

"What? Darlin', that whiskey's as good as my word. Don't let it go to waste now."

Not knowing how to respond to that, she retrieved her tablet instead and pulled up the YouTube app.

"Aw, what are you doin'?"

"I want to see what everyone else has already watched today." She smirked. "Don't you?"

"Nope."

"Well, feel free to take a peek if you change your mind." All she had to type into the search bar was *Johnny* and *Dwarf the Bounty Hunter's* newest YouTube channel pulled up immediately. "Look at that. You're the first thing that comes up."

"You sound way too happy about that." He downed the rest of his glass and popped the top off the bottle for a refill.

"No, it's a good thing. Oh, my God."

"What?" He drank more whiskey and couldn't bring himself to look at the tablet.

"They put this up six hours ago, and it already has almost two million views."

"Dammit."

"Johnny, this is good." Lisa selected the highest-viewed video "teaser" for the show's post-retirement season and let the ad at the beginning play all the way through. "Everyone's watching."

"That ain't never been a good thing." He glanced at the ad for some office networking software and snorted. "Why's that on there, huh? I ain't endorsin' anythin'."

"It's only an ad. Okay, look. Here we go."

The short video started with Pantera's "Domination" playing quietly in the background. Johnny sniffed. *At least they got the heavy metal part right.*

"Do you have any concerns about your ability to find and appre-hend this next bounty, given your previous record as a bounty hunter and then your rather long hiatus?"

Phil spoke from behind the camera that had focused on Johnny, "Stephanie," and two hounds beside a drastically enlarged neon-pink flamingo.

"I'm a dwarf. I coulda stayed outta the game for thirty years and still known exactly what I'm doin'."

"What?" He scowled at the tablet. "I specifically remember more colorful language than that."

"Which is why they voiced you over this shot." She pointed at the video, which changed to a wide, sweeping view of the swamp. Fortunately, that view stopped before the edge of the bounty hunter's home could come into view.

"I aim to clean up and throw the bastard out with the trash."

"Johnny doesn't discriminate." That was Lisa again, paired with a slow-motion clip of her as the redheaded Stephanie turning to shoot Johnny a winning grin.

"Oh, jeez." She rolled her eyes. "Such a flattering way to take all that out of context."

The bounty hunter chuckled. "I tell you what. That redhead's lookin' real sweet on me in that shot."

"Oh, come on."

"Naw, that ain't you, darlin'." He raised his glass at her again with a smirk. "I won't hold it against you."

The sound of the hounds barking in the background rose from the speakers and faded away as if Rex and Luther had been caught on audio disappearing into the swamp.

"Johnny." Rex trotted around the corner with his ears perked. "Is that us?"

Luther barked sharply, ran into the living area, and his head darted from side to side as he searched the suite. "You bring other hounds in here and not tell us?"

"It is us."

"No way, Rex. I sound way bigger than that."

"Join us for more sneak peeks of Dwarf the Bounty Hunter *as Johnny Walker and his coonhounds take to the streets of Baltimore, sniffing out justice and taking out the trash."*

"What the fuck?" Johnny scowled at the video. "That ain't in the interview."

The next image was a closeup of him, completely cutting out what had previously been captured of Luther pissing on the flamingo.

"That about sums it up."

The show's logo crashed into the center of the screen, the typography enhanced and animated with flames since the last time it had aired fifteen years earlier. Below it, smaller text appeared beside a pistol with an animated explosion bursting from the barrel—*You don't want to miss all this action. Subscribe Now!*

"For cryin' out loud." The dwarf took another long pull of his whiskey.

Lisa forced back a laugh and let the end of the video roll through to another short snippet the film crew had already posted. "Looking at this objectively, I'd say they did very well, although I can't help but notice it's only 'Johnny Walker and his coonhounds' and nothing about Stephanie."

"What? Do you want 'em to add, 'And his assistant?'" He grunted. "All the fancy images and puttin' in shit that ain't part of what they filmed. That asshole took a good thing and ruined it."

"It's been fifteen years, Johnny. The show has to change with the times."

"No, it don't." The next video started to play and he leaned sideways to swipe at the tablet and close out the YouTube app. "That's enough."

"Johnny." Luther sat at his master's feet and stared at the tablet. "Hey. Were we in there? Were we on TV?"

"I heard being on TV makes you look bigger. Like with tons of muscle and a longer tail," Rex added. "That true?"

Johnny gave the hounds a warning glance.

"Maybe it made him look bigger."

"Naw, Johnny's already got enough muscle."

When the dwarf turned toward Lisa, she was biting her lip in an attempt to hide a knowing smile. "What?"

"I know you won't come out and say it, but I think you miss having that show on all the time."

He rolled his eyes. "And Nelson up my ass every time a new episode aired? Naw. You're graspin' for straws."

"You didn't film any federal cases, did you?"

He avoided her gaze and knocked back the rest of his second drink. "Not that I recall."

"Huh. Because it was so long ago."

"Yep."

"It's a good thing Phil put up all seven seasons on the YouTube channel as a refresher course—"

"Don't you even think about it. If you wanna keep this partner arrangement, Lisa, you give me your word right now you ain't fixin' to watch all that behind my back."

Her eyes widened and a slow grin spread across her lips. "There it is."

"What?"

"This partner arrangement. You're finally getting it, aren't you?"

Johnny grunted and reached for the bottle of whiskey to pour himself another glass. "When I can use it as leverage? You bet."

CHAPTER EIGHT

They ordered room service for dinner with two extra pork chops for the hounds—as rare as the restaurant would make them—and went over the Senator Hugh case while they ate. Lisa poured herself another glass of the wine Johnny had grudgingly ordered at her request and leaned against the high-backed chair at the two-person dining table. "Okay, why do you still look like you bit into a lemon?"

He took his last bite and chewed thoughtfully. "No, I don't."

"Fine. Forget the lemon. What's on your mind?"

Luther whipped his head up from where he'd been licking the pork chop plate clean for the last ten minutes. "If you don't want that lemon, Johnny, I'll take it."

"Hey, what about more chops?" Rex licked his lips. "Those were amazing."

The dwarf snapped his fingers and pointed away from the dining table. "Go on now, boys. There ain't nothin' left."

"But she said lemon—"

"Git."

"Yeah, yeah, yeah."

Johnny shook his head, took a sip of whisky, and looked at Lisa over the rim of the glass. "What?"

"You look a little distracted, is all." She sipped her white wine delicately and gave him a patient smile.

"Distracted. Well, hell. I have you sittin' across the table lookin' at me like that and two hounds who don't know when to quit."

"Come on, Johnny," Rex protested and he and his brother padded into the huge separate bedroom for more exploring. "You've only been able to hear us for like— Wait. How long has it been?"

"Forever?" Luther suggested. "That feels right."

"And wrong at the same time."

The bounty hunter heaved a sigh. *Remember that those talkin' hounds saved your life and your sanity in those Portland tunnels. In and of itself, that makes up for everythin' else. So focus on the next.*

He thumped both forearms on the table and leaned forward to squint at his plate. "All right, darlin'. I'll talk."

Lisa chuckled. "Well, that wasn't very hard."

"You didn't even try, but I think your perspective ain't exactly somethin' I can afford to pass up." Johnny rubbed his temples vigorously. "Somethin's still sittin' not quite right about this whole 'filming a show' scenario."

"Oh." She sipped her wine again. "Do you have any idea what that is?"

"Well now, you showed me all that mumbo jumbo on the dark web with this asshole postin' as Lemonhead and tryin' to get his connections in with whatever idiots I bagged over a ten-year career of heavy hittin'."

"I did."

"The Red Boar's already got what he wanted, then. Ain't he? Aside from comin' after me." His frown deepened and he reached out absently to spin his dinner plate on the table. "It seems like we might end up wastin' more time than savin' it if you ask me."

"Hmm. Well, how about I ask you this." Lisa leaned toward him and studied his face. "What are you trying to say?"

Johnny looked slowly at her and froze. *So I'm that easy to read now, huh? Damn.* "I'm sayin' how do we even know the bastard's gonna be watchin' these shitty clips on that video site, huh? We're puttin' my mug and your...well, not your real face, but you're there. It's goin' up all over the Internet, however many idiots who still think I'm worth watchin' are tunin' in to watch again, and the Red Boar could be holin' up and schemin' with a group of even dumber criminals I apprehended however long ago. We have no guarantee."

Her smile widened. "That's been on your chest all day, hasn't it?"

"Huh." He sniffed and mumbled, "More like since you told me the plan."

"Okay. I get that." She set her glass down and stood from the table. "But come on, Johnny. I know how to cover my bases."

"I ain't sayin' you don't— Where are you goin'?"

Her redheaded, green-eyed, freckled illusion returned and she pointed at the hall. "To Stephanie's room. And when I come back, you'll give me ten minutes to show you why you're letting this eat you up for nothing."

She turned and disappeared swiftly around the corner of the living area to head toward the suite's door. It opened and shut again with a soft click, and Johnny could only stare at the empty kitchen.

Huh. If I didn't know better, I'd say she's fixin' to take the lead on this. Except that ain't how partners do it. Right?

He drummed his fingers on the tabletop and glowered at the empty plates from their dinner. Faint, rhythmic splashing came from the open doorway into the bedroom, followed by the hounds' whispered voices in the bounty hunter's mind.

"Come on, bro. You're taking way too long."

"I'm taking as long as I need to. You're supposed to keep watch."

"Yeah. I'm watching you and you're taking too long."

"You'll get your turn."

"Boys?" Johnny turned in his chair and the splashing stopped.

"Yeah, Johnny?"

"What's up?"

"I ain't gonna step in there and find y'all drinkin' outta somethin' that ain't made for mouths, am I?"

Rex and Luther nudged the door open with a creak so they could trot nonchalantly out of the bedroom side by side. Luther chuckled. "Why would you find that, Johnny?"

The smaller hound licked his muzzle but failed to catch the last few drops of water that spilled from the soaked underside of his furry chin.

The dwarf raised an eyebrow. "It's a hunch and usually, I'm right."

Rex lowered his head to lick the water drops off the floor. "All good, Johnny. Go ahead and look. You won't find anything in there you don't wanna see."

"Uh-huh. Close the door."

"What?" Luther looked behind him into the bedroom with pleading eyes. "It's nice in there, Johnny. Plenty of—hey."

Rex nudged the door all the way shut with his nose and snorted. "No swamp out here Johnny. No tide pools either, so…"

With a grunt, Johnny stood to walk toward the kitchen and check the large mixing bowl on the floor. "Well, I'll be. There sure is a nice big bowl of drinkin' water over here, though."

"What?" Rex darted toward his brother to nip at Luther's neck. "You told me it was empty."

"I thought it was."

Johnny pointed at them and shook his head. "Stay outta toilets. Y'all are better than that."

"We know that." Luther dodged another annoyed nip from his

brother and darted across the living area toward the huge armchair. He spun in two tight circles and curled in a ball on the floor. "Didn't someone smart say life's not worth living if you don't fill it with experiences?"

"That don't apply to the john, Luther." The dwarf ran a hand through his hair and sank into the fluffy cushions of the couch. "Don't do it again."

"Got it, Johnny. No more toilets. Hey, but what if they're outside?"

The steady lap of Rex drinking out of the actual bowl filled the suite.

When Lisa knocked on his door again, she had her laptop under her arm and a pert smile aimed right at Johnny. "Let's get comfy."

"For what?"

"For your first lesson in what's possible these days with the technology you refuse to touch."

"Come on, darlin'. I don't need to learn any of that."

"Tough. I'm showing you anyway. Mostly because you need to see how solid this plan is, and then you can get your head back in the game. We still have a Kilomea blackmailer to go after tomorrow and a Johnny-Haters Anonymous meeting after that."

He snorted. "Did you just come up with that one?"

"I've been sitting on it for a while. This felt like the right time." With a smirk, she sat on the couch and patted the cushion beside her. "Come on."

"Can't you simply tell me instead of making a big deal—"

"Sure I can." She grinned. "But I won't."

He sighed with a mixture of frustration and exasperation. "You're good."

"I know."

That drew a reluctant smile from him and he stopped to top his glass of whiskey off and retrieve her wineglass before he joined her on the couch. They both drank and Lisa opened her laptop to start his mostly willing lesson in modern technology, the Internet beyond Google, VPNs, and the dark web.

"What does all that have to do with makin' sure this bastard thinks I'm the idiot?"

"Basics first, Johnny." She grinned at him and pulled up a records search for her fake name—Stephanie Wyndom.

He squinted at the screen, then leaned forward to get a better look when she turned it on her lap to face him. "Did you steal someone's identity, darlin'?"

"Yep. I do it all the time."

He looked sharply at her and she burst out laughing.

"No, Johnny. Stephanie Wyndom isn't real and she never has been."

"That's a hell of a rap sheet for someone who don't exist."

"That's the point." Lisa scrolled through the hits her alias had pulled up—full name, birth date, and a photo of her nonexistent Florida driver's license. After that came multiple arrest records and case reports from Johnny bringing her in as a bounty.

"Well, look at that." He sniggered. "Public intoxication, grand theft auto, and arson. She sure is a mixed bag, ain't she?"

She nudged him with her elbow and took another sip of wine. "It's all part of the story. Stephanie had a substance abuse problem and cut a path of minor chaos across a few southern states in order to keep the habit going. And because she liked having nice things along the way."

"You just come up with that too?"

"No, but I like to think Stephanie thought she was classy." They both chuckled. "So here's the deal. Those old bounties of yours are getting together the night after tomorrow to brainstorm how to get some closure on all the grudges they hold against you. If I want in on that meeting, I have to send all this information to whoever sent me that link. And when they look up Stephanie Wyndom—because they will—they'll find this."

Johnny raised his eyebrows and shrugged. "It looks legit to me."

"Well, as far as the rest of the world and anyone on the Internet can tell, it is legit. We had one of the best teams put the background info together, enter it in all possible databases, and voila. She's a real half-Light Elf who had her joyrides and fleeting highs snatched out from under her by Johnny Walker."

"Twenty-four years ago, huh?"

"Well, it had to be before *Dwarf the Bounty Hunter*. Otherwise, she'd have her own episode to reference."

"And there ain't none."

"The Bureau's team is good, Johnny, but they're not that good." She scrolled through the rest of the documentation pulled up for Stephanie Wyndom and shrugged. "Whoever messaged me gave me five days to prove I'm legit. This'll get it done. And if the Red Boar and any of those other scheming thugs haven't heard about the show and the fact that you're in Baltimore for this next bounty, I'll make sure they hear about it at the meeting. Hell, maybe that alone will get the Red Boar to come out of hiding."

"Uh-huh." He scowled as something occurred to him. "And what are you gonna tell 'em when they see that redhead's face they've been watchin' on YouTube for days sittin' in front of 'em?"

"I'll think of something." Lisa downed the rest of her wine and grinned. "That's another thing we have in common, you know?"

"What's that?"

"Doing our best work on the fly."

The dwarf snorted. "Sure. Only I do it with my fists. Or guns. Or explosives. And you…make up stories."

"It sounds like the perfect team to me."

CHAPTER NINE

The next morning, Johnny and Lisa agreed to order room service separately to avoid a run-in with Phil and the film crew at the start of their day.

The last thing I need is to have my damn breakfast plastered all over the Internet with who knows what that idiot tries to pull outta anything I say. If I can't start the day right, the rest is a wash.

Lisa texted him a little after 9:00 am to ask if he was ready.

"Time to get on, boys. We have a Kilomea to bring in this mornin'."

"The big, hairy two-legs, Johnny?"

"Those guys stink. Kinda like Luther after he rolls in some other animal's shit."

"Hey, don't try to pretend I'm the only one."

"Yeah, but you do it way more."

"That's enough." With a grunt, the bounty hunter hauled his utility belt studded with exploding disks out of his duffel bag and strapped it on. "And yeah, it's the Kilomea. He's a low-level thug, so it shouldn't be anywhere near the hardest thing we've done. But make sure you stay sharp anyhow, understand?"

"Got it, Johnny."

"Any hairy bastard we see is an automatic suspect."

"No. Only the one we're goin' after."

"Right, right."

"Hey, Johnny." Luther stuck his snout against the underside of the door and sniffed deeply. "Didn't we already order room service?"

The dwarf snorted and marched toward the door. "Don't tell me y'all's memories keep gettin' shorter by the day."

"I'm not. I'm wondering why it smells like food and shoes and—"

"It's the TV people, Johnny." Rex yipped and sat to wait for his master to catch up.

With a growl, Johnny rolled his eyes. "Get on out the way, boys. Pretend they ain't even there. They want a shot of the real thing, let 'em have it."

"Wait, you mean like rip their arms off?"

"No, I think means don't rip their arms off this time."

Luther scuttled away from the door. "Weird. Doesn't usually mean that. You sure, Johnny?"

"Uh-huh." The bounty hunter opened the door, and both hounds raced into the hall and darted around crewmembers' legs and beneath equipment bags slung over shoulders.

"Take your shot, TV guys!" Rex shouted and pranced in a wide circle. "You might not get another chance."

"Hey, hey." Luther sniffed Cody's pockets. "If you share what you've got in there, I might be willing to do a private interview for ya. You know, only me. I could tell you things that'd make your pathetic excuse for hair stand on—whoa, whoa. Hey. Are those mints?"

"Morning, Johnny." Phil grinned as Johnny stepped out of his hotel room and closed the door behind him. "Are you ready to head out on this next—"

"To me, boys." He ignored the man altogether and headed across the hall and two doors down to Lisa's room. He knocked quickly on the door. "Time to go, darlin'. Your escort's here." He gave the film crew a begrudgingly accepting glance and muttered, "And the fellas with the cameras."

Her door whipped open to reveal Stephanie, her strawberry-blonde curls tied in a loose ponytail. "Good morning, Johnny. I'm ready when you are."

"Yep." He turned and stalked down the hall, followed closely by the fictional Stephanie, both hounds, and the filming crew. Clearing his throat, he leaned toward her and muttered, "Is Stephanie Wyndom carryin' this mornin'?"

The agent smirked and stared straight ahead at the elevators at the end of the hall. "Absolutely. She has no permit, though."

"She doesn't?"

"It doesn't fit the profile, Johnny. Why?"

"I'm makin' sure that if we find ourselves in a position that needs shootin', my redhead assistant has her ducks in a row." They reached the elevators, and he punched the call button before he glared over his shoulder at the film crew. "You know, ready for any situation."

"I won't draw a weapon on the film crew."

The elevator doors opened and he stepped inside with a shrug. "You never know what might happen."

Howie was already in the lobby waiting for them when they arrived. With a wrinkled grin, he pushed up out of the armchair and thumped his cane down with both hands. "There he is."

"Have you been waitin' down here long?"

"Only as long as it took your team to get up to the fourth floor and wait for you to come out of hiding." The old man chuckled. "Did they get anything good?"

"Only the cold shoulder."

"Well, let's hope heading off after this Kilomea gives them a little something else to focus on, huh?"

"I'm countin' on it, Howie."

The Kilomea's name was Yarren Brork, according to the case

file. Johnny slid behind the wheel of their rental—this one a black truck reminiscent of his four-by-four at home—with "Stephanie" up front, Howie in the back of the cab, and the two hounds in the bed.

The second Johnny peeled away from the curb of the Sagamore, the film crew scrambled to get situated in their rented vans to follow without losing sight of him.

He took a deep breath and draped his arm through the open driver-side window as he drove through downtown. "That's a breath of fresh air."

"Smells more like fish," Luther said from the truck bed. He poked his head through the open back window of the cab and sniffed in Howie's hair. "Or maybe that's this guy."

The old man laughed and ducked away from the hound's snout as he batted Luther's head aside. "What are you doing, huh? I may be old but I'm not senile. And no, you can't eat me."

Johnny whistled sharply and gave the hound a warning glance through the rearview mirror. "Where's the first stop again?"

"The house first, right?" Lisa asked.

"Sure. It might be a long shot on a Wednesday mornin', but I'm feelin' optimistic."

She laughed softly and pulled Yarren Brork's home address up on her phone's GPS app. "Do you want me to turn the navigation up?"

His gaze flicked to her and returned to the road. "I never liked the sound of that robot lady's voice, to tell ya the truth. You could do a better job of it anyhow. If that suits ya."

Lisa leaned away from him in surprise, unable to hide a smile. "Because you'd rather hear my voice telling you how many miles until the next turn?"

He shrugged. "Howie ain't much of a co-pilot. So yeah. I suppose I would."

"Johnny. Hey, Johnny." Rex thrust his head over the side of the truck bed. The wind whipped through his floppy ears and made his lolling tongue push across the side of his face. "The vans are catching up."

"Ooh, are you gonna try to race them again?" Luther asked.

"Everyone hang tight." The dwarf glanced in the rearview mirror at the hounds enjoying their windswept ride, then met Howie's gaze briefly through the reflection. *Racin' was for the back roads in the middle of nowhere. I gotta keep it legit in the city.*

They reached Yarren's neighborhood in Dundalk fifteen minutes later, and he parked the truck along the curb on the opposite side of the street a block before the Kilomea's house. The film crew's vans followed suit, and Phil hopped out of the first one with a huge, energetic grin.

"Here we go. Are you ready to see some action, people?"

Johnny grimaced at the man. "Y'all aren't seein' any of that personally. You hear me? The action's mine."

"Yes, and our job is to—" Phil jolted and stepped away when Rex snapped his jaws and uttered a low growl.

"You must have a death wish, two-legs."

"We can help you with that," Luther added and stared at the man over his shoulder as he and his brother followed their master down the street.

"Our job," Howie said and clapped a hand on the startled director's shoulder, "is to stay out of the damn way and catch what we can on camera."

"D-don't...tell me how to do my job." The director fixed the old man with a scathing glance.

"Of course not. I'm merely reminding you of a few key details. Why don't you sit back and watch a vet on this show working in his element, huh?"

"But I—"

"Let's move!" Howie uttered a piercing whistle and waved his cane in the air to get the film crew's attention. "I want mics and cameras no closer than fifteen feet from him at all times, got it? Dwarf can move if he has to, but only if he has the space."

"What about Stephanie?" someone asked.

"Sure, get in close as long as you keep to those fifteen feet." He chuckled and hobbled after Johnny, Lisa, and the hounds. "It's a good contrast to have an easy face next to all that hairy red scowling."

The Kilomea's house was exactly like every other smaller, older home in the mostly run-down neighborhood. A crooked fence bordering on rot, peeled and chipped paint on the siding, and the end of the gutter at the corner of the roof had twisted and now dangled a few inches below where it ought to have been attached. When they reached the front porch, Johnny rested a hand on the hilt of the utility knife at his belt and glanced at Lisa. "It's an easy bag."

"Nothing to be nervous about."

"I ain't nervous, darlin'. Only hopin' this Yarren ain't got some of the usual tricks and traps up his hairy-ass sleeve."

She stepped away from the door and nodded. "You do your thing, Johnny. I've got your back. It merely won't be with a badge."

"I've done most of my work without a fed and a badge so that's fine."

Luther stuck his nose against the bottom of the front door and sniffed. "Definitely Kilomea in there, Johnny."

"We could smell him from twenty feet away," Rex added.

The dwarf nodded and knocked three times—hard enough to show the occupant he meant business. "Yarren Brork. Open up."

When there was no reply or sound of movement from inside, the first thing he wanted to do was use a handful of his explosive beads to blow the doorknob and the lock off the door. *And then we get the whole damn world watchin' me breakin' and enterin'. Shit.*

Instead, he knocked again and shouted, "I only wanna...talk."

Luther cocked his head at the door. "Awful quiet in there, Johnny."

"Maybe he's sleeping," Rex suggested.

The bounty hunter scowled at the hounds. "Y'all said you can smell him."

"Well yeah. Everyone's house smells like them."

Lisa stepped off the front porch. "I'll see if I can get a look inside."

"Yeah, okay." Johnny knocked again. "Yarren!"

Moving across the front yard of mostly dirt scattered with a few patches of dead grass, "Stephanie" smiled at the second cameraman who stepped slowly toward her. "I'm merely trying to see who's home."

"Stephanie," Phil called and pointed at her. "Don't talk to the camera unless—"

Howie's cane whacked painfully against the younger director's shins. "Don't interrupt. Both of them have more experience in this than you. I can promise you that."

Fuming, Phil stalked away from the old man and nodded for the second cameraman to follow Stephanie.

As the hounds darted off to investigate the back yard sectioned off by a chain-link fence, Lisa rounded the side of the house and peered through windows either draped with sheer curtains or nothing at all. She doubled back to the front porch and shook her head. "I don't think he's home, Johnny. The carport's empty too."

"Damn."

"She's right," Luther called from the other side of the house. "And nothing out back but—squirrel! Hey! Rex, get it!"

The chain-link fence jingled as the smaller hound pounced against it and barked furiously.

"Dude, if you can't tell that's not a Kilomea, you should've stayed home." Rex trotted back down the side yard and ignored his brother's manic baying.

Johnny whistled. "That's enough, boys. We ain't findin' him here."

All Luther's noise stopped abruptly and he trotted to the front to rejoin his master. "Puffy-tailed bastard's laughing at me, Johnny."

Rex snorted. "Probably 'cause you're not doing your job."

"What? Hey, our job's to go after the hairy guy."

"Not a squirrel."

The dwarf strode down the narrow, cracked walkway in the center of the dead yard. "Next place to look?"

"Well, it is mid-morning on a Wednesday." Lisa shrugged. "We could try his place of employment."

"Uh-huh. That'll do."

When Johnny reached the sidewalk, Phil jumped on the opportunity and practically accosted the bounty hunter. "So the man you're looking for isn't home. Is that right, Johnny?"

"If it weren't, do you think I'd be fixin' to head out?"

Phil nodded toward Cody who still rolled the camera. "What's next then? Do you have a plan for—"

"Yeah. It starts with gettin' that damn camera outta my face." Johnny thrust a palm against the camera and jerked it down. The cameraman stumbled forward with a grunt.

"Hey!" Phil shouted. "You can't—"

"I wouldn't," Howie warned. "If you don't want Johnny to do something, don't tell him he can't."

The director scowled at him. "So he gets free rein to do whatever he wants?"

"Essentially, yes. It's part of what makes him so good at what he does." The old man smirked and hobbled down the street, his cane clicking on the sidewalk. "There's a reason I said fifteen feet."

Cody exhaled an exasperated sigh and turned his camera to check for damage.

"Keep it rolling," Phil snapped. "And get to the vans."

CHAPTER TEN

Yarren Brork worked at Canton Exports & Supplies in the Canton Industrial Area, which meant Johnny's appearance on the site—cameras or no—had a higher chance of making folks a little uneasy. He parked the truck at the far end of the lot and only waited for Lisa to join him before he stalked through the rows of other parked trucks and old sedans rusted and flaking from the saltwater and years spent driving on salted winter roads.

"What does he do here again?" the bounty hunter muttered and leaned toward Lisa to be sure his voice didn't carry behind him toward the mics. *Those damn cameras have me all jumpy. Who cares what I say?*

The agent darted him a sidelong glance but graciously picked up on his hesitation. "He's a shipment driver and has been at Canton Exports & Supplies for over twenty years."

"All right. So a few decades of hard labor, livin' in a fallin' apart house in Dundalk, and he only now starts pickin' up black-mail as part of his daily routine?"

She shrugged. "Maybe he's trying to pull himself up beyond his means."

"With a senator's pockets. Might be." Johnny sniffed and

headed around the side of the main building toward the sound of employee crews moving around, hard at work during what was still the beginning of a notably long shift. "Does that file say what Hugh was being blackmailed for?"

"Brork's demands. They weren't all that specific." Lisa frowned at him. "Blackmail is blackmail, and when it's against a political figure with ties to the Bureau…"

"Yeah, yeah. Real off-limits. I get it."

They rounded the back of the building and stopped at the edge of the open work yard. The loading-bay doors were open, and the yard teemed with undisguised Kilomeas. There were half a dozen huge, muscular men among them who looked human, but the dwarf caught the glint of one man's eyes flashing silver when he glanced at the two partners.

"Shifters, Johnny," Rex muttered and sniffed the air.

"Six of 'em," Luther added. "Maybe seven. Hey, how are we supposed to find one Kilomea in a whole horde of 'em, huh? They all stink the same."

"That's one reason I can talk and you can't." Johnny headed toward the workers hauling crates off the loading bays and stacking them in the backs of transport trucks.

Lisa glanced at the hounds and shrugged. "I'm guessing that was aimed at you guys."

"Lady, you have no idea." Rex trotted after his master and whipped his head from side to side as he entered the mass of workers.

Luther sat and stared at Agent Breyer. "I know you can't hear us, but Johnny's got it all wrong. We can talk."

"We should stick close, Luther. Come on."

"Huh." The smaller hound stared after her as she made her way around the edge of the workers. "You sure you don't speak hound?"

"I'm lookin' for Yarren Brork," Johnny said and raised his

voice over the noise without technically shouting. "Is he in today?"

"What's a dwarf doing here?" A Kilomea with a chunk of hair missing from his forearm stopped to study the bounty hunter. "You little guys are as strong as shit, I'll give you that. But most of these crates are half your size, man."

A handful of workers chuckled as they continued with their loading and stacking.

"I ain't here for a job," Johnny replied. "At least not doin' what you're doin'. Yarren works here, don't he?"

"As far as I know." A shifter with his uniform button-up removed and tied around his waist hefted another crate in his arms and grunted. "He didn't come in today, though."

"How come?"

"Beats me."

Johnny grunted and scanned the work yard. "Is the foreman in today?"

The working magicals chuckled and didn't pause in their hauling, stacking, grunting, and sweating.

Another Kilomea turned his head toward one of the open loading docks and bellowed, "Rocky! Got a dwarf out here asking for ya!"

"And a pretty little extra." The shirtless shifter slowed on his path past Lisa and studied redheaded Stephanie with undisguised appreciation. "You lost, sweetheart?"

She grinned at him. "Not at all, but you might be if you keep looking at me like that."

The workers burst out laughing. "It looks like you're losing your touch, Omar."

"Shit, son. I'd back away from that redhead real quick. Nothin' but trouble."

"Feisty." The shifter winked at her and sniggered. "I like it."

Boots thumped slowly across the closest loading dock, and Johnny looked up as a massive Kilomea descended. His eyeteeth were grotesquely crooked and a scar zigzagged from the top of his head down the side of his face before it hooked under his square, fur-covered jaw. The huge magical folded his arms, the same uniform button-up as his workers rolled halfway up his forearms. "What?"

Johnny acknowledged him with a nod. "Are you Rocky?"

"Yeah."

"I'm lookin' for Yarren."

A low growl escaped the forearm's throat and his shaggy fur ruffled in the warm, muggy breeze blowing across the work yard. "He called in today. Yesterday too. Personal issues."

"Yeah, that's one way to put it."

"Hey, aren't you that bounty hunter?" A shifter asked and pointed at Johnny before he hefted another crate. "The one with the show, yeah?"

"Are you a fan?" the dwarf asked.

"Not really."

"Good."

"It looks like he brought the whole damn crew with him, though." A Kilomea with thick black hair tied in a topknot nodded toward the side of the building. "Boss?"

Rocky hopped off the end of the loading bay with a loud thump.

Luther skittered away from the huge magical and snorted. "Jeez. Look where you're stepping, huh?"

The foreman peered around the side of the building to see Cody and Dave inching toward the work yard, followed by the rest of the crew. He shook his head. "No cameras."

"It's part of the show returning," Lisa said and stepped toward him. "You can request that we keep everyone's identity anonymous if you like. Blurred faces and everything—"

"No cameras."

The bounty hunter smirked. "I'm right there with you, brother. Get back to the lot."

Cody stepped forward and turned to pan the camera.

"Man, you got shit in your human ears?" Rocky stormed toward the cameraman with another growl.

Cody stepped back but didn't stop filming.

"You want us to step in Johnny?" Rex asked.

"Yeah, we'll chase off anyone. I'll get the big guy. He almost squashed me."

"Naw, let 'em work it out." Johnny folded his arms and tried not to grin.

"This is private property," Rocky roared, "and I don't give a shit about your home videos. Keep moving."

Howie uttered a piercing whistle. "Everyone out front!"

Phil stared at Rocky with wide eyes, then gestured around him toward the work yard full of magicals without any illusion at all. "Do you know how many shots there are of businesses with nothing but magicals working out of—ow! Jesus, what are you doing?"

Howie yanked the man by the ear and turned toward the front of the building. "It's either my hand on your ear or your arm ripped out of its socket, Phil. Would you prefer the other option?"

"Ah-ah-ah!" The director shrieked as Johnny's old friend yanked him away.

Then, Howie banged his cane against the chain-link fence lining the driveway behind the building. "Let's go, people. We can catch Johnny on his way out."

Cody kept filming but almost dropped the camera when Rocky lurched toward him again and pounded a fist into his other hand. The man tucked his equipment protectively under his arm and turned to scatter with the rest of the crew.

"Pain in my ass," the foreman growled. "All of 'em."

The dwarf nodded. "On a different day, I reckon you and I would get along just fine."

Rocky grunted and turned toward him. "Why are you lookin' for Yarren?"

The bounty hunter spread his arms as if to indicate that the answer was obvious. "Bounty. I'm tryin' to do my job like the rest of y'all. He's been out for two days?"

The Kilomea's tongue flicked against one of his crookedly protruding teeth. "Yep. He hasn't called off a shift in ten years so I assumed it was something important. What did he do?"

"Trying to change his circumstances, I reckon."

"There's nothing wrong with his circumstances."

"Did he say anything about why he took the personal days?" Lisa asked and stepped toward them. "Any sign that something was off before he called in yesterday?"

Rocky turned toward her and studied her in an offhand way. "You practicing to play a cop role in that movie of yours?"

She lowered her head and pressed her lips together to suppress a smart quip. "I'm simply curious."

"Who are you?"

"My assistant." Johnny cleared his throat and raised a hand to warn Lisa to hold off. "But she's on the right track with the questions."

Rocky growled. "He's a good worker and never complains about a shift or a heavy load. Always shows up to clock in and stays late if he has to. But times are hard."

"How's that?"

"If you can't tell by looking around, dwarf, you're not gonna find it." The Kilomea hawked and spat at the chain-link fence.

"Whoa!" Luther darted toward the slimy projectile but stopped short when Johnny snapped his fingers.

"Do you have any idea where we might find him?"

"Someone's paying you to take him in for something, huh?"

"I'm tryin' to do my job."

"Yeah." Rocky shook his head and turned to stride toward the loading bays. "I got nothing else to say."

Johnny wrinkled his nose and shrugged. "Then we're done here. Fellas." He nodded at the magical workers who had watched the exchange between the bounty hunter and their foreman. Some of them nodded in return. A few cast crooked smiles and winks at the redheaded Stephanie, but most simply returned to their work.

Lisa followed him down the drive toward the front parking lot. "You didn't try very hard to get more information."

He shrugged. "Yarren's boss ain't gonna give him up just like that if he has no reason to doubt the guy. And I ain't fixin' to take on a squad of hairy bastards and half a dozen shifters so they can tell me they don't know where he is. These are workin' folks, darlin'. They ain't done nothin' wrong as far as I can tell."

"I agree with you there." She looked over her shoulder, but the open yard behind the building was now out of view. "But something doesn't feel quite right."

"Because those fellas ain't fixin' to turn in one of their own?"

"No. Because the foreman said Brork hasn't called in or missed a shift in ten years. So the guy's been visiting Senator Hugh on his own time after work to make his threats."

"Maybe it's somethin' of a weekend hobby, then."

"Sure." She frowned. "But blackmailing a senator repeatedly takes considerable guts, time, and planning. Not to mention the fact that Hugh's statement in the case file said Brork's been after him for weeks. And the guy starts missing work only now?"

"It might be he's startin' to crack down a little harder. So we showed up at the right time."

When they reached the lot, Phil clapped and twirled a finger in the air for the film crew to get everything in their next shot.

Rex growled when one of the team moved toward them. "You heard the old guy, two-legs. Fifteen feet."

Luther went straight up to Cody and snarled, which made the cameraman step back quickly despite the fact that he kept rolling with the camera centered on Johnny and Lisa. "Hey, Johnny. Did we get upgraded to bodyguard status? I'll chase him anyway. Just say the word."

The dwarf forced himself to not look at either of the two cameras closing in on him and Agent Breyer as they returned to the rental truck.

"The bounty's not at home and not at work," Phil shouted and jogged in a wide circle around the cameras and mics and low-growling hounds. "Where will you look for him next?"

Johnny stopped beside the truck, jerked the driver's door open, and grunted. "You'll have to keep up and find out."

CHAPTER ELEVEN

Senator Richard Hugh lived in Guilford, and after the case file's description of Yarren Brork's multiple visits to the senator's home in the last few weeks, that seemed like the next best place to look.

Johnny killed the truck's engine in front of Hugh's large, Victorian-style house and nodded. "If the Kilomea ain't inside, I reckon Mr. Senator will be more'n happy to illuminate whatever we're missin'."

"Do you think he'll know where Brork is?"

"Maybe." He shut his door, whistled for the hounds to jump out of the truck, and hooked his thumbs through his belt loops as he started up the clean, smooth driveway. "Not that I trust a word comin' from a politician's mouth, but there's an art to readin' between the lines."

The doors of the film crew's vans rumbled shut as everyone took their places to follow Johnny toward the front door.

"Stop, stop, stop." Howie pointed at them with his cane. "Not here."

"This is part of the show, old man—"

"Sure. If you want to get your asses majorly sued by a Maryland-raised senator. Turn the cameras off." Howie snapped his fingers at Cody. "I mean it."

"And how are we supposed to get enough for this episode?" Phil blustered. "If we keep getting told to turn the cameras off, we won't have anything to—"

"Oh, come on and quit your yammering." The old man rolled his eyes. "We stay here, and I'll make sure Johnny stops to answer some questions before we move on. Fair enough?"

Phil rolled his eyes and scowled at Johnny, Stephanie, and the hounds walking up the driveway. "All right. Everyone stays. Keep the senator's house out of it. We'll wait."

"Whoa-ho-ho, Johnny." Rex sniffed at the rows of hedges along the driveway. "This place has everything."

"It's huge." Luther snapped at a small white butterfly flittering from flower to flower in the bushes. "Hey, if we get this Kilomea, do you think the two-leg who lives here will be grateful enough to give us snacks?"

"Only way to thank a hound, Johnny."

"Yeah, and belly rubs."

"Heads in the game, boys." Johnny's boots thudded onto the wide covered porch with a two-person swing hanging from chains at the far end. "We're here for a chat. If Yarren happens to be here at the same time, we'll catch him in the—"

"Back up, asshole!" The muffled shout came from inside. "This will not go well for you if you don't start listening!"

Johnny pounded on the door with a fist. "Richard Hugh?"

Someone roared inside the house, followed by the thump and bump of a scuffle before something shattered.

"Hey! What the hell? This wasn't part of the deal—"

A gunshot went off, and Johnny snorted. "Fuck privacy, then."

He pulled two black explosive beads from his pocket, crushed them, and stuck them on either side of the doorknob. When they detonated, the brass knob popped in its setting. He kicked the door in before the piece of hardware landed on the porch.

Out on the street, Phil circled his finger in the air and took off running. "We gotta get this, people. Let's go!"

Johnny and Lisa raced inside and the hounds darted through the foyer with them. "Definitely Kilomea here too, Johnny."

"Yeah. Unless it's the senator."

Johnny turned at the sound of light footsteps trailing behind him. Cody darted through the doorway first, his camera rolling, quickly followed by Dave with the boom and two other crewmembers trying to squeeze through all at the same time. "Do you have any brains at all? This is real violence. Get the fuck outta here!"

Two more shots were fired at the back of the house, followed by more shouts. Johnny sneered at the film crew, then spun to race toward the noises with Lisa and the hounds.

"Get him down, man!"

"This fucker's lost his mind!"

"Drop the gun. Hey, hey—"

Removing her Stephanie illusion, Lisa drew her firearm from her shoulder holster beneath her lightweight overshirt. The second she and Johnny reached the end of the long hallway and darted into the massive living room in the back, she raised her weapon and shouted, "FBI! Drop your weapon and put your hands in the air!"

"Get them!" The shouting man pointed at two Kilomea and a half-wizard fuming at him from across the living room. "Get those animals out of my house!"

"Animals? You're the one who—"

"Hey!" Lisa shouted. "I said drop your weapons!"

But there were no weapons to be dropped. The only firearm lay in the center of the living room between the portly Senator Hugh and his blackmailers.

The half-wizard hissed and summoned a fireball in one hand before he hurled it toward Hugh. Lisa's fireball was faster and struck the assailant in the wrist to make his attack fly wild. His spell streaked into the bookshelf behind the senator's head and he turned toward her with a snarl.

Both Kilomea roared and turned toward Johnny and the hounds. "We got 'em, Johnny."

"Which one's the one we want?"

"Which one of you is Yarren?" Johnny shouted.

The closest Kilomea with flecks of white tipping the fur around his face charged and swung a huge fist to knock the bounty hunter aside. He ducked and spun behind the giant magical to deliver a perfectly aimed blow to his kidney.

The other blackmailer bellowed and flailed, dragging Luther through the air by the hound's jaws clamped around his wrist. His opposite leg kicked out and struggled against Rex's vicious grip as the bigger hound whipped his head and jerked his target's ankle in every direction.

Lisa ducked another fireball from the half-wizard and raised her firearm again. "This isn't the way you want to go! Hands up!"

Rather than comply, he darted behind the long white leather sectional and hurled a fireball at Johnny.

The dwarf yanked the detonating beads out of his pocket, crushed a handful, and slapped some of the gooey substance on the back of the white-tipped Kilomea's legs and the rest on his huge back before he leapt away, drew his utility knife, and flicked it open.

In a series of sputtering pops, the crushed beads detonated one by one and threw the large magical forward with a grunt. He collided with the glass coffee table and shattered it to spill shards over the Persian rug and the wooden floors.

Ducking another fireball, Johnny raced after the downed Kilomea, leapt onto his back, and wrapped a thick forearm around his target's throat. He pressed the tip of the blade against the side of his neck and leaned down to mutter, "If you ain't Yarren, I ain't here for you."

"What the hell do you want?"

"Ah, shit!" The second Kilomea stumbled back into the half-Elf, still flailing with two fifty-five-pound coonhounds attached to his limbs. Both magicals fell in a pile of fur, teeth, and grunts.

Rex and Luther leapt off him and skittered out of the way before they turned to snarl, their hackles raised. "Can't crush us that easily, man."

"Yeah." Luther licked his muzzle repeatedly and snorted. "But I think you might have fleas."

"Don't move." Lisa hovered over the recovering half-wizard and the hound-bitten Kilomea. "I mean it."

"We almost had it taken care of," the half-wizard snarled. "And you fucked the whole thing up."

Johnny looked at the guy and flexed his arm around the Kilomea's throat. *This big guy had better be the right guy.* Instinct told him it was Yarren. "Sure. Y'all almost had the senator murdered right here in his home. Is that what you were takin' care of?"

"What?" The downed Kilomea raised his hands in surrender to Lisa's firearm and shook his head. "Man, you have this whole thing—"

"These brutes have been stalking me for the last three weeks!" Hugh shouted and fumbled with his thin-framed glasses to straighten them on the bridge of his nose. "Take care of it!"

"Well, hold on now." Johnny turned to Hugh and flicked the point of his blade toward him. "We have this under control, Senator. You let us—"

"If they're still breathing, it isn't under control!" Hugh stormed across the living room and snatched the wayward pistol off the floor. His house shoes crunched across the shattered glass of his coffee table as he approached Johnny and the Kilomea he'd tackled. The man lifted the gun toward the Kilomea's head and thumbed the hammer back. "I can't even pay someone to do a job the right way."

"Johnny, watch out!" Luther ran up the seated Kilomea's back and launched off the magical's shoulders toward the angry senator.

The dwarf rolled aside, ducked beneath Hugh's outstretched arm and the pistol at the end of it, and delivered a sharp blow to the underside of the man's forearm. The weapon jerked up to the ceiling and fired to rain plaster and wooden splinters around the living room. Luther's front paws landed on the senator's chest a second before Johnny disarmed the man with a deft twist of his wrist. The firearm skittered across the floor and took shards of glass with it.

"And stay down!" Rex shouted from behind the couch as Luther landed on Senator Hugh's chest. The impact knocked the man's glasses completely off his face, and he wheezed at the extra weight pinning him down.

"Point a gun at the wrong two-leg again, asshole, and you'll get much more than that!" Luther snarled in the man's face and snapped his jaws an inch from the senator's nose.

"That's enough." Johnny snapped his fingers, and the hound stepped off the wheezing man's chest. When the Kilomea behind him stirred, the bounty hunter turned sideways and pointed his knife at the magical's throat again. "You too. Every one of y'all's lost your damn minds."

Groaning, Hugh slapped the ground beside him until he finally found his glasses and fumbled with a shaking hand to put them on. "You," he seethed at Johnny. "You're the one they sent?"

"Maybe. And you're the one who should be grateful for a hand, not reachin' for someone else's gun to shoot a guy when he's down."

"That's his gun!" the half-wizard shouted. "He pulled it on us."

Johnny glanced at Lisa and nodded. "Go ahead and check 'em, darlin.'"

"Arms up." With one hand, Lisa kept her service weapon trained on the half-wizard. With the other, she patted him down, then gestured with her weapon for him to stand back. "You too, big guy."

The second Kilomea nursed his hound-shredded forearm as he rose to his feet with a grunt and slowly raised both arms. "We didn't come here to shoot anyone. Honest."

"Someone had to take it to a whole new level," the half-wizard muttered and glared at Hugh.

"They're clean," Lisa said.

"All right, enough." Johnny reached toward the senator and offered him a hand up.

The man scoffed and pushed to his feet without assistance. "Every single one of you can't send your kind to do anything right the first time. Hell, not even the second or third time."

Johnny blinked at him. "What was that?"

"You heard me. Even the damn FBI's been compromised. And now you're taking the side of these brainless, invading ingrates!"

"You piece of shit," Yarren roared and launched himself toward the senator, both hairy, claw-tipped hands stretched toward the man's throat.

"Hey!" Johnny punched the Kilomea in the gut and whipped his knife up to point the tip at Senator Hugh's throat. "Now I'm here to keep y'all from tearing each other apart. And I ain't gettin' paid for that."

Hugh snarled at him. "Do your job."

"Oh, sure. I aim to do exactly that, Senator, and without you gettin' in the way. Luther. Keep an eye on our host."

"You got it, Johnny. He tries anything funny, I'll jump him again."

"Ha-ha." Rex barked behind the couch. "'Cause you jumped on him."

"You got it over there, darlin'?" Johnny nodded at Lisa.

"Yeah." She adjusted her grip on the pistol. "Rex has my back."

"You know it, lady."

"Anyone moves," the dwarf added, wagging a finger from

Hugh to the three magicals who'd invaded the man's home, "I can't promise that any of y'all are leavin' this house in one piece. Understand?"

No one responded, but that was all the answer he needed. With a grunt, he headed down the hall toward the garage.

"W-where are you going?" Yarren growled after him.

"Findin' a way to make sure everyone's comfortable. We're gonna hunker down and have us a little chat. Sit tight."

CHAPTER TWELVE

"Whoa, Johnny." Rex sniffed the leg of the solid oak dining chair and sniggered. "When you said sit tight, you meant literally."

The dwarf grunted as he finished tying the thick knot of rope behind the chair, which groaned at the sharp tug. The unidentified Kilomea seated in it grimaced and stretched his hands where they'd also been tied behind his back. "Do you think you can go any tighter?"

"You're a big fella." He slapped a hand on the magical's shoulder and nodded. "I'm sure you've been through worse." He dusted his hands off and glass crunched as he crushed it beneath his heavy boots when he moved across the living room. Now that everyone was secure, he dropped onto the cushion of the expensive leather couch and crossed one leg over the other. "There. Now you have got a fair chance to say what needs to be said without tossin' around fists or spells." His next pointed look was aimed at the senator. "Or bullets."

Hugh struggled against the rope tying him tightly to his chair. "This is outrageous! You people broke into my home, damaged my property, and now you're interrogating me like I'm one of your suspects?"

Strapped to the chair beside him, the half-wizard inclined his head toward the senator and muttered, "Technically, you're the only *person* in the room."

"Don't argue semantics with me, you low-life alien scum."

"Whoa, now." Johnny slung an arm over the back of the couch and raised his eyebrows. "It sounds like someone has a few things to say about magicals. And it ain't pretty."

"You have no idea who you're messing with, you pathetic excuse for a—"

"Luther."

The smaller hound darted toward the senator and nipped lightly at the man's ankle with a snarl. Hugh shrieked and tried to lurch away, but the rope held him firmly. "That means stop talking, numbnuts."

"I think we've had enough outta you for the moment, Senator. What d'ya think, darlin'?" Johnny turned toward Lisa who was seated beside him on the couch.

She tapped the barrel of her service weapon against her thigh and tilted her head. "I think Senator Hugh has had his say, yes. At least, we know his side of the story."

"We sure do." The dwarf pointed his knife-tip at Yarren, who sat strapped to the fourth chair at the end of the half-circle Johnny had positioned them in. "If you have somethin' to say, now's the time."

Yarren's eyes widened, and he glanced at the half-wizard beside him, then his fellow Kilomea on the other side of Senator Hugh. He exhaled a massive sigh that ruffled the white-tipped ends of his thick facial hair. "It wasn't supposed to happen like this."

The bounty hunter snorted. "A sentiment shared by every fella findin' himself tied up in someone else's livin' room. So what's the deal, huh? 'Cause the way I heard it, you've been terrorizin' Senator Hugh here for a little longer than only the last few days. And someone mentioned blackmail."

Hugh scoffed. "Don't say it like it's so *blasé*—"

"One more word outta you until I say, Senator, and you'll be sharin' that chair with my hound."

"Yeah. On your back," Luther added with a low growl.

"But the rest of y'all, feel free to chime in whenever it feels convenient."

Soft, slow footsteps whispered down the hall. Cody appeared first with his camera, followed by his sidekick with the boom, Alicia with the bandana, Phil, and two other crewmembers. Howie's cane clicked across the wood, and when he peered around the corner and saw Johnny on the couch, he spread his arms and shrugged.

Lisa immediately pulled her Stephanie illusion up and slipped her service pistol into its holster.

"Who are those people?" Hugh demanded. "Get them out of here! This is my home. You're on private property."

Johnny sniggered. "Naw, they can stay. I think it's a good idea to get all this on film anyhow."

"What the hell for?" The senator jerked against the ropes, tried feebly to free himself, and failed miserably. "No one said anything about you filming your sick little freakshow!"

"Oh, you ain't seen my show?" Johnny shrugged. "Huh. Your loss. Now, fellas. I believe you were 'bout to get down to it, yeah?"

"We might as well get it over with, Yarren," the half-wizard muttered. "We're strapped to fucking chairs and I don't see another way out."

"Percy?"

The other Kilomea sighed heavily. "We don't have a choice, man."

Yarren nodded slowly and closed his eyes for a moment. "Fine. This whole thing started when we heard about some of the new bills this senator was tryin' to get passed. They were only at the Maryland level, sure, but I live here. We all live here, and I couldn't simply sit back and wait for these politicians to start overturning lives left and right. We deserve as much of a chance as the next guy. It doesn't matter where we're from."

Lisa and Johnny exchanged a glance, and she leaned slightly forward on the couch. "What bills?"

"It's fucking segregation is what it is," Percy growled.

"What is?" Johnny asked.

"This douchebag and all his stuck-up political bozo friends wanna make slaves outta magicals in this state—"

"That's absurd!" Hugh shouted. "You're still getting paid—a-ah!"

Luther jumped into the senator's lap and snapped in the man's face. "Strike one!"

"Get this mongrel off me!"

"Johnny, what's a mongrel?"

The dwarf ignored his hound and the senator and focused instead on the disgruntled magicals' story. "Keep talkin'."

"The bill would pay magicals half state minimum wage. Max."

"Now, I know the two of y'all Kilomeas are some fairly hairy fellas as all Kilomeas are." Johnny scratched the side of his face and squinted at them. "But y'all have illusions at your disposal, don'tcha? Spells or whatever the hell does it."

"Sure we do," Percy replied with a slow nod. "But an illusion doesn't do shit if every employer in the state gives a mandated blood test to every damn worker—the kind that identifies whether or not you have magic in that blood. Understand?"

Johnny leaned toward Lisa and muttered, "Do you know about anythin' like that?"

"It's the first I've heard of it."

"Huh." He studied Yarren carefully. "That don't sound like an appetizin' new bill to me, man. I'll give you that much. But comin' to the senator's house now and again to give him a little shakedown ain't the way to change lawmakin'."

"That's not what happened," the Kilomea protested.

"Don't you dare try to worm your way out of this." Hugh seethed helplessly. "All the evidence is stacked against you. The FBI sent this damn dwarf here to take you away and get you out of my hair. If you were innocent, they wouldn't have—"

"This damn dwarf said enough outta you, Senator." Johnny whistled, and Luther jumped into the man's lap again and this time, toppled him backward.

Hugh shrieked when his head and his twisted hands behind his back met the wood floor. "D-don't! Don't l-let that filthy animal touch me!"

"Who are you talking about, huh?" Luther hopped back and growled in the senator's face. "Me or one of these other guys? Either way, you'd be wrong."

"Yeah, we're hounds, dipshit!" Rex added with a bark, although he stayed between Johnny and the three magicals tied to their chairs around Hugh.

The dwarf gestured toward Yarren. "Keep talkin'."

"I went to his office first," the Kilomea continued. "I made an appointment and everything and brought the petition we'd made up with signatures from the guys at Canton Exports & Supplies and nine other companies up north. All of us are hard-labor workers, regular magicals simply trying to live our lives."

"We had a few thousand signatures too," the half-wizard added. "Once we got friends and neighbors to pitch in."

"The first thing Senator Hugh asked me when I stepped in his office was whether or not I belonged here." Yarren glared at the senator's feet dangling over the edge of the upturned chair. "Whether I was human. I'm not gonna lie about who I am to anyone and he turned me out for it without even getting to the petition at all."

Hugh growled indignantly. "It's not your place—"

"Shut up!" Johnny roared. He tossed his utility knife at the man's head, and the tip buried itself a quarter of an inch into the wood floor just shy of Hugh's right ear. "That ain't a miss, Senator. That's a warning."

The man's face drained of all color and he stared at the ceiling.

"So you came to blackmail this bigoted human thinkin' he'd kill the pay-cut bill?"

"No, man. The guy sent someone after my family." Yarren shook his head. "That's where I draw the line."

"How exactly?" Lisa asked.

"They caught my brother as he was coming off work. Two assholes in suits beat the living shit out of him and gave him a message for me—that Senator Hugh said to drop the petitions and stay the hell out of politics."

Percy shook his head and growled. "Fucker."

Johnny's eye twitched. "Is that it?"

"No. We found the guys who beat Maurice and followed 'em—me, Percy, and Evan. You might not think it, but Ev's pretty decent with a camera."

"Good enough. The newspapers will pay for a few shots, I bet," Evan added with a gruff nod.

"This asshole's goons beat seven different magicals to a pulp in the last three weeks," Yarren continued. "We have shots of 'em all and pics of his victims too—the ones who are trying to stand up for their right to be here like we are."

"Until we pounded those bastards' faces into the cement." Percy growled with satisfaction.

"Yeah. We finally got 'em." Yarren swallowed thickly. "And we came here to talk to this poor excuse for a leader in person and show him the pictures. We tried to tell him we know what was happening and would go to the press if he didn't do something about it."

"That piece of shit pulled a gun on us," Evan shouted. "We don't even have guns."

"He doesn't give a fuck about what happens to any of us,"

Percy added. "We came to make this peaceful, man. And he doesn't wanna listen."

"Senator?" Johnny turned slightly on the couch cushion to stare at the soles of the man's house shoes. "Now would be the time for you to say somethin'."

"You'll all be behind bars when I'm done with you!" Hugh spat the words with ugly virulence. "And I'll shoot these fucking dogs myself."

Luther cocked his head. "Okay, see, I still can't tell who you're talking about."

"I think I've heard everythin' I need to hear." Johnny stood from the couch and strode toward the senator's overturned chair. He squatted beside the man's head that glistened with beads of sweat and fixed him with a hard look. "You made your bed on this one, didn't ya?"

"I'm protecting the good people of Maryland from being taken advantage of. You Oriceran freaks have magic. What the hell do you need money for?"

The dwarf sniggered. "You'd hate to see my place back home." He grasped the back of Hugh's chair and hefted it upright again. The man yelped in surprise and the chair creaked beneath him. Johnny bent down to take hold of his utility knife and jerk it out of the floor.

"Oh! That's the best damn decision you've made since you got here," Hugh snapped. "Now get these goddamn ropes off me."

Johnny stepped toward Evan and sliced through the ropes binding the half-wizard to his chair. "Go on. Get up."

"For real?"

The bounty hunter cut Yarren and Percy free as well and nodded toward Lisa. "Y'all are gonna hand over your numbers to this good-lookin'…redhead over here."

She looked up at him with wide eyes. "They are?"

"You bet. In case we need to contact y'all in the future."

"Um…what?" Yarren stood slowly and the severed ropes

dropped around his body as he stared at Johnny. "You came here for me, didn't you?"

"Sure. But what I got was the truth. I see no reason to take y'all in as peaceful as y'all have been. Well, for the most part. And whoever has those photos needs to send 'em along when y'all finish exchangin' numbers, understand?"

"Yeah." The Kilomea glanced at his friends as they all moved slowly toward Lisa, frowned at each other in confusion, and rubbed their wrists. "I... Thanks, man. I don't know what else to say."

"You've said enough. Sorry y'all had to be tied up for anyone to hear it."

"I want all of you out of my house." Hugh snarled with barely suppressed rage. "This is a violation—"

"Y'all get in here and get a good shot of this magical-hater, huh?" Johnny pointed at the senator with his blade, then flicked the utility knife shut and returned it to his belt. "As close as you like. Maybe even get that pulsin' vein in his temple."

Without waiting for anyone else's permission, Cody stepped nimbly across the broken glass to zoom in on Senator Hugh. The man tried to jerk away from the camera but was held fast in his chair. "Let me out, dwarf!"

"Naw. You need some coolin'-off time to think about your choices." The bounty hunter stepped past the film crew and nodded once at Yarren and his buddies who shared their numbers with Lisa. "It's time to get on, boys."

"Aw, Johnny. Can't I at least bite a chunk out of him?" Luther snarled at Hugh, then darted out of Cody's way.

"What about his gun, Johnny?" Rex asked as he leapt onto the leather sectional and trotted down the length of it. "He wasn't using it the right way."

Johnny snapped his fingers and waved for his hounds to catch up without turning to look at them.

"Untie me this instant!" the senator bellowed. "This is why none of you deserve the same rights. You're monsters."

The dwarf snorted.

"You...you can't do this!"

"Watch me." He threw the knob-less front door open with a bang and stepped out onto the front porch.

CHAPTER THIRTEEN

After Lisa got all the information she needed from the magicals Johnny had deemed perfectly innocent, she joined him on the sidewalk beside their rental car. Yarren, Percy, and Evan hurried down the street toward their vehicle and glanced over their shoulders. The half-wizard raised a hesitant hand in thanks and farewell, and he nodded.

"Johnny."

"Lisa."

She turned toward him and folded her arms. "You took a federal case and flipped it completely on its head."

"Uh-huh."

"The Department will lose their shit when they see this report."

He glanced at her and sniffed disdainfully. "I'm the one callin' the shots, darlin'. I always have been and always will be."

"That's not the way they see it."

"I ain't worried 'bout how they see it. And I ain't workin' for the Department. I work for myself. I sure as shit didn't come out of retirement to be the Bureau's lapdog."

Lisa raised an eyebrow. "You won't get paid for a bounty you don't bring in either."

"If I did, it'd make me as bad as Senator Earthist in there."

Despite the odd turn of events, she couldn't hold back a laugh. "Earthist?"

"Well, it ain't entirely racist, is it? If he had his way, you and I would both be outta here with every other magical."

"Huh." She glanced at the front door of Hugh's house as the last of the film crew hurried down the long driveway and gathered beside their vans, waiting for the next adventure. "You could probably coin that phrase, you know."

"I don't want nothin' to do with it. But I do wanna take a look at those photos Yarren and his pals snapped of Hugh's muscle. Did you get those?"

"They told me I'd get an email later today. Is this something you want to take to the Department?"

"With recorded proof of their story and the senator makin' an even bigger ass of himself? Sure."

"Well, that little snippet of video has you letting three magicals—including the bounty you were sent after—go free while you left a senator tied up in his living room."

Johnny snorted and stepped around the front of the rental truck to open the driver's door. "Let 'em see, darlin'. I don't give a damn 'bout what the Department might make of it."

They both climbed into the cab and he looked in the rearview mirror at Rex and Luther sniffing the open bed.

"Besides, the whole damn Bureau owes me much more than lookin' the other way on this. I ain't opened my mouth about Dawn's murder and Operation Deadroot and the fact that they let me think her murderer was walkin' round free for fifteen years. They'll be gettin' a helluva bargain when we're done in Baltimore."

"Oh, yeah?" Lisa closed her door and buckled up.

"You bet. A two for one special. The Red Boar on a silver

platter and the video of Senator Asshole incriminatin' his own damn self. Maybe then they'll stop sendin' me bullshit cases with the wrong name fillin' in that blank line under *Bounty*."

"And that's all you want?"

He shrugged and started the engine. "After we're done here, I reckon I could ask for whatever I want simply to keep them thinkin' they have me in their pockets."

"Like what?"

"I dunno yet. I'll hafta think about it."

The back door to the cab opened and Howie's cane thunked onto the back seat. With a groan, the old man pulled himself into the cab and flopped down with a heavy sigh. "Well, wasn't that exciting?"

"It's been a while for you, huh?" Johnny smirked at him through the rearview mirror.

"Something like that. Listen, Johnny. I told that over-eager director that I'd get you to stick around and do another Q&A after you were done with this house."

"Why'd the hell you tell him that?"

"Well, mostly to get him to stay the hell out of your way."

"Huh." Johnny leaned toward his window and looked through the side mirror.

Phil stood in front of his van and saw the dwarf looking at him. He spread his arms. "It'll be quick!"

"But they didn't stay outside until we were done." He shrugged. "So you're off the hook with your promise. I think they have enough for a whole extra episode with what they caught inside just now. Close your door, Howie. We're gettin' outta here."

For a moment, the old man looked as if he couldn't put two and two together. Then, he shrugged. "Yeah. Yeah, I guess that works."

His door clicked shut and he strapped himself in.

"So should we tell them where we're going?" Lisa asked.

"Naw. They'll get the hint."

"Do you know where we're going?"

He smirked at her, then took his black sunglasses from the center console and put them on. "We have the whole rest of the day to kill, darlin'. Is there any chance you made a list?"

She laughed. "Tell me you're not serious."

"Maybe."

They left their rentals at the hotel and walked through Baltimore city with the film crew tagging along behind Johnny, "Stephanie," and the hounds. Howie made sure to keep the crew no less than ten feet away, but even the old man who used to run *Dwarf the Bounty Hunter* back in the day wasn't fully prepared for the one week in August that couldn't have been much stranger.

"Oh, my God!" A woman shouted from the corner of the street on South Sharp Street. "Is that the bounty hunter?"

Johnny tried to ignore the shouts, gawking, and pointing, but when they reached the Baltimore Convention Center, he could no longer restrain himself. "What the hell is goin' on here?"

Lisa responded with an uncertain chuckle and scratched her head. "I honestly have no idea."

"Johnny. Hey, Johnny." Luther stepped closer to his master and lowered his head, his ears and tail pressed down flat. "Are those horses walking on two legs?"

"I've never seen horses like that, Johnny." Rex barked twice. "I think they can talk."

"Look! Look—I knew it!" A man wearing a black costume with a horse head, rainbow-colored hooves, a tail, and fluttering sheer wings pranced toward them. "Guys, come on. Look who it is!"

"What the fuck is this?" the dwarf muttered.

From outside the convention center, a whole swarm of people followed the black-horse down the sidewalk toward the bounty hunter and his hounds. "Oh, my God. You're Johnny Walker, right?"

"I heard your show was coming back. It's for real! Are you filming in Baltimore?"

"Of course they are. Look at all the cameras."

"Excuse me. Excuse me." A woman dressed in a shimmering white sequined jumpsuit and a wig of purple curls shoved through the crowd closing in on the dwarf. Her eyes were plastered with blue makeup and glitter, and she brushed the wig over her shoulder and threw her head back to reveal a white unicorn horn in the middle of her forehead to round the ensemble off. "Johnny?"

He studied her for a moment with a confused scowl. His gaze lingered on the extremely low cut of the white-sequined jumpsuit that almost exposed her whole chest. "Who's asking?"

The woman tossed her purple hair again and grinned. "I'm Rarity."

"That's not your real name," another horse weirdo shouted.

"It's close enough, okay?" The woman stepped toward the dwarf with her hands clasped in front of her chest, batted her lashes, and somehow widened her eyes at the same time. "I've been a huge fan ever since I was a little girl."

The bounty hunter raised an eyebrow and muttered, "Are you sure you still ain't?"

A high-pitched giggle escaped her. "Oh, my gosh. It would make me so happy to get your autograph. Can I? Please? *Please?*"

"I don't do autographs, darlin'. Sorry."

"Well, maybe you should start." The woman pressed closer. "You brought the show back, right? Maybe now's a good time to change things up a little."

"Johnny…" Luther crouched lower at his master's side. "They don't smell like horses but they're closing in."

Lisa forced a laugh back as the people of Baltimore in outrageous horse cosplay formed a huge crowd around the bounty hunter. "It's all on camera, Johnny," she muttered. "Part of a good distraction, right?"

He grunted. *The Red Boar's gonna see me signin' autographs for a buncha crazies. Sure. That'll draw him out.*

Shaking his head, Johnny sighed heavily. "Just the one then."

"Yes! Oh, my God. Thank you!" The woman screeched in delight and bounced up and down in her shiny purple heels.

Rex cocked his head and stared up at her. "Johnny, that lady's gonna fall out of her suit."

"It's a lady?" Luther whined.

"Got a pen or somethin'?"

Lisa shook her head.

"Oh, no, no." The purple-haired woman reached into her dangerously low-cut jumpsuit and pulled out a purple marker. "I always have something on me."

"Is that right?" Johnny cleared his throat and took the marker from her. "Glitter?"

"It's the only way to go." She winked at him, then turned and bent slightly forward and pointed at the small of her back just above the tail of purple hair sprouting from her suit. "Right here, please."

Lisa rolled her eyes and chuckled. "Wow."

"How about a better—"

"No, that's exactly where I want your name." The woman looked over her shoulder at him and grinned. "Forever."

Holy shit. With wide eyes, Johnny scribbled a sloppy signature quickly that didn't look anything like what he used for official documents, then thrust the marker at the woman and raised both hands in surrender. "There. Done. Now go back to...whatever you were doin'."

"You're amazing!" The woman spun and dropped a heavy kiss on the dwarf's cheek. "This is the best thing that's ever happened to me!"

She pranced through the crowd, practically skipping in her purple heels.

"Dammit." Johnny scowled at the horse-costumed people

around him—the brightly colored wigs, the fake hooves, the face paint in rainbows and stars, stripes, moons, and hearts. The next woman who shoved toward him had added a cowboy hat to her ensemble.

"Sign my hat?" She crouched on all fours in front of him and whinnied.

"What're you doin'?"

"Please?"

"Johnny…" Lisa pressed her lips together and pointed at the huge banner hanging over the front doors of the convention center.

He looked at it intently for a moment and scowled. "What the fuck is BronyCon?"

The woman with the cowboy hat handed him a sharpie as she stood, then removed her hat and handed that over too. "My Little Pony." She grinned. "You have no idea what this is, do you?"

"No, and I ain't fixin' to find out." He snatched the hat and marker from her, scribbled, and shoved them back. "That's it. No more."

"Friendship is magic." She flashed him a peace sign, put her hat on, and skipped through the crowd, squealing in delight.

"No." Johnny pushed through the first row of people in front of him who chattered loudly amongst themselves and asked for autographs. "We're out. To me, boys."

"But Johnny…" Rex panted heavily and stared at the horse-dressed people towering over him as they cooed and scratched behind his ears and along his back. "They like hounds. Oh, yeah. Scratch right there—yeah, yeah, yeah."

Luther turned in a tight circle, his eyes wide, and barked at a man with his face painted black with yellow stars. "Johnny, I want out. Hey, back up, horse. Guy. Whatever."

The dwarf responded with a piercing whistle, and both hounds extracted themselves instantly from their quirky fans.

Lisa wove through the cosplayers to catch up with him. "So what do you think?"

"Right now, darlin', my mind's been wiped blank." He snorted and shook his head. "I don't get it."

"Is this weirder than Portland?"

"Don't you try to turn this around. I ain't goin' back to that damn city. And we're avoidin' the convention center like a plague."

She laughed and glanced over her shoulder at the crowd of people who stared after them and pointed. The film crew moved around the pedestrians to hurry after the bounty hunter. "Well, on the bright side, *Dwarf the Bounty Hunter* has one of the most eclectic fan bases I've ever seen."

"Those ain't fans. Those are crazy people."

"You think so?" They turned the corner toward McKeldin Fountain, and Lisa regarded him speculatively. "Let me guess. You don't even dress up on Halloween."

He sniffed and glanced at the sculpture that looked like a hunk of giant rocks stuck together on their left. "That's months away and we ain't talkin' 'bout it."

CHAPTER FOURTEEN

They took a brief trip to see Oriole Park at Camden Yards, then paid a visit to the Maryland Science Center and the Gallery at Harborplace. Wherever Johnny Walker showed his face, the fans came out of the woodwork.

"I can't believe it. He's back!"

"I told you he wasn't dead, Maggie. He only wanted to get out of the spotlight for a while."

"Oh, my God. They've been putting videos up for two days, and he's still out here filming?"

"This is even better than the last season. He has dogs with him!"

"And a sexy sidekick too."

"Hey." Johnny pointed at the man and cocked his head. "Watch your mouth."

Lisa laughed as they headed down East Cromwell Street after a walk along the water in Riverside Park. "So you're trying to defend Stephanie's honor now too, huh?"

"What?" He scoffed. "Just because you're showin' up on everyone's damn smartass devices don't give folks the right to say whatever they want to your face."

"It's not my face, though, Johnny."

"Huh. You're still in there."

The crowds thinned by necessity when Howie began to swing his cane from side to side and spouted warnings about interference with the filming. "Do you want to be sued for this? No? Then back the hell up, buddy. Johnny has work to do!"

"Okay, now I get why you wanted the old guy around." Lisa chuckled. "Was he your bodyguard too back in the day?"

The dwarf ran a hand through his hair and grimaced. "I don't need a bodyguard, darlin'. That's crowd control."

"But he has a cane this time."

The aforementioned cane whacked on the sidewalk behind them. "Move along, people! You'll see it all when the episode airs. Get back!"

"Yep." Johnny glanced at the row of marquees stretched across the restaurants in front of them. "And he can handle it. Are you hungry?"

She. "Are you?"

"I could eat. It would take my mind off all the crazies tryin' to run me down to sign their babies."

"That might be taking it a little too far. No one's offered their baby today."

"Naw, I'm talkin' about Season Four."

"What?"

Luther and Rex turned to face away from Johnny and growled at anyone who tried to approach them or even pass them on the sidewalk.

"You know what this is like, Johnny?" Rex wagged his tail and barked when a woman walking her golden retriever passed on the other side of the street. "Hey, how's it goin'? Johnny, this is like going to the dog park when someone brought their bitch in heat."

Luther uttered a low whine. "Yeah, Johnny. And you're the bitch."

The dwarf snorted and glanced at the smaller hound facing away from him. "Have you got that outta your system?"

"I wanna get this city outta my system, Johnny."

Lisa folded her arms. "Are they doing okay with all this attention?"

"Totally," Rex replied. "We can handle anything."

Luther yipped. "Not okay, lady. Johnny, let's go back to the hotel."

The dwarf studied the menu within the clear case hung on the outer wall of Rye Street Tavern and shrugged. "Comfort food. Exactly what we need if you're ready for dinner."

Lisa scanned the sign over the restaurant's front door, then peered through the closest window. "This looks nice."

"I think it is."

Turning slowly toward him, she inclined her head. "Is that how you ask every redhead out on a date?"

"I ain't askin' a redhead darlin'. Not a real one, anyway."

Her eyes widened over a cautious smile. "So you're asking me on a date."

He chuckled and opened the door for her. "Are you hungry or what?"

Laughing, she stepped inside the restaurant and the hounds trotted through the door before Johnny joined them.

Luther chuckled. "You didn't say no, Johnny."

"Uh-oh." Rex sniffed at the floor. "Johnny, we know we're the best hounds and everything, but you didn't have to ask us on a date too."

"I didn't," the bounty hunter grumbled.

Thinking more about the hounds and less about public access, Johnny asked for a table on the back patio, which was strung overhead with soft white lights as sunset cast an orange glow over Baltimore. Two other tables had customers, but they were far enough apart that he could finally get some air.

"Finally. Quiet."

Rex and Luther sniffed around in the green lawn behind the patio, their tails sticking straight up in the air. "Sure is nice, Johnny."

"Yeah. Where'd all the people go?"

The dwarf leaned back in his chair and sighed. *Well, it would be quiet without them hounds goin' on. Still, I'll take those two over those damn pony folks any day.*

Lisa sipped her water. "I'm surprised a place like this has your one and only drink."

"What are you tryin' to say?"

"Only that this seems a little more…upscale."

Johnny grunted. "Just 'cause it ain't expensive don't mean it ain't quality."

"Hey, I'm not here to judge. I'm merely surprised."

Their server returned with their drinks on a tray and set Lisa's gin cocktail down first. "Gin Campari Sour for the lady. And your Johnny Walker Black, sir."

"I appreciate it." He glanced at his usual four fingers of whiskey in the rocks glass and nodded. "There's more where that came from, right?"

"Yes. Your manager made it perfectly clear we were to reserve the entire bottle." The server grinned and cleared his throat. "And can I say, Mr. Walker—"

"Johnny."

"Right. Can I just say what an honor it is to serve you tonight?"

He lifted his drink to his lips. "Go ahead."

"I grew up watching your show, and after I heard you were coming back for one more season, I finally got my wife to sit down with me and start watching *Dwarf the Bounty Hunter* all over again. We're almost through Season Two."

The dwarf frowned at him. "When did you start?"

"Oh, Monday night." The man smiled a sheepish smile. "The

perks of streaming old favorites for binge-watching at home, right?"

"Uh-huh."

"She already loves it."

"Good for her."

As Johnny sipped his whiskey, Lisa and the server exchanged an awkward glance. "All right. Well, you heard tonight's specials, so I'll give you two another minute to look at the menu."

"Thank you." She nodded and forced herself not to laugh when he retreated into the restaurant again and glanced over his shoulder in awe at the bounty hunter seated in his section. With a smirk, she leaned forward over the table. "Your manager?"

Johnny set down his glass with a contented sigh. "Sure. Howie wears any number of hats."

"I thought he was your old director."

"Yep. And crowd control. PR. Manager." He pointed at her. "That fella can do more than a crew three times the size of what Nelson thought he was so smart hirin' for this. Asshole."

Lisa removed the sprig of rosemary from her glass and took a sip. "And curator of Johnny Walker's one and only drink."

He raised his glass. "Howie knows what he's doin' and I ain't gotta ask."

She leaned back in her seat and smirked as she nursed her cocktail.

"What?"

"What?"

Johnny raised an eyebrow. "You're lookin' at me funny, darlin'. Even when you're a redhead with green eyes and freckles, I know that face."

Lisa laughed. "You do?"

"You bet. It means those wheels up there are turnin' and you ain't decided whether or not to let it out. So go ahead. Spill."

"Okay. I think all this…" She gestured around them at the city of Baltimore in general. "Being here with a film crew, seeing your fans, having your manager back to make sure whatever restaurant you go to has a bottle waiting for you—"

"You're playin' it up, darlin'." He sipped his whiskey again.

"I think you like it."

"Huh."

Lisa leaned forward, propped both elbows on the table, and rested her chin on the backs of her hands. "I think you're back in your element, and you simply don't want to admit it."

"Naw. My element is out on the swamp in my airboat with a rifle in my hands."

"Sure. But there's no rule against belonging in more than one place."

Johnny looked at her in surprise and snorted. "Are you tryin' to use all that head-shrinker crap on me again?"

"No, Johnny." She grinned. "I'm merely calling it like I see it. And sure, I'm playing the reformed convict Stephanie Wyndom through the whole thing, but I'm still glad I'm here to see it."

"Huh." He looked out across the back patio to where Rex and Luther stood with their snouts pressed against the grass. "I guess I could say the same."

"The perks of having a partner who gets it, right?"

"You're seriously pushin' this partner business, ain'tcha?"

Lisa shrugged. "Well, you haven't tried to correct me lately. I'm simply making sure it's real."

"Well, you can't go waltzin' around as Stephanie callin' yourself my partner."

"Oh, I know."

Their server returned to take their orders. Lisa chose the grilled shrimp scampi, and Johnny went with two plates of pork chops for the hounds, the Maryland rockfish with shrimp and grits for himself, plus an order of a dozen oysters on the half-shell to start. When he ordered the latter, Lisa leaned back in her chair with wide eyes. "And another whiskey when you can."

"Absolutely." The man left to put the order in, and he shook his head. "You're lookin' at me like I ordered baby seal. They're oysters."

She smirked. "You know what oysters are known for, right?"

If the word aphrodisiac comes outta her mouth, I'm done. "Sure." He downed the rest of his whiskey. "Bein' delicious, same as them shrimp and grits. If a restaurant up here can pull off that kinda southern cookin' the right way, I aim to stop by a time or two."

"Oh, yeah? You'd come to Baltimore merely for the shrimp?"

"It ain't my first time in Charm City, darlin'." He grimaced as he looked out over the city skyline beneath the sunset. "But fuck comin' back in August. If I never see another Yankee done up like a damn horse, it'll be too soon."

She chuckled and shifted a little in her chair. "BronyCon. I had no idea that existed."

"It shouldn't." He raised his glass toward her. "To skippin' over what gives ya nightmares."

Lisa startled and stared at his raised glass.

"Darlin', not joinin' a toast is worse than leavin' a fella hangin' for a high-five."

"You've never given me a high-five."

"It's only a comparison. Come on."

She clinked her cocktail glass against his, then tipped it back for a long drink.

"Whoa, now." Johnny chuckled. "If I didn't know better, I'd say you're havin' second thoughts about this dinner."

"What? No, of course not."

"Then what's all that about?"

Lisa took a deep breath and set down her drink gently. "Are you trying to hit me with all the head-shrinking business now?"

"I'm sure I'd do a piss-poor job of it." His smile faded, and he set his drink down too. "But you look like you got somethin' on your chest. And I got ears, so…"

"Nightmares."

"Say again?"

Her mouth twitched into a tight smile. "That's what you said. 'To things that don't give you nightmares,' right? It...caught me off guard."

"Huh. Look, I ain't sayin' I know you inside-out, darlin', but I wouldn't've pegged you for the kind to start feelin' down for a *lack* of bad dreams."

"Nope." Lisa stared at the table, then met his gaze. "It's the opposite, unfortunately."

"Oh." Johnny tugged his beard and narrowed his eyes. "From Portland?"

"Yeah. Honestly, I got more sleep the first night here than I could pull together over the last two weeks. And I guess it was easy to forget I'd been kept up at night by...different things."

"And I brought it up again like an asshole." He gestured apologetically and leaned back in his chair. "I didn't mean nothin' by it."

"I know you didn't. I'm fine."

"You look as pale as a ghost, darlin'." Johnny snorted. "Granted, I reckon most of it's just that illusion—"

"Very funny."

"Do you wanna talk about it?"

"Not really." Lisa picked her drink up again and forced an easier smile onto her lips. "It's simply another reason I'm glad to be here—along with not taking in paid bounties and running around Baltimore as the 'sexy sidekick' in a show no one thought they'd ever see again."

He laughed and slapped a hand on the table. "It wasn't my first plan."

"No, the show was my plan."

"Yeah, all right. Give yourself a pat on the back for that one. But I tell you what, darlin'. I reckon havin' a better-lookin' face than my ugly mug up on folks' screens all the time has a helluva lot more to do with them crowds today."

"Wow. You're laying it on thick."

"Next time, we'll have to bring on Agent Lisa Breyer as a permanent replacement."

She grinned at him. "And watch your ratings plummet."

"I don't give a damn about all that. I'd rather see you rollin' around with me instead of Stephanie, is all."

CHAPTER FIFTEEN

Their server brought out the oysters and Johnny's second drink, which drew the hounds from the back lawn to sniff around the table.

"Johnny, you got oysters?" Rex licked a small drop of lemon juice on the patio. "Get any extra for some hounds?"

"No way, bro." Luther backed away from the table and sat, staring at the plate of shells. "You gotta be careful with those, Johnny. Remember that time we helped Ronnie haul in a bushel and I ate some?"

Rex tittered. "Oh, yeah. The Wood Elf said he'd shoot you himself if you didn't stop humping his leg."

"It hurt."

"Your feelings?"

Luther crouched and uttered a low whine. "No…"

When their dinner arrived with Lisa's second drink and Johnny's third, they were both laughing at a story from one of *Dwarf the Bounty Hunter's* last few episodes.

"I caught him right here under the arm." Johnny poked his armpit. "And he skipped along after that speedboat like he forgot the damn water skis. I took him to the pier like that and hauled him right in."

She wiped a tear from the corner of her eye and shook her head. "That's insane."

"Naw, darlin'. It's only the show."

He set the two plates of pork chops on the patio and whistled. Both hounds raced toward him from the far side of the lawn.

"Hey, Johnny! I think there's—ooh. What is this?"

"It's like bacon, bro." Rex sniffed his plate before tearing into his meal. "Very weird-shaped bacon. Keep talking, though."

"Wait, what was I saying?"

"I don't know, but this is delicious!"

With a chuckle, Lisa picked her fork up and studied her dinner. "I'm surprised by how easy it was to get that out of you."

"Get what out?" Johnny shoved a spoonful of grits into his mouth and closed his eyes. "Damn. They got this right."

"That story." She looked at him with a coy smile, her fork poised over her shrimp. "I thought I would have to pry any of it out of you."

"Well, you already looked through my record with the Department."

"Yeah, but those were federal cases. I had no idea about all the extra jobs you took on the side."

"It's a good thing those ain't in my Bureau file." He snorted and tossed a whole shrimp into his mouth, tail and all. "It makes a different kinda record for all the rest, but it's hard to believe those damn episodes are still floatin' around out there."

"Part of me wants to go through and watch them."

"Oh, sure. Invite our waiter and his wife over while you're at it. Y'all can have a big time of it."

She laughed and took the first mouthful of her pasta. "Oh, wow. This is incredible."

"Good." Johnny smirked at her and held his water glass down by his chair for the dogs.

Rex looked up first and licked his muzzle. "Thanks, Johnny."

"Hey, don't drink it all," Luther muttered. "You're not the only hound on the patio."

"Still, it ain't nothin' like the grub Darlene makes back home or the kinda eatin' I can find just down the street on any given day."

"You don't think this is better?" Lisa asked.

"Naw, I ain't sayin' that. It's not better, but there is somethin' to be said for a new take on a good thing."

"So you're enjoying yourself."

"I might be." He drained the last of his second whiskey, picked up the third, and brought it to his mouth. "Are you?"

The small smile playing on her lips made him narrow his eyes. "Are you asking as the bounty hunter, Johnny? Or as the guy who asked me out to dinner?"

He cleared his throat. "Well, there ain't two of me, darlin'."

"Yes, and both worlds are better because of it."

"Aw, now come on." Johnny chuckled and leaned toward her. "You tryin' to tell me you wouldn't be happy to see two of me?"

"No, one is more than enough." Lisa stared at him as she sipped at her cocktail. "Honestly, I like only the one."

"Uh-huh." *Shit. If it ain't the whiskey, it's the goddamn oysters. What the hell am I gettin' myself into?* "Well, I'll tell you what, darlin'. Beneath that redheaded exterior of yours—"

She laughed and batted her eyes.

"—is a woman I'd be proud to call my partner."

Lisa blinked in surprise. "That sounds conditional, though."

"Naw, only me thinkin' out loud." *You can stop talkin' anytime, Johnny. The last thing you need is to get tangled up even more in this. Right?*

"Well, I'm glad that's what you can see under this mask." Chuckling, she gestured at her Stephanie face.

"There's more. Ain't just Agent Breyer I see, neither."

"Oh, really?"

"Um...Johnny?" Luther turned around to sniff the air behind his master. "Maybe you should—"

The dwarf snapped his fingers and kept staring at Lisa.

"But seriously, Johnny," Rex added. "You're not gonna—"

"Hush." Johnny grabbed his rocks glass and held it on the table. "Bein' an agent is what you do, darlin'. It ain't who you are."

"And you think you know who I am already, is that it?" She smiled, her eyes a little glassy after almost two tall cocktails.

"Sure. Under all the rest of it, I see—" A flicker of movement reflected in the window beside their table caught his attention. "Those bastards."

Her smile disappeared. "Excuse me?"

Johnny's chair scraped loudly as he pushed it away and stood to whirl around. Cody was zeroing in on them with the camera and the man with the boom followed closely behind and tried to get a good angle with the mic.

"Oh, jeez." Lisa sighed.

"Tried to tell you, Johnny," Luther muttered.

"You just couldn't hear past the goo-goo eyes, could you?" Rex added.

"Private dinner, assholes." Johnny pointed at the camera. "Get lost."

Phil popped his head up from behind a bush on the other side of the back lawn. "These are the kind of moments we need to see too, Johnny."

"No, they ain't. Y'all weren't invited."

"We don't have to be," Phil continued as he walked around the bush. "We're getting shots of your life. And viewers are going to love seeing Johnny Walker on a date with the beautiful Stephanie—"

The dwarf grabbed his half-full water glass and chucked it at the guy. Phil dodged it with a yelp, and the glass shattered and sprayed all over the patio.

"Johnny, please," Lisa protested.

"Get lost, dipshit." He snarled, snatched his utility knife from his belt, and flicked it open.

"Johnny!" Howie hobbled down the sidewalk at the side of the building. "Fuck. They told me they went back to the hotel."

"I don't care where they go, but they need to get outta here real fast before there's a permanent director position for you to fill, Howie."

"I know, I know." The old man leaned against the wall of the restaurant to catch his breath. "Phil, get the hell back here—"

"Are you threatening me with a knife, Johnny?" Phil's hands raised despite the fact that he was trying to play it brave.

The dwarf glanced at the camera still rolling while Cody stepped lightly toward him. "Last warning."

"That's good, that's good." Phil nodded furiously. "Get some of that anger—"

The bounty hunter kicked one of the hounds' plates off the patio and it thunked into Cody's shins.

"Aw, shit, man!" The cameraman lowered his gear to glance at his legs. "What the hell?"

"Yeah, Johnny, what gives?" Luther sniffed around the patio where his missing plate used to be. "I wasn't finished with that."

"Get out!"

Their server darted out of the restaurant and onto the patio. "Is…is there a problem here, Mr. Walker?"

"There will be if these dumb shits don't get out."

"I'm sorry, guys. Patio seating is for paying customers only."

"We're with Johnny!" Phil shouted.

"No, they ain't."

The man nodded. "Then I'm going to have to ask you and your…friends to leave."

"We got it, we got it," Howie muttered, waving the man away, and his cane clicked on the paving as he hurried toward Phil. "And this scheming idiot's about to get the fun side of my cane if he doesn't do what I say."

The director glanced from Johnny to the old man and clapped his hands. "That's a wrap, people. It's time to go."

"Yeah, and ice my damn shins." Cody rubbed his leg and grimaced at the dwarf. "We're only doing our jobs, man."

"Move."

Howie pulled the cameraman away with him and nodded at Johnny to assure him that everything was taken care of.

Rex and Luther stalked after the retreating film crew and continued to utter low growls until the party crashers disappeared around the corner. Luther stopped at the shattered plate on the patio and sniffed. "Oh, look. Leftover mashed potatoes."

The bounty hunter stalked to his chair and slumped into it. His elbows thumped onto the table, making silverware clatter and drinks slosh in their glasses. Without a word, he snatched his spoon up and shoveled the rest of his grits into his mouth.

Lisa stared at him. "Are you okay?"

"I'm eatin'."

"Is there anything else I can get for you?" the server asked.

"To-go boxes and the check, pal. That's it."

"Johnny, we don't have to leave—"

"Well, I ain't stayin' here." He downed the rest of his whiskey and growled. *That's the closest I got to sayin' somethin' real, and those fuckers had to come in and ruin the whole thing.*

"I'll be right back with those." The server nodded and hurried inside.

When they got their check and the boxes, Johnny added the leftovers furiously to the containers, eating pieces here and there as he did so.

"Truly," Lisa said in an attempt to diffuse the suddenly tense situation. "It's okay."

"No, it ain't, darlin'." A huge chunk of rockfish went into his mouth. "Now the whole world's gonna see me and Stephanie Wyndom sittin' at a fancy spot laughin' it up and gettin' cozy."

"What's wrong with that?"

He pulled his wallet out and placed enough hundred-dollar bills on the table to cover the tab and leave a thirty-percent tip. Then he smacked his hand down on the surface, picked up the to-go boxes, and stood. "'Cause it ain't no one else's damn business and it ain't you."

The bounty hunter stalked around the corner, and the hounds whipped their heads up from more sniffing to follow him.

Lisa sat in her chair for a moment longer and frowned in surprise as she drained the rest of her cocktail. *I wonder if he even knows what he said.*

CHAPTER SIXTEEN

They reached Johnny's huge hotel suite without being badgered by the film crew again. He slumped in the high-backed armchair built for a giant and stared at the area rug beneath the coffee table.

Lisa looked at him from her place on the couch and raised an eyebrow. "Will you be pissed off about one filmed dinner all night?"

"If it suits me, sure."

"Hey, Johnny." Luther stared at his master from the edge of the kitchen and took slow, cautious steps toward the counter beside the fridge. "Johnny..."

"I don't think he can hear us, bro."

"Well, make sure."

"Johnny!" Rex barked. "Anyone home?"

The dwarf rubbed his mouth and continued to stare at the rug.

"He's totally gone. Hurry."

Luther leapt up and put his front paws onto the counter beside the to-go boxes Johnny had neglected to put in the fridge.

He darted a wary glance over his shoulder at his master, then buffeted both boxes onto the floor with his snout.

"Yes," Rex whispered.

"Victory! We—ow. Quit nipping me."

"Then quit shouting or you'll break him out of his pissed-off concentration."

Luther sniggered. "Probably thinking of all the ways he could blow up that guy with the crazy hair."

"Howie?"

"No, the other one. Hey, look. Shrimp!"

"Shh!"

Lisa turned to look into the kitchen, but the corner of the hallway blocked the conniving hounds from view. *If Johnny's not stopping them, I won't say anything.* She took her laptop from the couch cushion beside her and opened it on her thighs. "Well, how about something else to take your mind off it, huh?"

"I ain't watchin' more IdiotTube videos."

She snorted. "No, I was talking about next steps with this dark-web Johnny-hater meeting. But feel free to sit there and sulk."

He looked at her with wide eyes and finally heard the barely contained snuffling and chewing coming from the kitchen. "Boys?"

"Uh…yeah, Johnny."

"Shit. Stop for a sec. What're y'all up to?"

Rex trotted into view and his claws clicked on the kitchen's tiled floors. When he met Johnny's gaze, he licked his muzzle and stared. "Hanging out. Grabbing a drink. You know, the usual."

Luther's head-butted the cabinet as he licked the destroyed pieces of to-go boxes across the floor. "Ow."

"That don't sound like water," Johnny muttered.

Rex sniggered. "Does it surprise you that he can't find the water bowl, Johnny?"

Luther smacked his head against the cabinet again when he looked up to stare at his brother. "Hey—"

Rex whipped his head toward the far end of the kitchen. "Wait. Luther. Did you hear that?"

"What?"

"I think it's a mouse. In the cabinet." The larger hound darted out of his master's view to pounce on the to-go boxes.

"Ha-ha. Who's dumb now? I already checked that one, Rex. There's no mouse—"

"The other cabinet," Rex snarled.

"Oh, right… Yeah, get it."

"Johnny?" Lisa leaned sideways to try to catch his attention. "I'm about to make another big move, so if you want to see what's happening here—"

"Yeah." He pushed out of the armchair with a grunt and stepped slowly across the living area and frowned at the entrance to the kitchen. "Did you see those hounds get up to somethin'?"

She logged into her laptop and shook her head. "I've been watching you the whole time."

"I like her, Johnny."

"Shh. Focus."

With a shrug, Johnny sank onto the couch beside her and glanced at the laptop screen. "Next big move, huh?"

"For us, at least. Honestly, this is my first time *interacting* on the dark web instead of…you know. Poking around."

He looked curiously at her. "For what?"

"Well, we can start with the time I entered a dark-web auction and bid for a twelve-year-old girl with your money."

"But that wasn't the first time."

"No. I did some digging for the Department a time or two before they assigned me to Amanda's case with you." She stopped typing and looked up at him staring at her. "Okay, fine. Twenty-one cases where dark-web scouring was a priority."

"I didn't say a thing."

"Yeah well, you didn't have to. Stop looking at me like that." Lisa pursed her lips to hide a smirk as she pulled up her VPN and dove into the dark web. Then she retrieved her phone and brought up the picture of the anonymous Johnny-haters private invitation.

The dwarf grumbled and shook his head. "You can't simply do all that with one damn piece of equipment?"

"What?"

"What's your phone gonna do?"

She turned the device to show him. "This is the link to upload some perfectly legit fake documents."

"Huh."

Lisa typed the hyperlink into the URL bar that displayed .onion domains and pressed the Enter key. Another horizontal flash of white light darted across her screen a second before the link's direct page came up.

"Is that somethin' you should worry about?" Johnny asked and wagged his finger across the screen. "That little flash?"

"Honestly, I have no idea." She shrugged. "But I don't keep my laptop synced to my tablet or phone. So if someone thinks it'll be fun to hack into my system, they'll find nothing but my book-marked websites and a few random poems."

"Say what now?"

She waved him off. "It's only me playing around. It's nothing."

"Stuff hypothetical hackers would see and run away from?"

"Very funny."

"I thought you had a handle on keepin' folks outta your... systems anyhow." Johnny glanced at the photo of the private message on her phone. "Don'tcha?"

"Well, I know enough to be fairly certain I'm about eighty-five percent safe. I think." Lisa paused to look at him. "But I'm not a pro, Johnny. Yeah, technically I've done this and gotten paid for it, but it's not—"

"Slow down, darlin'." He chuckled. "I get the gist."

"Right."

"Now, how come you're only doin' this now?" He nodded at the screen. "I thought you had the whole thing set up and ready to go."

"Yeah, I could have. But I didn't want to seem desperate by putting all this up immediately."

"Uh-huh. Tryin' to fit in with the cool thugs, huh?"

"Yes, Johnny. My greatest ambition in life is to make criminals you put behind bars like me." With a chuckle, she read through the list of information the private criminal-screening invitation wanted from her and sighed. "Here we go."

Name: Stephanie Wyndom
Age: 47
Height: 5'11"
Weight: 127 lbs
Gender: Female
Race: Half-Light Elf
Hair Color: Strawberry-blonde

"Naw, darlin', don't put that in there."

"What? Why?"

"Come on? Who says that about their own damn hair, huh? That'd be like writing your age in as, 'I'm forty-seven a half, but all my friends tell me I don't look a day over thirty-five.'"

She elbowed him in the ribs. "I do not sound like that."

"Sure. I was imitatin' Stephanie." He gave her a crooked smile. "There ain't no way you're forty-seven."

"I'll overlook that potentially unintended insult and tell you that none of the things I'm putting in here are real. How's that?"

"Not all of it…"

She laughed. "Wow. I made a mistake in asking you to come watch."

"All right, all right. I'll shut it." Johnny stood and went to the round side table beside the huge armchair for the whiskey he'd poured as soon as they got back to the hotel.

Squinting at him, Lisa changed her last entry and moved on.

Hair Color: Red

Eye Color: Green

Identifying Marks: None

Birthplace:

"Huh." She picked her phone up and signed into the secure server for the Department's shared files to open the case documents with her fake identity detailed in one place.

"What's wrong?"

"Nothing. I had to remember where Stephanie was born."

He moved closer to her again and snorted. "That's one of those things most folks don't forget. Are you sure you're ready to head out and meet these bastards tomorrow night?"

"Johnny, it's one detail. One. Now I know I was born in Milwaukee, Wisconsin, and I won't forget it."

"No wonder you turned to a life of booze and crime."

Lisa rolled her eyes and kept going.

Birthplace: Milwaukee, Wisconsin

Most Recent Arrest: 2015

Reason for Requesting Access:

She paused at the last one. "I need to make this good."

"You already know what they wanna hear, darlin'. Go ahead."

"Well, give me a minute, okay? It has to look real."

The dwarf nudged her shoulder lightly with the back of his hand. "Why don't you answer it with a poem?"

"Stop."

Reason for Requesting Access: I want to see that fucking dwarf draw his last breath.

"Well, shit." He rumbled a deep laugh that drew a smile from her. "Tell 'em how you truly feel."

"No, I'm telling them how they feel. Is it too much?"

"I ain't gonna make you change it.'

"Great. That's everything but the picture. So…" Lisa picked up her phone again and dove into the FBI-manufactured documents of Stephanie's nonexistent life to pull up the doctored mugshot. "That'll work."

"You're gonna send 'em your mugshot from the day I never took you in?"

"Well, it's not like we had the time for a photo shoot." She paused to study the fake image of Stephanie in an orange felon uniform, her light-red hair mussed and sticking out in all directions. "It looks like the real deal to me."

"Sure. But the picture's on your damn phone."

Lisa turned toward him with wide eyes. "Honestly? Oh, you're serious about that."

"What?"

"Johnny, how do you stay in touch with the rest of the world on a regular basis?"

"I don't." The dwarf shrugged and took another sip. "No TV and no FacePage or Tweetie or whatever the hell."

"Oh, jeez." She closed her eyes and forced back a laugh. "Please tell me you at least know what email is."

"'Course I do. But why the hell would anyone email me?"

"Oh, I don't know. Maybe to send an image file from their phone to your computer, for instance." Which was exactly what she did with Stephanie Wyndom's mugshot. "If you don't know how any of this stuff works, why do you have a smartphone?"

"My last phone went overboard durin' a hunt. The guy at the phone store pulled one over on me when he said he could put all my saved numbers into the new one."

"It's called the—you know what? Never mind."

"Sure." He frowned at her and kept drinking.

Lisa dragged the photo from her email and dropped it into the upload box on the private chat. "And that's the end of it. Let's see if good ol' Stephanie stands up to the test."

She clicked the send link, and the web page went completely blank.

"Is that it?"

149

"I guess so. I have no idea what comes next, so we'll simply roll with it." Lisa clicked around through the pathways she'd taken four days before and made her way easily to the site she wanted: *Dwarf the Bounty Hunter: The Official Site – Your One-Stop Shop for All Things Johnny Walker, Bounty Hunting, and the Best Oriceran-Hosted Show on Earth!*

"Aw, not this again." Johnny leaned back on the couch with a grunt. "No one even knew about Oriceran when that damn show was runnin'."

"But it seems it became a cult classic sometime between the reveal of magic and…now. I'm checking to see what the official fans have to say about the show."

"Ain't my idea of a fun night, darlin'."

"Well, you don't have to look with me."

"I won't." He stood and made his way out of the living area toward the kitchen across the hall.

At the sound of his approaching boots, Rex and Luther skittered out of the kitchen.

"Hey, Johnny." Rex licked his muzzle and darted under the dining table before he curled in a ball on the floor.

"Don't mind us," Luther added as he ran toward the bedroom. "We're only—aw, man. Johnny, do you have to keep this door closed all the time?"

"Y'all got no business in there unless we're all passed out for the night."

"What?" Lisa called.

"Only the hounds." He refilled his whiskey glass and frowned at the empty counter beside the fridge. "Lisa?"

"Yeah?"

He opened the fridge door, peered inside briefly, then closed it again and turned. "Did you do somethin' with those leftovers?"

"Nope."

"Huh." He took another sip, thoroughly confused, and turned

slowly to scan the kitchen. *I'd say the hounds got into my supper, but they ain't neat about stolen food.*

"You sure you brought it in, Johnny?" Luther asked and stretched out on his side in front of the closed bedroom door.

"Yeah, maybe you left it at the restaurant."

"You were mad as hell, Johnny. Makes sense if you forgot. Happens to the best of us."

"Y'all mind your own, ya hear?"

"Sure, Johnny." Rex licked his forepaw.

"We'll hang out," Luther added as he rolled onto his back. "Chill. Keep you company."

"Oh, whoa." Lisa laughed and then clamped a hand over her mouth to suppress the rest of it. "This is insane."

"I think we already settled that when you said there's a damn website with my mug all over it."

"If it wasn't crazy before, Johnny, it is now." Grinning, she scrolled through the newest posts on the page that had been recently created specifically for *Dwarf the Bounty Hunter* Season 8, Episode 1: *Back in Black*. "Did you know they'd already named the first episode?"

"Nope and I don't care."

"But you like AC/DC, right?"

"What're you on about, darlin'?"

"*Back in Black*, Johnny."

"Huh." He sat beside her on the couch again and couldn't bring himself to look at the laptop. "Nelson's PR team did somethin' right, at least."

"And people are freaking out. There's a whole page dedicated to the episode that hasn't even come out yet. Look at this."

"Nope."

"There are almost ten thousand comments simply speculating about what you're doing in Baltimore. Everyone knows. And they're all talking about—oh."

Johnny leaning his head back against the couch cushion. "Well, don't that sound promisin'. What is it?"

"Some…uh, rather choice descriptions of Stephanie."

He chuckled.

"Oh, look. Someone wrote a piece of fan fiction."

"Get outta here."

"No, I'm serious. It's… Whoa. Erotic fan-fiction. Again, with Stephanie."

"Darlin', you oughtta close outta that before you start losin' your mind."

"Okay, well, I'm not reading that. But I'm enjoying this. Sure, no one knows it's me, but all this means our plan's working."

"Your plan." Johnny raised his head to drink more whiskey. "I gotta give credit where it's due. You thought all this up on your own."

"Yeah, in the middle of the night after being awake for twenty-two hours straight."

He frowned at her. "Seriously?"

"I suppose I found a way to be productive on an insomniac's schedule. Don't worry about it. I've been getting six hours for the last few nights, so I think it's getting better."

"Whoever told you six hours was enough needs to have their head checked. I get eight. Nine if I bagged some prize-winning game the day before."

Luther sniggered. "Eleven if you brought a lady over the night before."

"Ooh, yeah. Johnny, remember that one time when we went to that party and you got shitfaced? And we had to walk you home? I'm very sure you slept a whole day after that."

"And you did way more than whiskey that night, didn't you?"

The dwarf snapped his fingers and took a huge sip. *And that's why no one else hears the hounds but me.*

"Well, either way," Lisa continued, oblivious to the hounds

heckling their master, "it's getting better. So I'm not too worried about it."

"Sure. Have you tried any—"

"Oh, hello..." She nudged his shoulder and pointed at the screen. "Incoming message."

"From the same guy?"

"There is no way to tell. But probably."

Your face is all over the internet. Explain.

Below that came a screenshot of the Johnny Walker fan site with a frozen video frame capturing Stephanie Wyndom grinning at the bounty hunter. A text box for her to send an immediate reply opened at the bottom of the message.

"Shit. Do you have an answer for that?" he asked.

"Sure." Lisa started typing.

"You don't sound all that reassurin', darlin'. It might be we oughtta—"

"Shh. Let me think."

He snorted and leaned slightly toward her to read her on-the-fly explanation over her shoulder.

You saw my face in other places too. Twenty-four years is a long time to remember what that asshole did to me. The opportunity came my way, and I took it. They wanted a pretty face on the show this time around, so that's all they see, but I'll be here as long as it takes to find everything he loves and cares about. I thought meeting up with some like-minded ex-bounties would help me connect the dots in the end.

Johnny whistled. "Are you sure you didn't already have that floatin' around in the back of your mind?"

"No, my lies are much better when I don't plan them." She grinned at him. "Otherwise, I forget half of it."

"Like where your alias was born?"

"Johnny, they won't ask me to confirm everything I sent them directly. Especially not when they can double-check for themselves. It's fine."

The text both she and the anonymous messenger had sent to each other disappeared, then whoever was on the other side of the chat started typing again.

Come alone. No human weapons.

Below that was an address. Lisa used her phone to snap a photo before the message box disappeared with another flash of white light across her screen. "Got it. We're in."

"All right, darlin'. I'm impressed."

"Good. You should be." She left the dark web, closed the VPN down, and signed out of everything before she turned her laptop off. "Now, we're one step closer."

"Well, you can spin a story by the skin of your teeth, I'll give you that. Do you reckon you can hold your own tomorrow night in a room full of vengeful pricks?"

The laptop clicked shut, and she turned to raise an eyebrow at him. "Why wouldn't I be?"

"If you ain't been sleepin'—"

"I'm fine." Lisa stood and tucked her laptop under her arm. "But speaking of sleep, yeah. I should probably go do that. You too."

"Uh-huh."

"Goodnight, Johnny."

"'Night, darlin'." He raised his glass toward her, then paused. "Hey, when those idiots start filmin' us again tomorrow, you should throw a few nasty looks my way."

She looked at him over her shoulder with a confused smile. "What?"

"You know. Like you can't wait to kick my ass so everyone gets a good look at it."

"Ha! I'll see what I can do. It shouldn't be that hard."

CHAPTER SEVENTEEN

Johnny managed to bypass the film-crew plague the next morning when he ordered room service for breakfast and stretched out in the huge suite with a perfectly black cup of coffee. Rex had gone through the entire extra order of bacon brought up for him, and the larger hound now stared at the second plate in front of his brother. "You gonna eat that, Luther?"

"I don't know." Luther lifted his head off the floor and sniffed the bacon. "I don't feel all that hungry."

The newspaper Johnny had been reading—fortunately without any mention of him or the damn show—slapped down on his lap before he turned a sharp frown onto the coonhound. "What's wrong with you?"

"Dunno, Johnny." Luther belched and rolled over onto his side. "Maybe I'm feeling a little bloated."

"You do kinda look like it." The dwarf glanced at Rex. "What'd he do?"

"Don't look at me." The larger hound lowered himself to his belly and licked the bacon grease off his plate. "It's Luther. Could be anything."

"Uh-huh. And that's what I'm worried about. Are you hurtin', boy?"

"Not really. Only..." Luther farted and rolled onto his back, his forepaws dangling limply beneath his chin. "Waiting."

"Well, hurry up about it." Johnny drank his coffee and took a deep breath. "I have no idea when we'll be—"

A sharp knock came at the door to his suite. "Johnny?"

"Interrupted by the biggest pain in my ass all year." The dwarf sighed and set his coffee and newspaper down on the dining table.

"Johnny, it's Phil. Come on and open up, will you? I want to go over a few things with you before we—oh. Good morning."

Johnny grasped the suite door tightly and stepped in front of the open space to block the rest of his room. "What?"

"What are you planning to get into today?"

"I don't have any real plans, to tell ya the truth."

Phil smoothed his wildly scattered hair away from his head. "Great. Then we can—"

"But they don't include you."

"I know, Johnny. But look. We've seen more hits on the YouTube videos and more trending hashtags than I even imagined was possible. And that's only the last few days. So we want to get a little more up close and personal today, you know? We haven't done any more Q&As since the first one at your house. Our viewers are screaming for more. We need to give it to them."

"Screamin'." Johnny regarded him dubiously. "Is that right?"

"Literally and virtually, yeah. So why don't you go ahead and get ready to go out? See the sights. Go shopping. Do whatever you need to do—"

"I'm good."

Across the hall, Lisa's door opened, and redheaded Stephanie stepped out with wide eyes. "Already, huh?"

"Yeah, we wanted to get a head-start," Phil said quickly over his shoulder. "Look, this is merely us following you and your dogs around Baltimore—oh, and Stephanie. Right now, the most important thing is that we recapture that 'day in the life of Johnny Walker' effect. You know, the same thing you were doing back in the day. No bounties to go after and no traveling, merely a dwarf out on the town doing whatever he does between."

Johnny sniffed and darted Lisa an exasperated glance. "This ain't a regular day in my life, Phil."

"Yeah, yeah, I know that." The director stepped toward the door and leaned toward him to whisper, "But our viewers don't."

"And you wanna make all those folks think I live in Baltimore?"

"No, they already know you're from the south. This is for character, Johnny. It's been fifteen years. A lot happens in fifteen years, and if we want this to be a success, everyone out there watching needs to feel as if they've known you for the last fifteen years—that they can reconnect with you, right? That you haven't changed all that much."

"Filmin' me walkin' around the city ain't gonna make a difference."

"It's not the worst idea," Lisa said as her hotel room door shut behind her.

"Aw, not you too."

"Oh, come on." She smiled at Phil in a friendly way, but the man was too intently focused on pleading for Johnny to notice. "Hey, why don't we walk down to the waterfront? We don't have to have an actual plan, but I heard the view's nice. We could do the Q&A down there, maybe grab a drink, and see what happens."

The bounty hunter grunted, his expression obstinate. "What happens is I stay right here."

"Johnny." She peered around Phil's unruly hair and raised her eyebrows. "You never know who might be watching, right?"

After a moment, he scowled and twisted to shout over his shoulder. "Come on, boys. We're goin' down for a day in the fuckin' life."

"What?" Rex trotted down the hall. "Life of what?"

"A dwarf that don't exist. Luther!"

"I'm good, Johnny. Truly, I could lay here all day. You go ahead—"

He snapped his fingers. "Get on right now. If I ain't stayin' in this hotel suite, neither are you."

"Okay, okay…" Luther grunted and pushed to his feet. When he waddled down the hallway, his head swung slightly from side to side and Rex sat with a low whine.

"You look awful, bro."

"Thanks."

"What you need is just a chance to run it off. The park's a good idea." Once the hounds were out the door, Johnny turned to head toward the elevators.

Phil met Lisa's gaze and mouthed, "Thank you."

"This is essentially your one shot," she whispered. "So don't blow it like last night, okay?"

"Oh, I'm the bad guy here? He threw a plate at my cameraman."

"Where's Howie?" Johnny called from where he stood beside the elevator.

Phil scowled. "Waiting downstairs in the lobby. He said something about cookies."

"Ooh, hey, Johnny. You think they have any hound cookies?"

The dwarf snorted. "This ain't Portland, Rex."

"Yeah, yeah, but if Luther and I happen to find some cookies laying around, you think—"

"Dude…" Luther let out a heavy sigh and sat. "Don't talk about cookies. Or eating. Or moving. I can't handle it right now."

"There is something wrong with you."

They walked just shy of a mile and a half down to Federal Hill Park in the warm morning air. The smell of the ocean and fish mingled with scents from the restaurants open for breakfast and the thick, almost burned aroma of roasting coffee beans.

More strangers stopped to stare at the bounty hunter and his entourage. Some of them waved and shouted hello while others simply pointed. One man tried to flag Johnny down to get an autograph, but Howie was there to remind the guy that they were on official *Dwarf the Bounty Hunter* business. Maybe another time.

"Okay, Johnny. Stop right there." Phil pointed at him. "Yeah. Right there."

Johnny turned with both hands shoved into the pockets of his black jeans. "On the grass?"

"Oh, yeah. It's perfect. Like you're part of the city with the bay in the background and all these people. The lighting's great. And look, you fit right in. All the locals are doing it. Benson, grab those lawn chairs, huh?"

One of the crew slid two nylon folding chairs out of their cases and followed Phil's instructions in setting them up. The dwarf didn't move.

"You look like you're about to be sick," Lisa muttered as she joined him in front of the chairs.

"Naw, I think that's Luther."

The smaller hound waddled across the grass, stopped to sniff a dandelion, then lowered himself to the ground and rolled onto his side. "I'm fine, Johnny. Stop looking at me."

"All right, now Johnny, Stephanie, go ahead and take your seats."

Johnny looked over the rims of his black sunglasses and raised an eyebrow at Howie. The man shrugged and gestured apologetically. *Yeah. I already knew this was gonna have to happen sooner or later.*

He and Lisa sat, and Phil's hands fluttered excitedly toward them as Cody and the boom assistant took their places around the lawn chairs. "And how about taking off those sunglasses, huh?"

"No."

Phil scoffed. "It doesn't do well for the shot, though. It would be much better if we can—"

"At least you have the damn shot, man. Take it or leave it."

The director's mouth dropped open, then he took a deep breath and nodded at Cody. "Go ahead and start the new reel."

Johnny folded his arms and watched the pedestrians milling around Federal Hill Park. Half of them slowed to stare at the filming in progress. *This is gonna be one hell of a short season.*

"Are we rolling? Great. Here we go." Phil pointed at the bounty hunter and nodded. "So now that you've been in Baltimore for a few days, Johnny, how do you feel?"

"I'm ready to get back to my swamp."

The director's shoulders slumped and he shook his head as he whispered, "Try to be real here, okay?"

"He thinks I ain't serious about this whole thing," Johnny muttered, leaning slightly toward Lisa. "What the hell does he want from me?"

She grinned and watched Phil gesticulate in what amounted to a bunch of nonsense she didn't understand. "Ratings."

"Ridiculous."

"What's been your favorite part of Baltimore so far, Johnny?" Phil continued.

"I have a nice hotel suite," he muttered. "It's bigger than the others."

"You mean bigger than the places you used to stay when you were going after bounties fifteen years ago?"

Shit. "Yeah. 'Course that's what I meant."

"You like big hotel rooms. Okay." One of the crewmembers sniggered, and Phil cast him a scathing glance. "What else about the city draws you in?"

"Besides a job?" Johnny sniffed and scanned the park and all the pedestrians. *This is ridiculous.* "You know, Baltimore's got... charm. Right? It's an old city with considerable opportunity for folks who can see it for what it's got. I guess."

"Great. Tell us about your run-in yesterday with a few magicals at the...in Guilford."

Johnny rolled his eyes but of course, no one could see it beneath the dark sunglasses. "I don't have much to say. We were lookin' for our guy, and it turned out we had the wrong criminal. That's it."

"Will you continue the search over the next few days?"

Lisa leaned toward him and muttered, "Now would be the time to play up the whole 'sit back and relax' part of this."

"Naw." Johnny folded his arms and stared at the camera. "I been called off the job after a few key details came into play. So I reckon I'll stick around here for a few more days, see the sights, enjoy all the...city folk."

He gestured toward a large crowd walking through the streets downtown and almost ate his own words when he saw the damn pony people in bright colors among them. *Does it ever end?*

"And you can say you've been enjoying yourself while you're here, right?" Phil asked, his eyes widening as he geared up for more questions.

"Sure."

"Baltimore has kicked it up a notch when it comes to the fine-dining scene. Like where you and Stephanie went out for dinner last night." Johnny's hands balled into fists in his lap. "We only got to see a little of that moment between you two. It looked like you were having fun."

"Yeah, until someone showed up and ruined a perfectly good night. Are you serious with this shit, man? This ain't 'a day in the life.' It feels more like puttin' me on a witness stand."

"Just roll with it, okay?" Phil whistled at the cameraman and twirled his finger before he pointed at the bounty hunter and his "assistant." Cody and the second cameraman closed in. "The next question's for you, Stephanie."

Lisa crossed one leg over the other and leaned back in the chair. "Okay."

"How easy is it to get on Johnny's good side?"

She laughed in surprise and tossed her red curls over her shoulder. "I'm sorry, what?"

"Well, you know him fairly well. Yes, you're on the show as an assistant, but I'm talking about knowing him well enough to go out to dinner last night. It looked like you two were having quite the evening. Is that something you have to work at, or does it come naturally to you?"

Jesus, Phil. Lisa stared at the camera as Cody stooped and stepped toward her, zooming in. *Way to pop the seriously unexpected questions.*

"Well…" She glanced at Rex sniffing around Cody's feet and raised her eyebrows. "That's a little personal—"

"Oh, it's fine," Phil cut in, nodding vigorously. "We love personal. So do all Johnny's fans."

"Okay. I guess first I should say that my interview for this show wasn't the first time Johnny and I met."

"Keep going."

"It was a long time ago. That first meeting." Lisa turned toward Johnny and pulled up a fake smile she tried to make look as uncomfortable as possible. *He said make it look like I hate his guts. Here we go.* "Johnny changed my mind about many things. Mostly about where I was headed and the kinds of choices I was making. Now, I…want to pay him back for everything he brought into my life."

The dwarf snorted and looked away from her to stare at the camera.

"Do you think you'll accomplish that?" Phil asked.

"Oh, I certainly do." Lisa smirked at the camera and cocked her head. "Maybe sooner than he realizes." *That'll pin the nail in the coffin. Stephanie Wyndom's on a quest for revenge.*

"Johnny, you have a rough history with personal relationships."

The dwarf lowered his head to stare at Phil over the rims of his glasses. "What the hell are you goin' on about?"

"I'm merely taking a dive into your past. You're still the same Johnny Walker, but now you have fifteen years of a whole different kind of experiences under your belt, namely retreating down south for voluntary retirement way before the end of your time."

Johnny shook his head. "I ain't talkin' about the last fifteen years. Or what happened before them."

"This is important."

"No, it ain't." Johnny leaned forward and pointed at Phil. "Change it to somethin' else or we're done."

The director stepped back and twirled his finger in a "keep going" gesture. "This is good stuff, Johnny. Vulnerable. Raw. Let's stay here for a while—"

"You can stay. I'm checkin' out if you don't start blabbin' about somethin' else."

"I'm trying to draw your essence out." Phil stepped forward again. "You have something of a budding new relationship with Stephanie here. You have two coonhounds with you now, which is new since the last time fans saw you in action. Do you ever worry about what might happen to people who get close to you?"

Johnny whipped his sunglasses off. "You piece of shit."

"There it is." Phil grinned. "Let's explore that."

"Naw, we're done."

Luther trotted past his master and sniffed wildly at the grass. "I figured it out, Johnny."

Rex stared after his brother. "He's not listening to you, dummy. What are you doing?"

"Fixing it."

"Johnny, wait," Phil shouted and gestured for the dwarf to sit again. "We're only getting started on the juicy stuff. Tell us about your kid."

Rex whined and swung his head to stare at the director. "Uh-oh."

Luther hunkered in the grass beside the film crew. "You stepped in it now, two-legs."

Johnny glared at Phil. "Move on."

"Oh, come on. The world hears nothing from Johnny Walker for fifteen years and now he's out and about again. Dating, raising coonhounds, getting back into the swing of things as a caregiver, right? What's her name again?"

Lisa glanced at Johnny and tried to hide her concern and to keep smiling for the camera. *He's about to explode.* "Maybe there's something else I can answer—"

"Not right now, Stephanie. I want to hear what Johnny has to say about stepping into his role as the protector again. That's what happened, right?"

The bounty hunter sniffed and stared directly ahead at nothing.

"We saw the bedroom at your house when we started filming a few days ago. Let's talk about the girl—"

Johnny lurched from his chair, grasped the back of it, and hurled it across the grass. He stormed past Cody and flipped the camera the middle finger before he strode away.

"Johnny?" Lisa stood and frowned at Phil. "I guess that's the end of it."

"Aw, come on. We were getting to the good parts—"

"Come on, boys." Johnny whistled and Rex barreled after him across the park.

"You okay, Johnny?"

"We're done with this filmin' shit. It was a bad idea."

"Wait, wait. Luther! Come on!"

"Yeah, yeah. Give me a minute." Five yards away, the smaller hound finished squatting in the grass and turned to sniff what he'd left behind. "Oh, shit. What is that?"

"You don't know?" Rex looked at Johnny, then sidetracked to

check his brother's unburdened treasure. "Uh...Johnny? I don't think this is normal."

The dwarf stopped in his tracks, turned, and hurried to where the hounds were investigating a particularly large pile in the grass. He frowned and bent over for a closer look. "What the hell?"

"Right?" Luther looked at his master and panted, his tail wagging furiously. "But lemme tell ya, Johnny. I feel so much better!"

"You don't say." He folded his arms. "And y'all got no idea what that is?"

"Nope."

"Absolutely none."

"Is he gonna die, Johnny?"

"Well, not now that he passed what I reckon is two whole Styrofoam to-go boxes."

"Whoa, what?" Luther poked his head toward the pile again. "How'd you come up with that?"

"Dude, you ate the boxes." Rex snorted and shook his head. "New low, Luther. Even for you."

Rolling his eyes, Johnny nodded toward the street to indicate that he intended to return to their hotel.

"Johnny?" Luther looked from the evidence to his master. "Johnny, are you mad?"

"Not as long as we leave all the shit here at the park." *That includes shitty questions and useless director morons.*

CHAPTER EIGHTEEN

Johnny spent the rest of the day holed up in his hotel suite and refused to step out again for anything. Rex lay curled in front of the armchair, and Luther sat at his master's feet, staring at the dwarf. "Johnny. Johnny. Hey, Johnny."

"Boy, what do you want?"

"Only to tell you I feel so much better. And that I hope you're not...mad at me?"

With a grunt, Johnny reached out to scratch behind the hound's ears and shook his head. "You can't help what's in your nature."

"Hey, wait a minute." Rex whipped his head up to stare at them. "Don't pin his stupidity on the whole canine race. I didn't eat Styrofoam."

"But you ain't gonna try to tell me y'all didn't share the leftovers."

The larger hound sighed and lowered his head to his forepaws again.

"Uh-huh. That's what I thought."

"So we're good, Johnny?"

"As long as you don't do it again. Or make a mess like that inside."

"Yeah, no problem." Luther twisted to lick between his legs. "Feelin' pretty empty right now, actually."

"I bet."

A knock came at the door, followed by Lisa's voice. "Johnny?"

"Yeah, I'm comin'." He sighed and strode toward the door. When he opened it, she thrust a bag of store-bought popcorn toward him and slipped inside his room.

"I thought I'd give you some space," she said, turned to walk back down the hall, and grinned at him. "But you've been in here all day, you have no inclination to leave again, and I'm not gonna let you sit here all on your own and throw yourself a pity party without some company."

Johnny sniffed. "It ain't a pity party, darlin'."

"Oh, yeah? Then why didn't you answer any of my texts?"

"What texts?"

"See? You were so caught up in being pissed off that you didn't even notice. There were four, by the way. I began to think maybe you'd had a heart attack and I should come make sure you're still alive."

"That's dumb," Luther said as he scratched behind his ear. "If Johnny died, the whole building would know about it."

"Yeah, you wouldn't be able to shut us up, lady," Rex added. "Except for the fact that you can't hear us."

"Sorry," Johnny grumbled as he flopped down onto the couch. "I wasn't thinkin' about the damn phone."

"I know. Which is why I brought popcorn."

His thick eyebrow quirked when she joined him on the couch. "I ain't makin' the connection."

"Well, we have a couple of options for killing time without stewing in misery about it." She set her laptop on the coffee table and waited for Johnny to open the bag of popcorn. "Yep. That's a start. We can talk about your buttons getting pushed out at

Federal Hill Park if you want. I won't force you, but I'm here for that. Or we could try to find a movie or something on that giant flatscreen over there that seems reserved for giant hotel suites. It's much better than mine. Or we could take a look at what the film crew's already posted for today, and I can be a hell of a lot more prepared going into this meeting tonight knowing what's been put out there for the general public to consume faster than we can film it. Take your pick."

Johnny rolled his eyes and leaned slightly away from her. "What about the option where you go do any of that on your own and I can get some peace and quiet?"

"Come on. We both know that's not what you want." Lisa plunged her hand into the open bag of popcorn, took a small handful, and ate it a few pieces at a time. "Watching YouTube videos it is, then."

"Darlin', that ain't the kinda thing that's gonna lift my spirits." He cleared his throat. "If they needed liftin' anyhow."

"You can think of it as research, Johnny. I need to be prepared for this meeting, and I could use your help pulling out a few nuggets here and there to use in case I need them." Lisa opened her laptop and pulled up the YouTube website. "Any insight into what the rest of the world is seeing of Johnny Walker and Stephanie Wyndom. Okay?"

"Fine." Johnny snagged a handful of popcorn and shoved it into his mouth. Small pieces toppled into his beard and stuck there as he stared at her screen. "It sounds more like torture to me, but if it helps you at this meetin'—"

"That's exactly what it'll do."

The first short *Dwarf the Bounty Hunter* clip that pulled up was from their interrupted dinner the night before at Rye Street Tavern. Johnny scowled and pointed at the screen. "These guys need to stay out of other folks' business."

"They're only trying to do their job. Which I'm sure you realize you don't exactly make very easy."

"Filmin' a private dinner ain't got nothin' to do with bein' a bounty hunter."

"Johnny, I don't think all the people who watched your show and became die-hard fans like this were into it for the bounty-hunter aspect."

He frowned. "What the hell else is there?"

"You." Lisa shrugged, then turned the volume up.

"Although Johnny and Stephanie crossed paths for the first time almost twenty-five years ago and under wildly different circumstances, Season Eight brings more than a new opportunity for fans and admirers to relive the excitement that was Dwarf the Bounty Hunter.*"*

Phil's voiceover filled the suite, and Johnny crammed another handful of popcorn into his mouth. *"This time, it offers an opportunity for love. Two lost souls finding solace in each other, brought together by nothing more than a shared dedication to justice and taking down the criminals no one but Johnny Walker is capable of bringing in."*

"Jesus Christ." The dwarf scoffed and turned away from the laptop. "Last time we filmed the show, there wasn't anything like this bullshit recorded over some sappy shot. It's all speculation."

"Yep. Speculation the fans are eating up like candy. Look at all these views, Johnny. And the comments."

"Naw, I'm good."

"'Good for him,'" she read aloud. "'Johnny's been on his own for way too long. He deserves a nice girl like Stephanie.'"

"For fuck's sake—"

"Oh, look at this one. 'If he doesn't hold onto that hot piece of ass, he's dumber than he looks.' Huh."

"Folks are gettin' way too involved in this." He shook his head. "And if they're spoutin' off that kinda bullshit, I ain't fixin' to have that kinda fan followin' me around in the first place."

"Well, this is the kind of stuff that keeps people's attention, I guess."

They went through more short clips already posted—the beginning of their trip into Senator Hugh's house, a brief glimpse of the stop at Canton Exports & Supplies to speak to Rocky and his work crew, Johnny and Stephanie throwing sticks to the hounds at the Baltimore Waterfront Promenade and laughing, Johnny shoving a pedestrian out of the way when the man tried to feed Rex a dog treat. There were a fair number of clips of him shoving someone, although most of them involved members of the film crew.

The last one they opened was a panned-out shot of Johnny surrounded by dozens of cosplayers in brightly colored horse costumes outside the convention center. It showed his scrunched-up face as the woman in the white-sequined jumpsuit bent over to get his autograph, while Rex and Luther crouched warily among the sea of people who looked only halfway like horses. Lisa stood a few yards away, smirked at the whole thing, and looked more than a little amused by Johnny's palpable discomfort.

"Even on the job and in the middle of hunting his newest bounty, Johnny Walker still has a soft spot for engaging with his fans. Not one to turn down a beautiful woman in a pony costume, this bounty hunter doesn't care who you are, where you're from, or what eclectic interests you hold. If you're a fan of Johnny Walker, he's a fan of you. Join us next week for the Season Eight premiere of Dwarf the Bounty Hunter: Back in Black. *And don't forget to subscribe to—"*

"All right, turn that shit off." Johnny stood from the couch and crossed the living area to retrieve his half-full whiskey glass from the dining table. "They made us both look like a couple of idiots."

"Stopping to make someone's day by signing their…tail doesn't make you an idiot." Lisa fought back a laugh when the dwarf spun and glared at her. "Come on. It's funny."

"Sure. Damn hilarious."

"Okay, look. I know you're still on edge about finding the Red Boar. I know we're close. This will all work out, Johnny."

He downed the rest of his whiskey and opened the bottle again to pour another.

She closed her laptop and set it on the coffee table. "You believe me, don't you?"

"I know you believe it." He darted her a sidelong glance and grunted. "Dammit, fine. Yeah, I believe it too. You set up somethin' I wouldn't have even considered on my own, darlin', but this ain't my usual style."

"Oh, I know. Which is why this will work. Every criminal out there who's had a run-in with you since you started knows exactly what your usual style is." Lisa snagged the bag of popcorn and placed it on her lap. "They won't expect this."

"'Cause I ain't got the patience to sit around and wait through all this pomp and circumstance for a fuckin' show when that ain't why I'm here!"

Rex and Luther both snorted at their master's outburst. "Jeez, Johnny. You don't have to yell."

"Yeah, we're all right here in the same room." Luther lowered his head to paw at his ear. "And we can hear you just fine when you whisper."

Johnny took a long drink, glanced up at Lisa's open, patient smile, then cleared his throat. "Sorry."

"You don't have anything to be sorry about. I know it's hard to wait. Especially since you've been waiting fifteen years without any idea that this was coming."

"Shit." He vigorously scratched his head. "You got me all worked out, don'tcha?"

"Hardly. But I like to think I know enough." She jiggled the bag of popcorn at him. "We still have a few hours to kill. I'll let you choose the movie."

"Ha. Helluva consolation prize, darlin'."

CHAPTER NINETEEN

When 10:00 pm rolled around, Lisa and Johnny were fully ready to stop flipping through available cable channels on the hotel TV. She glanced at her watch and nodded. "It'll be time for me to head out soon. The Johnny Haters Anonymous meeting is in an hour."

"Great. I'm comin' with you."

"Johnny—"

"I know. You're gonna tell me it's a bad idea. I'm gonna agree. Then I'll say I'm comin' anyway 'cause I ain't lettin' you head off all on your own into a den of shitbrained thugs who wanna see me hang. You'll try to stop me, which we've already proven ain't possible any way you try to sling it." He stood and sniffed. "So let's cut through all the formalities and get to the part where we make ready to head out together, all right?"

The agent stared at him and pressed her lips together to hide a smile. "How long have you been rehearsing that one in your head?"

"Since about halfway through *Die Hard*. Love the film, darlin', but I already know how it ends."

"Okay. Fine. I don't have enough bandwidth right now to argue with your plan."

Johnny smirked. "'Cause you know I'm right."

She stood with a soft chuckle, shook her head, and pulled up her redheaded Stephanie illusion. That done, she took her cell phone from her pocket and placed it on the coffee table.

"What are you doin'?"

"Leaving my phone here if you're coming with me—and staying hidden the whole time. Let's be clear about that."

"Yeah, yeah. I'll be a fly on the damn wall."

"A fly who stays outside, Johnny."

He grunted.

"As long as you can do that, I don't have any reason to keep my phone on me. And honestly, I'd rather not. That service account isn't registered in Stephanie Wyndom's name, and I'm very sure anyone who can send me a private message like that over the dark web won't have any problem at all discovering that my phone belongs to someone else."

"Well, now there's no way in hell I ain't joinin' ya."

"But you stay outside—"

"I get it, darlin'. I hear you loud 'n clear."

"Good." Lisa looked at both hounds curled up in front of the armchair and raised an eyebrow.

"What?" Luther lifted his head to stare at her. "I didn't do anything."

"Don't look at me." Rex sighed and closed his eyes. "It was probably Luther."

Agent Breyer didn't have to say it out loud. Johnny had already had the same thought. "Lisa and I are headin' out, boys."

Luther leapt to his feet, his tail wagging furiously. "All right! Yes! You know how hard it is to stay cooped up in the same room all day without a change of scenery?"

Rex stared up at his master with wide eyes.

"But no hounds on this particular outin'. Sorry."

"What?" The smaller hound snorted and trotted after Johnny as the dwarf headed into the huge bedroom.

Lisa glanced at Rex and shrugged. "It's better this way tonight."

"Yeah, I know you know I can hear you, lady. But it's not fair when I can't argue."

"What do you mean no hounds?" Luther whined. "Johnny, we're a team!"

"I aim to stick to the outside where no one's gettin' a whiff of a dwarf spyin' in on their secret hate meetin'," Johnny muttered. "I ain't gonna risk the two of y'all gettin' found out too."

"Aw, man. We can be quiet, Johnny."

"Yeah, you already know that," Rex added from the living area. "We're great huntin' dogs."

"That ain't the point this time, boys. No huntin' and no sniffin' out. Only watchin' and waitin', and that'll be hard enough for me." Johnny took his duffel bag from the closet and heaved it onto the bed to root through the gear he'd brought.

"This sucks." Luther jumped up to settle both forepaws on the bed and sniffed at the black duffel bag. "You won't be gone forever, will you?"

"Or we'll shrivel up and die in here, Johnny."

The dwarf snorted. "Few hours tops. Y'all ain't got nothin' to worry about."

"Except there's no grass in the hotel, Johnny. What if we have to...go?"

He smirked at Luther, then crossed the bedroom and opened the bathroom door. "Do it in the shower." He turned to leave, then remembered the toilet and closed the lid with a loud clack. "And stay outta the john."

"Johnny, did you tell them to do their business in the shower?" Lisa called from the living area.

"Uh-huh."

Rex chuckled. "She's getting very good at guessing the rest of the conversation when she can only hear half. Hey, lady. Try to read my mind. What am I thinking right now?"

Lisa stepped toward the open bedroom doorway to watch Johnny rummaging through his bag.

"Figures." Rex snorted and lay his head back down on his forepaws. "No one even wants to try."

Leaning against the doorway, Lisa watched Luther sniffing around the opposite side of the bed. "We can take them out before we go, Johnny."

"No, we can't." Johnny strapped the belt loaded with explosive disks around his waist, then pulled out the pistol he'd repurposed into a tranquilizer. "How much you wanna bet Phil and his damn crew put someone out in the hall to watch for either one of us leavin' this suite?"

"What? They wouldn't do that."

"Feel free to check, darlin'. I'm sure you'll find somethin'."

"No…" With a frown, she turned hesitantly away from the bedroom doorway and hurried across the suite to check through the small peephole in the front door.

Johnny smirked and took a six-inch square device from the bag.

"Wow." Lisa reappeared in the doorway and ran a hand through her currently red curls. "I honestly didn't expect that."

"Someone camped right outside the door?"

"Yeah. Cody with his camera and the woman they have with them. The one with the bandana. What's her name?"

"I have no idea." Tucking the tranquilizer into its holster which he'd slung over the belt of disks, Johnny carried the black device into the living room. "But we ain't gettin' out that way without the whole damn team refusin' to let us go on our own."

She wrinkled her nose. "If we told them what we were doing, though—"

"Darlin', those idiots followed us into an active shootout at the senator's house. They ain't concerned about gettin' into a little danger—or startin' it—as long as they get their damn shot.'"

"So we have to sneak out of our hotel. Is that what you're saying?"

A dark chuckle escaped the dwarf as he slid the dining table away from the window. He jerked the window open as far as it would go and punched the screen out. "Sneakin' out. Sure. It's one thing I've always been good at."

Lisa stared at the open window that allowed in a full, bay-air breeze with nothing in the way. "Seriously? We simply climb through the window like a couple of thieves?"

"'Course not. Like a couple of professionals who need to go get a job done without the paparazzi makin' a mess of the whole damn thing." Johnny returned to the center of the living area and set the square black device on the floor in front of Rex. "And this is for y'all."

Luther stepped up immediately to sniff at the device. "What is this, Johnny? Doesn't smell like treats."

"Doesn't look like anything for hounds at all," Rex replied.

"I got a job for y'all, boys. While you're stayin' here."

Rex perked up at the idea of being more useful. "What's the job?"

"We can do whatever you want, Johnny. We're your hounds."

"It's a pedal." Johnny nodded at the device. "Anyone comes knockin' on this door lookin' for me, y'all make sure to press the damn thing, understand?"

"Press?"

"You mean paw?" Luther did exactly that and stepped on the black device.

"I ain't interested."

"Oh, shit!" The smaller hound sprang away from the pedal with a yelp. "Johnny! How the hell did you get inside that little box?"

The dwarf chuckled. "It's only my voice. It's looped with a few

Johnnyisms if you gotta use 'em but make sure you keep the barkin' up real loud too, all right? It keeps most folks too confused to realize Johnny Walker's repeatin' himself with the same six lines."

"Huh." Luther sniffed the pedal, then pawed it again.

"Get outta here before I come throw you out."

Rex tittered. "That's a good one, Johnny."

"Yeah, definitely you."

Lisa smiled at the dwarf in confusion. "You came to Baltimore prepared to use that, didn't you?"

Johnny raised his eyebrows. "'Course I did. I used this all the damn time back when Nelson thought it was his inalienable right to knock on my door at any damn hour he pleased. Granted, that was before I had a couple of coonhounds to put the fear of Johnny Walker in him. It'll do fine for the film crew."

"You can count on us, Johnny." Rex stood to sniff the device. "No one will know you guys snuck out. Promise."

"Yeah, we won't say a thing," Luther added. "Not like anyone would hear it anyway. They won't get past us, Johnny."

"All right. It's only a few hours, boys. Y'all be good."

"You got it, Johnny."

"We're on it like my paw on this—" Luther stepped on the pedal and backed away.

"I ain't fixin' to repeat myself. Now git!"

"Ha-ha. Johnny, that is you."

The dwarf shooed his hound away from the pedal. "Not until we're gone, huh? I ain't tryin' to explain why I was havin' conversations with myself all night."

Lisa glanced at her watch. "We need to get going."

"Yeah, yeah. All right. Do you wanna take the lead out the window, or should I?"

She glanced at the open window with Baltimore's cityscape lit up across the darkness outside and shrugged. "Be my guest."

"Well it's my suite, so it's technically the other way round. But sure." Johnny crawled onto the windowsill and moved gingerly along the small ledge toward the first-story roof protruding from the back of the building.

Lisa ducked through the window behind him and looked into the parking lot. "At least we're only on the fourth floor."

CHAPTER TWENTY

After Johnny disappeared around the corner of the building with a promise to stay out of sight and not cause any trouble, Lisa glanced at the marquee over the front door. *A staffing agency's main office isn't too bad. At least they're not holding this Johnny-hater meeting in the basement of a church or something.*

She opened the front door and stepped inside in her full redheaded Stephanie illusion. The front room of the staffing agency was empty and all the lights turned off, but some were on down the hall, so she followed them and the sound of low, agitated voices.

When she stepped into the room off the hall, the conversation stopped. A dozen heads turned toward her—magicals and humans—and the massive shifter seated at the head of the long conference table nodded at her. "Look who finally decided to show up."

A witch in a thick black hoodie snarled at Lisa. "Did you have a hard time getting away from your new boyfriend without him noticing?"

The agent took the last empty chair around the table and didn't bother to meet the witch's gaze. *We were right. The Red*

Boar's not here but I'm willing to bet that shifter's his mouthpiece. She sat and nodded at the shifter. "I hope you didn't get started without me."

"You're not the one who put this together, Stephanie." He sneered when he said her name. "Merely another invite."

She glanced around the table at the disgruntled ex-bounties and recognized most of them from their photos under the episode descriptions on the Johnny Walker fan site. *This is surreal.*

"Man, that fucking dwarf must've lost most of his brain cells if he brought an ex fucking con on with him for this joke of a show," a half-Kilomea grunted. He picked at his long eyeteeth with the pointed end of a shish-kabob stick, his takeout box open and empty on the table in front of him.

Lisa shrugged. "He lost a lot of things fifteen years ago."

"Not nearly as much as the rest of us." A crystal woman seated across the table tossed her long braids over her shoulder. "That's for damn sure."

"And not nearly as much as he deserves," the agent added with a firm nod. "That's why we're here, isn't it?"

Two gnomes closest to the shifter at the head of the table—one with an eyepatch and the other with his left ear missing—lowered their heads together for a whispered conversation. The one with the eyepatch sneered. "Do you expect us to believe you've been running around Baltimore with that damn bounty hunter for days and don't give a shit about what happens to him?"

She gestured toward the shifter. "I sent all my details exactly like the rest of you. At least I assume the vetting process was the same given that we all found each other in a place where most people—and magicals—do what we can to stay anonymous. I don't know about you, but I'm very sure the shifter, whoever he is, wouldn't have told me how to get here if I didn't check out."

"Kellen," the shifter grumbled. "If you need a damn name, call me that."

"Okay, Kellen." She folded her arms and glared at the gnomes.

"I thought we were here for the bounty hunter with his head so far up his ass he still thinks he's Oriceran's gift to Earth, not to interrogate me."

A few ex-cons chuckled at that. The gnomes huddled together again for another unheard conversation but didn't say anything else.

At least that got their attention. Whatever Johnny's picking up with that spy bug, I'll have to remind him later that I don't mean any of this.

"But I'm having a hard time buying all this," the witch in the hoodie added, her glare still extremely hostile. "We've all seen the clips that stuck-up prick put all over the Internet. It looks like you two are cozier than you want anyone to believe. And I don't think I believe you."

"And that's why I'm on the show with him now and you aren't. Because I'm smart enough to know that the best position to turn on someone and rip their life apart from the inside out is from right next to them. Up close and personal. The dwarf trusts me enough for that. And when I'm sure he trusts me with his life, that's the best time to strike." Lisa leaned sideways in her chair and raised an eyebrow at Kellen. "I assume you guys didn't do a meet-and-greet before I arrived."

"It's not exactly something we need," a half-wizard interjected and smoothed his oiled hair away from his temples with both hands. "Our identities were plastered all over the TV for months after that shithead dwarf put us away. But you haven't shown up anywhere."

"Look, he didn't break into bounty hunting when he started that stupid show," Lisa told him. "That was merely something he added to his fucked-up resume. And I happen to be on his bounty list that predates his idiotic scrounging for ratings and his sucking up to the goddamn FBI when they pulled him in as a regular contractor. It doesn't mean I don't want to see him bleed any less than the rest of you."

"So prove it, then," the Crystal woman said. "I wanna hear

what you think you know about him that earns you the right to sit here and call the rest of us idiots."

"Fine." Lisa folded her arms. "What do you want to know?"

"When did he bag you?"

"2016."

"Doing what?"

"I'd lifted a new Mercedes in LA and got it as far as Kansas City before I ran out of my stash and had to re-up." Lisa sneered at the other ex-cons. "The fucker picked me up right after that and didn't even give me the chance to get right again. He took all eighty bucks worth of what I'd just scored too."

"How the hell'd he even find out about you?" one gnome snarled.

"The owner of the Mercedes dealership was a wizard and must have gotten word of the bastard's skills through the grapevine. You know how it was before Earth even knew about us and magic."

The cons grumbled amongst themselves and glanced at Kellen for confirmation. The shifter shrugged. "Like she said, she checks out."

It's a good thing I spent time researching my fake past. Lisa pressed her lips together in irritation. "So can we quit focusing on my fuckups and get down to the real issue here or what?"

"You're not running the show, Light Elf," the half-wizard snarled. "So shut the hell up and let the big dogs handle the meeting, huh?"

"Oh, sure. All you big dogs have considerable personal information about Johnny Walker already, right?" She gestured to include those present and smirked. "You've merely been waiting however many years to use it in a fun group setting. I get it."

"This bitch's head is as big as the dwarf's," the witch spat. "You think you're better than the rest of us."

"Well, you assholes aren't exactly making it hard for me."

The woman leapt from her chair and leaned over the table

and black-and-silver light illuminated in a sharp-tipped vortex within her palm. She snarled at Lisa. "Say that again."

"Sit down!" Kellen barked. "All of you need to shut the fuck up. This isn't about who's got the biggest criminal sack, understand?"

With a hiss, the witch snuffed out her unused attack spell and slumped into her chair.

The shifter shook his head and glared at every face around the table. "We're here because the guy I answer to who reached out to all of you on that fan site wants to hear what each of you brings to the table. If you don't have anything useful to add to what he's looking for, you can get fucked. Understand?"

Those present subsided, the silence punctured only by a few grumbles.

At least I'm playing the part. Lisa focused her gaze on the shifter. "You're talking about Lemonhead, right?"

"You saw the message boards," he replied flippantly. "It was a ballsy move to insert yourself there without having any real ties the way the rest of us do."

"I saw an opportunity and I took it." She shrugged. "And it worked, obviously."

"Uh-huh." The shifter studied her speculatively, then slid both his hands onto the table and drummed his fingertips on the surface. "So why don't you take this as another opportunity to tell us what you know about Johnny Walker. What makes you useful?"

Lisa glanced at his drumming fingers and tried to hold back a smirk when the thick silver ring on the shifter's finger caught the overhead light and flashed red. The shape carved on it was the same profile of a boar she and Johnny had seen on so many drug baggies and tattooed on a random low-level drug dealer in Portland. *If he's been on the Red Boar's payroll this long, I bet at least one of those red stones is a real ruby.*

"Sure." She took a deep breath and scanned the faces of the

other criminals around her. "It wasn't on the YouTube clips, and it won't be on the episode, either as per Johnny's orders. But I know where he lives in Florida. I've been inside his house."

The witch scoffed and shook her head. "But you won't tell us where?"

"Everglades City, right on the main strip and backed up to the swamp. I'd give you an address but I didn't think I'd have to bring that information with me. And no, I haven't memorized it."

"But we're not in Florida," the gnome missing an ear piped up. "We're in Baltimore. The fucking dwarf's in Baltimore. We shouldn't wait until he goes home and gets nice and cozy before we move."

"And that's why I'm here—why we're all here, right?"

The gnome scowled at her.

"Look. Here's everything I know." Lisa tapped her fingers on the table. "Those dumbass dogs are as close as he gets to having family. Johnny lost his mind after his kid was gunned down fifteen years ago. I know you all know about that. And he hits the bottle every night like it's still fifteen years ago. He tries to fill his time pretending to be useful with all his stupid fucking gadgets, but he's still hung up on how badly he failed to keep his kid from eating a bullet.

"And if you intend to keep asking me about all those clips of me and him, then yeah. I'm playing the 'go straight to Johnny's heart' card. Hell, I may even be the first living being on two legs instead of four that he's opened up to in fifteen years. And when he opens up all the way, which he will, his guard will be completely down."

It took everything she had to not grimace at the way she twisted Johnny's pain and his past merely to make it look real in that context. *He knows what I'm doing. I only hope he doesn't get so pissed about it that he forgets the plan.*

"Why you?" Kellen asked. "Specifically, I mean. Why would he take some Light Elf he bagged in '16 under his wing for this failure of a show trying to crawl its way back into the public eye now?"

"Because I told him what I thought he wanted to hear." She forced herself to not look at the boar ring on the shifter's hand when he lifted it to stroke his chin. "His team was holding interviews for an assistant in this stupid thing so I called in and got myself a slot to talk to the bastard. I told him to his face how he'd ruined my life back then and sent me off to spend ten years behind bars, and that I'd come full circle to recognize how he saved me."

The witch snorted.

"Yeah, I know. It sounds like a load of shit." Lisa nodded at her. "And it was. But he was so desperate to feel like he'd done something good in his life that I had him eating from the palm of my hand after the first five minutes. I told him I wanted to work with him on the side of justice and all that crap, and that I admired him for what he was doing and how he got the job done. I convinced him that I decided this was the best way to repay the dwarf who tore my life apart and helped me to turn it around and he still believes that's exactly what happened."

The other thugs sniggered around the table. The witch didn't seem all that convinced, but she assumed the woman had come in there looking for someone to tear down anyway and it happened to be aimed at Stephanie Wyndom.

"Fair enough." Kellen leaned forward at the head of the table and folded his hands. "It sounds like we have an in, then."

"Sure. And we get to go over all this with Lemonhead too, right?" Lisa gestured toward the other criminals. "He wants to see the dwarf burn as much as we do, doesn't he?"

The shifter smirked. "He couldn't make it tonight. I could. And I know he'll be especially grateful to hear more details from someone who's done more than spend the last decade or two stewing over a revenge plot. It looks like you're the only one who's taken any action."

"Yeah. I spent enough time doing jack shit behind bars." She grinned.

"I bet. So where's he staying?"

Lisa paused for a second. *Careful. This could turn south very quickly.* "We're both at the Sagamore Pendry right now with the whole film crew."

"Uh-huh." Kellen pulled his phone out and typed something into it. He didn't look up at her when he asked, "What room?"

Shit. "424. Fourth floor. Right across the hall from me in 427."

The shifter's gaze flicked up to meet hers and he nodded. "Well, that's a start."

Yeah, and we'll have to move quickly to get whoever's staying in those rooms the hell out of there before the Red Boar shows up. At least we'll have the element of surprise.

"We should go after him tonight," the half-wizard said. "Now."

"Yeah." The gnome with the eyepatch pounded a fist on the table. "While he's curled up with his dumb mutts and has no idea this Light Elf turned on him."

A round of shouted agreement rose from the other criminals and some of them banged on the table in their excitement.

Kellen studied Lisa with a raised eyebrow, and she shrugged. "I wasn't planning on tonight, but I sure as hell won't object if that's the way you want to go."

"Then let's grab that bastard in his sleep and tie him up like the fucking animal he is," the Crystal woman shouted and pushed from her chair.

"No." Kellen turned a warning gaze onto her and pointed at her seat. "Sit."

"You want us to wait even longer?" the witch hissed. "I thought we were here to do something—"

"We will do something but not tonight." Kellen slipped his phone into his pocket and stood. "I'll take this information to Lemonhead, and he'll call the shots from there. The rest of you sit back and wait for us to reach out."

"This is ridiculous," the one-eared gnome growled. "Why should we wait for instructions from some asshole who won't even show his face here when we already have everything we need?"

The shifter hissed at him and his eyes flashed silver in warning, although he didn't shift. "Because unlike the rest of you, Lemonhead has outsmarted Johnny Walker at every turn, and the dwarf hasn't laid a hand on him, although not for lack of trying. And because if anyone moves on that dwarf without getting the go-ahead from me first, you won't live to see the day when we take the bounty hunter down ourselves. If Johnny doesn't kill you for moving in on him before it's time, Lemonhead will. And I could be wrong, but I assumed everyone in this room would be a little smarter than they were when a fucking dwarf with an over-inflated ego tossed you behind bars the first time. On camera."

The other thugs grumbled and shifted in their seats, but no one argued any further.

Lisa glanced furtively at those around the table. *They know Lemonhead's reputation, at least. Probably not the Red Boar, but it doesn't matter if they know who they're taking orders from. We do.*

On the fourth floor of the Sagamore Pendry, Phil waved his crew onward down the hall toward the front door of Johnny's suite at the very end. Cody stalked quietly behind the director, followed by David with the boom mic, Alicia in her bandana carrying lighting gear, and Fred and Brad as backup.

"We'll go at this from a different angle, people," Phil whispered and pointed at Johnny's door. "He's had all day to simmer down from that little outburst at the park. And I'm willing to bet he'll be much easier to handle at the end of the day."

They stopped outside the door and he knocked briskly three times. "Johnny? It's Phil."

One coonhound barked inside, then the other.

The director smirked. "Well at least we know he's awake. Johnny! Come on, man. Only a few more questions. You've been in there all day."

The dogs barked wildly.

"I ain't interested," the dwarf shouted.

"I know things went a little south earlier today," Phil said. "But I'd like to get a final wrap-up of the day, Johnny. We've come up with a few talking points we think the viewers would enjoy hearing straight from you."

"Get outta here before I come throw you out."

Phil stepped away from the door and glanced at his crewmembers. "Hang tight. I'll get him to come around," he said quietly, then resumed his usual tone. "Okay, Johnny. I'll be honest with you. I know I pushed a little too hard when we began to dive into your past. That's okay. This new season isn't about your past, though. It's about the present. And we merely want to highlight—"

Paws thumped against the door and scratched furiously as one of the hounds barked over and over.

Staggering back in surprise, Phil stared at the door. "Jesus. He needs to bring those attack dogs under control."

"I don't like havin' to repeat myself," Johnny called from inside. "It's none of your business."

Phil sighed, took his phone out of his pocket, and pulled Lisa's number up. He glanced at Cody. "Are you rolling right now?"

The cameraman nodded without saying a word and panned the camera toward him.

"Not me, man. Focus on the door. He might still answer." Phil made the call and lifted his phone to his ear.

Lisa's cell rang inside Johnny's suite.

"This ain't what I call fun," Johnny said as the hounds barked wildly.

"Johnny, we know Li—we know Stephanie's in there with

you. I can hear her phone." Phil knocked again. "Come on and open up."

"I'd rather be huntin'."

Phil frowned. "Well, yeah. We get that. But we're here now, so—"

"You look like you're about to shit yourself. Get movin'."

"What?" The director called Johnny's number next, but it went straight to voicemail.

"Johnny, what's going on?"

"I ain't interested. Get outta here before I come throw you out."

"Yeah, you already said that." Phil scratched his head.

"I don't like havin' to repeat myself. It's none of your business. This ain't what I call fun."

Alicia cocked her head and scowled. "I don't think that's him."

Phil pounded on the door again. "Johnny! You better open this door right now or I'll call the front desk and tell them your dogs are on a rampage in that suite!"

"I'd rather be huntin'."

"Dammit. Did he seriously record himself on a loop?"

"That's definitely what it sounds like," David muttered.

"I know what it sounds like." Phil whirled around and scanned his team. "Todd, go down to the front desk and...Todd?"

The other members turned around to search for their second camera guy.

"Where the hell is he?"

Dave shrugged. "I thought he was here."

"Shit."

CHAPTER TWENTY-ONE

Johnny tapped the earpiece that synced with his spy bug and scowled at the plain brick wall as he listened in on the private meeting inside the staffing agency office. *I oughtta head right in and wring that fucker's neck, whoever he is. Make him rat out the Red Boar right here and now.*

He took a deep breath and pressed a hand against the wall. *This isn't the time. She did it right. After this, we'll either find the asshole knocking on the wrong hotel door, or she'll get all the details on his next move. And we'll be ready.*

The shifter's voice continued in Johnny's headset. "And I could be wrong, but I assumed everyone in this room would be a little smarter than they were when a fucking dwarf with an over-inflated ego tossed you behind bars the first time. On camera."

The shuffle of slow footsteps rose from behind the dwarf, and his hand went to the hilt of his utility knife at his belt. *A whole city full of idiots.*

Johnny whirled, drew his knife, and flicked it out. "You picked the wrong night, asshole."

"Whoa, whoa." The man Johnny recognized from the film crew took one hand off his phone—which he kept aimed at the bounty hunter's face—and raised it in surrender. "Hey, man. I'm only here to catch the action."

"Are you fuckin' kiddin' me?" Johnny stormed toward the man and tried to slap the phone out of his hand. "Turn that shit off. You ain't even supposed to be out here."

"And you aren't supposed to leave without telling us. That's the deal, right?"

"Deal's off. Gimme that."

"No." The guy ducked away from Johnny and lifted the phone again. "What is this place anyway?"

"None of your business. Dammit, you… What's your name?"

The guy raised an eyebrow. "Todd."

"I swear on Sheila's diesel engine, Todd, if you don't get that damn phone outta my face and hightail it back to that hotel, I'll—"

Static crackled in his earpiece, then multiple voices rose again from inside the meeting.

"You hear that?"

"Someone's outside."

"I bet this Light Elf bitch brought backup with her."

"Hey," Lisa said, her voice even and level. "I've been nothing but straight with you guys."

"Then go check it out," the shifter said. "Alone. We'll wait."

"Shit." Johnny hissed and lunged for Todd. He managed to wrap an arm around the guy's neck and pulled him close. "Gimme that fuckin' phone."

"No! Get off me!"

The front door to the office building opened, and Lisa stormed outside. She rounded the corner to see Johnny holding Todd in what was almost a sleeper hold. "Hey! What the hell do you think you're doing?"

Johnny frowned at her, and she nodded toward the building with wide eyes.

Yeah. We're puttin' on a show, then.

"Hey, I just came to see what's going on in there," Todd started. "And now this—"

"Shut up," Lisa spat. "I don't know who you are, but you picked the wrong night and the wrong place to play super spy."

"What are you—ow! Ah! Get off me! I'm—" Todd choked and crumpled when Johnny stabbed a pressure point at the base of the man's neck with two fingers.

Lisa shot a fireball at Todd's feet for added effect, and the unsuspecting cameraman stared at her with wide eyes.

"Why are you—"

The click and hiss of Johnny's tranquilizer gun unloading a full dose into the guy's neck were fortunately quiet enough to not travel through brick walls. Todd thumped to the sidewalk beside the building when Johnny released him and the dwarf looked at Lisa and shrugged.

"Stupid," she muttered.

The front door burst open again and this time, released the full dozen criminals gathered to bash on Johnny Walker and plan his demise. The dwarf darted into the shadows and used the thugs' clamoring footsteps to hide the sound of his own as he headed toward the back of the building.

"Did you get him?"

"Who the fuck was it?"

"I bet she let him go. She's too soft."

Lisa snatched Todd's phone from where it had toppled to the sidewalk and turned and raised an eyebrow at the criminals. "Some dipshit thought he'd come take a look at what's happening. I got him and his phone. So we're good."

"Is he a friend of yours?" the witch asked with a scowl.

"Yeah, I wipe out all my friends with magical attacks and leave them dead on the side of office buildings," Lisa quipped. "Come on. I've never seen him before."

Kellen guided the front door closed gently and peered at Todd. "So you got him."

"It sure looks like, doesn't it?" She folded her arms and glared at the shifter. "Does anyone else want to keep questioning whether or not I am who I say I am?"

"No, you're all right." The gnome with the eyepatch hawked and spat and the wet glob landed just in front of Todd's face. "Now you get to clean up your mess."

"Yeah, and I will." Lisa turned toward Kellen. "So what's next?"

"The rest of you fuck off and wait to hear from me." He sneered at Todd, then turned and roared at the criminals, "*Now.* Do I need to throw you out on your asses or what?"

The dozen thugs scattered away from the office building and disappeared into the shadows beneath Baltimore's city lights in the middle of the night.

Lisa sighed and rolled her eyes. "I need at least ten minutes to get rid of the body."

"Do what you gotta do." The shifter stepped toward her and handed her a burner flip phone. "Then wait for the call."

"Do you hand these out to everyone else too?"

"No. You're the one with Johnny Walker eating out of your hand. Lemonhead will wanna talk to you. So take the phone, Stephanie. Wait for the call. And don't fuck this up."

"Yeah, I get it." She took the phone and stuck it in her back pocket beside Todd's smartphone. "Anything else?"

Kellen nodded at the body on the sidewalk. "Make sure no one sees you."

"This isn't my first time, but thanks for the tip." She waited for the shifter to leave, but he stood in front of the building and made a call on his phone instead. *Shit. He wants to see me toss a dead body that isn't even dead too?*

"It's Kellen." The shifter shot Lisa a sidelong glance, then stepped away across the front of the building. "Yeah, all of them."

Lisa turned toward Todd as the man's fingers twitched and he groaned quietly. *No, no, no.*

"Yeah, hold on." Kellen turned toward her with a questioning frown. "Is there a problem over there?"

"No. The skinny asshole's heavier than I thought." She waved him off and tried not to stare at Johnny creeping toward the corner with his tranquilizer gun in hand. When she took Todd's arm, he groaned again.

"All right, what the hell?" The shifter strode toward her.

"Back off. I got it." She snarled belligerently to cover up the sound of Johnny dosing the cameraman with a second tranquilizer. Kellen fortunately didn't seem to notice.

"Have you ever done this before?" he asked.

"I said it wasn't my first time. I'll handle it."

Johnny whipped a disk from his belt, activated it, and launched the explosive with a sidearm toss up and over the side of the office building.

"Do you know any severing spells?" the shifter asked.

"What?"

"I have a good one for choppin' up big hunks of meat and making them disappear a hell of a lot easier than—"

Johnny's disk exploded on the other side of the building, rattling a trashcan and setting off the alarm of a car parked on the other side of the cross street.

"What the fuck?"

Lisa gritted her teeth. "I'd offer to come check it out with you, but I have my own cleanup right here."

He growled and turned toward the site of the explosion. "Hurry the fuck up already. And keep that phone on you."

"Yep."

Kellen jogged across the front of the building toward the car's blaring alarm and lifted his phone to his ear again. "I don't know. Some asshole playing with homemade explosives, probably. You never know in this city…"

His voice faded away as he went to investigate.

Lisa looked up at Johnny as he crept toward the twice-unconscious Todd. "We need to hurry," she whispered harshly.

"And I gave us a diversion. You're welcome, darlin'." He squatted beside the cameraman, slung the man's torso over his shoulder, and stifled a grunt as he stood. "Now, we get the hell outta Dodge."

Two dogs started up a furious round of barking across the street, accompanied by the car alarm that still blared in the middle of the night. The partners took the cross street on their side of the building to get out of sight. From there, they stuck to back alleys and stayed far away from open bars and restaurants and the pools of light from the streetlamps as they headed toward the hotel.

By the time Kellen returned to the front of the office building, they were already three blocks away. "No, it's fine," he said into his phone as he peered into the shadows. "It's taken care of. Yeah, I'll be there in a while."

CHAPTER TWENTY-TWO

Todd recovered from his second dose of knock-out juice a block away from the hotel. He groaned and shifted and his eyes fluttered open. "Hey, what the fuck—"

His elbow flailed and collided with the back of the dwarf's head.

"Shit. Stop."

"Let me go. What the hell?" The man wriggled so much, Johnny finally lowered his shoulder and let him tumble onto the sidewalk with a thump.

"Ow…"

"Look here, Todd." The bounty hunter pointed at the man who stared at him in wide-eyed shock. "You ain't got no business followin' anyone in the middle of the night. Especially us."

"I was only trying to—"

"Don't matter what you were only tryin'. You almost fucked up a seriously high-level, top-secret, federal goddamn case, ya hear? You're way outta line here, pal."

Todd blinked quickly, then looked at Lisa. "Where's my phone?"

"That's what you're worried about?" She shook her head and pulled his phone out. "Unlock it."

"Why?"

"Because I said so, and if you don't, Johnny will inject another of his tranquilizers into your neck, and you can spend the rest of the night passed out here on the sidewalk." She leaned down, her gaze hard, and offered him the screen of his phone. "Do it."

"Jesus. Okay." He unlocked the device and she pulled it away and went through the video clips. "Come on. What are you doing?"

"Getting rid of the evidence you don't have clearance to carry around with you." Lisa deleted the last three videos on his camera, then tossed him his phone. "Don't do that again."

"Shit. That was good stuff—"

"It ain't your place." Johnny grasped the man's upper arm and hauled him to his feet. "And you're walkin' a thin line already."

"It's my job, man."

"And when I say back the fuck off and get rid of the cameras, I mean it!" Johnny snapped. "You're lucky you're walkin' away from this with a groggy head and a few bruises."

Lisa folded her arms. "Or that you're walking away from it at all. I'm merely glad no one wanted to stick around to watch me rip you apart limb from limb."

What little color remained in Todd's face drained instantly. "What?"

"We managed to make them think I killed you. So now you'll have to hide your face behind more than a camera phone until this is done."

"I don't get it."

"You don't need to. Get back inside." Johnny shoved the man toward the front doors of the hotel and grunted. "And I need a drink."

Todd stepped off the elevator on the third floor to head to his hotel room, and the two partners continued to the fourth floor on their own.

"Johnny, we need to put some kind of security on those two room numbers I gave." Lisa swiped her fake red hair away from her forehead. "In case they decide to move on the hotel first."

"It didn't sound like that was part of the plan, darlin'. You wouldn't have been handed a burner phone otherwise either."

"True." She reached back to pat the phone in her pocket. "Do you think they put a tracker in this too?"

"I'm bettin' on it. Which is good." He smirked. "It shows 'em your story panned out. We're in the Sagamore Pendry, and that's part of what they wanted to know."

She sighed heavily. "Right. Now I guess I wait for the call."

"Yep." Johnny reached for her hand and gave it a quick squeeze before he released it. "You did a damn fine job of it, darlin'. Even when it came to spoutin' hateful shit about 'the fuckin' dwarf.'"

"Oh, yeah. That was fun."

They chuckled, and the elevator doors opened with a soft ding. "Now I'm fixin' for a nightcap and a full night's—what the hell?"

A large group of people had gathered at the far end of the hall —Phil, the film crew, the on-duty hotel manager, and two other hospitality staff members.

"Mr. Walker?" The manager knocked on the door with a nervous grimace. "Sir, we're getting noise complaints now about your dogs and you need to open up."

The hounds bayed inside and scratched at the door in agitation.

"Mr. Walker?"

"Get outta here before I come throw you out."

"Sir. I'm merely trying to understand the situation. And...and if you don't open this door right now, I'm within my rights to open it for you."

"Don't worry about all that, now," Johnny said as he strode down the hallway. "I'm back."

The manager startled and turned quickly to see the dwarf heading toward him. He looked at the suite door and his mouth opened and closed in confusion. "I…you… Who's—"

"It's all right. Nothin' to keep goin' on about." Johnny retrieved his wallet and gestured at the crew. "If y'all were lookin' for Todd, he's back in his room puttin' ice on a few choice parts of himself. It's time for the rest of y'all to move on."

"Johnny…" Phil looked like he was about to explode.

"Now. I'll make it worth your while tomorrow, huh? But get out of here. These folks have had more than enough to deal with for one night."

With a growl of frustration, Phil gestured for the crew to head out before he stormed toward the elevators, shaking his head.

Johnny opened his wallet, pulled out a handful of twenties, and distributed them to the manager and the two staff members the man had brought. "I'm sure this ain't the kinda emergency you fellas are used to runnin' up against on the regular."

"I… Well, no, Mr. Walker."

"Johnny. Thanks for your concern. And this is for your troubles."

The manager took the cash with wide eyes. His staff members exchanged a confused glance but pocketed the money instantly. "Right. So…who was that yelling at me inside your suite?"

"Naw, that was my voice all right." Johnny leaned toward the man and gave him a conspiratorial smirk. "I hate to leave 'em alone in there, but when I ain't got another option, the recordin' helps the hounds feel a little more comfortable. Otherwise, they tend to get unruly, you understand."

"Unruly?" The manager stared at the suite's door and frowned. "Worse than that?"

"You bet." He flashed his key card at the door, pushed it open, and nodded at the hotel staff. "Enjoy your evenin', fellas. Stephanie, why don't you step inside with me for a spell?"

"Sure." She smiled politely at the baffled hotel manager. "Thanks for everything. Have a good night."

"Yes. Yes…y-you too…" The man stared after them until Johnny shut the door and slid the lock into place.

"Johnny!" Luther barked and raced across the suite toward the front. "Finally! You were gone forever."

"Yeah, and we had to cover for you the whole time. Those two-legs out there are so gullible."

"Did you bring us any treats, Johnny?"

"You know, for a job well done?"

"In a moment, boys. Y'all did all right with the pedal." He set the tranquilizer gun on the half-wall of the kitchen. Then, he stooped to pick up the pedal device and switched it off before he tossed it onto the bed through the open bedroom doorway. "I need a minute."

He went to the kitchen to pour himself his usual four fingers of Johnny Walker Black and returned to slump onto the soft leather couch with a heavy sigh. "Well, that was somethin'."

"It sure was." Lisa joined him on the couch. "Your little spy-bug thing doesn't pick up visuals too, does it?"

"No." The dwarf raised his eyebrows. "What did you see?"

"The shifter. Kellen? He had a boar-shaped ring on his left hand. A few red gemstones and everything."

"The damn mouthpiece, right?"

"It looks like it." She grinned. "And Stephanie Wyndom has an in none of the other Johnny-haters were offered."

"With the phone. Well shit, darlin'. You brought this all together to get it workin' out just fine."

"Thank you."

"No, I mean it."

"And you didn't try to bust the door down even once."

He snorted. "I wanted to."

"I know."

They sat on the couch for a few moments in silence as Johnny sipped his whiskey and thought over everything they'd heard. "We got an in. And until we bag the Red Boar, whoever he is, the feds can keep footin' the bill and thinkin' we're still on the Hugh case." He turned toward her with a grin and raised his glass for a toast, then paused. "Aw, shit. Do you want a drink? I didn't even—"

"No, it's okay." Lisa laughed and waved him off. "I'll toast empty-handed with you."

"Naw, that ain't a toast. It's bad luck to toast with water, darlin' and even worse luck to do it with a handful of nothin'." He stood and headed toward the kitchen.

"Johnny, you can pour all you want but I'm not drinking your whiskey."

"Just sit tight."

She sighed and shook her head.

Luther padded toward her and rested his chin on her knees. "You got any treats for us, lady?"

"Hey, Luther." She scratched behind his ears and chuckled. "It sounded like you guys had a real blast with that pedal, huh?"

"She doesn't have treats, bro," Rex said from where he'd curled in front of the armchair. "And she can't hear you."

"I know. But hey, the ear-scratching's real nice. Yeah, yeah, lady. Keep that up."

Johnny returned from the kitchen not with another rocks glass full of whiskey but with a wineglass. "Here you go. And don't even think about tellin' me you ain't into wine, 'cause this is the same damn bottle you ordered up here the other night."

Lisa took the glass and stared at him. "I took that bottle to my room with me."

"Yep. And I had another brought up." He sat on the couch and turned to face her with a crooked smile. "Now we can toast like partners oughtta."

"Well." She grinned and lifted the wineglass. "To partners."

"And to Lisa Breyer's master plan. Hell, I'll even toast to Stephanie fuckin' Wyndom while we're at it."

They clinked their glasses together, and Lisa took a large sip of her wine. "Thanks for this."

"The toast or the wine?"

"Well, the toast was nice, Johnny. The wine's even better."

"I'll take your word for it." He sipped his whiskey and met her gaze. "A person oughtta have their drink of choice stashed away just for this reason. Reasons for celebratin' come few and far between in my experience. I aim to be prepared when they do come around."

She stared at her drink and tried to hide a smile. "And how often do you stock whatever kitchen you're in with a bottle of someone else's drink?"

Johnny snorted. "You got me, darlin'. This is a first."

"Oh. Well then, I'm flattered."

"You should be. Just don't let it go to your head. You dropped a couple of real heavy bombs in that meetin' about me."

Lisa almost choked on her next sip of wine but managed to compose herself. "Johnny, you know that was all part of me getting them to trust me, right? I didn't—"

"You didn't mean a word, I know. Or at least half of it." When he grinned, she chuckled with relief and shook her head. "That was top-level lyin', darlin'. Well done."

"And we're this much closer to finally getting your justice."

"Not mine. Dawn's."

She set her glass down on the coffee table and turned on the couch to face him. "Of course it's for Dawn. And it's also for you. After everything the Bureau did to cover up one hell of a mess they made, you deserve to get this all cleaned up. Don't leave yourself out of the picture."

"Huh." Johnny sniffed and looked away from her. "I can't argue with that one."

"So don't even try."

He downed the rest of his whiskey and grunted. "Once we clean up the streets and take that Red Boar fucker in, I'll still have a bone to pick with the whole damn FBI."

"Well, I didn't expect you to walk away from that. And you don't have to tell me what that entails, but—"

"Naw, I ain't exactly worked it out myself yet. But I'll know how to handle it when the time comes. And then I'll go back to my swamp."

Lisa chuckled and shook her head. "Of course. And do what?"

"Whatever feels right."

"It's the best way to be if you ask me." She tucked her hair behind her ear with a hesitant smile. "But I do hope you decide to keep working for the Department. Even after whatever giant ass-kicking you decide on dishing out when all this is over."

"Ass-kickin's the least of it, darlin', although I ain't too sure why you'd want that."

Lisa scooted closer and studied the dwarf's brown eyes, her smile growing. "Because if you're done with federal cases, that means I'll have to go back to DC and I'm not sure I want to do that."

"Oh, so now you're such a huge fan of the swamps you can't stand leavin'?"

"And a few other things."

She stopped him from saying anything else when she leaned forward and kissed him softly. Before Johnny could wrap his head around what was happening, Lisa pulled away and grinned. "But you still have time to think about it."

The dwarf cleared his throat and watched her stand.

"Goodnight, Johnny."

"Yeah. 'Night."

She pulled up her redheaded Stephanie illusion to make the trip across the hall, and he didn't move until he heard both his suite door and the door to her hotel room close behind her.

"Whoa-ho-ho, Johnny!" Luther trotted toward him with wide eyes. "What did I *watch*?"

"Seriously, Johnny?" Rex's head whipped from his master to the hallway. "She made a move. *She* made a move! Why are you sitting there?"

"It's about damn time. Go get her!"

The dwarf snapped his fingers and both hounds fell silent. "It's late, boys. I'm turnin' in."

Luther gasped and froze and stared at his master as Johnny rose slowly from the couch.

Rex snorted. "Are you feeling okay, Johnny?"

"I'm fine."

The larger hound padded after him as he headed swiftly to the bedroom door. "You sure? Come here and let me smell ya, Johnny. 'Cause if you're turning down a lady like that, I think there's something wrong with you. Hey, come on. Stop walking away—"

The bedroom door closed in the hound's face, and Johnny said from the other side, "Night, boys."

"Johnny," Luther said warily. "Johnny? Seriously, I think you need to see a two-leg vet or something."

The bounty hunter flopped on the king-sized mattress and stared at the ceiling with a sigh. *There ain't nothin' wrong with me. I like her, is all, and now I know for sure.*

CHAPTER TWENTY-THREE

The next morning, Johnny woke up at 6:15 am with more energy than he could remember at that hour. He hopped out of bed and jumped into the shower, whistling the whole time. When he'd toweled off and pulled on another pair of black Levi's and a button-down shirt, he combed his hair, winked at himself in the mirror, and thrust the bedroom door open.

"Beautiful mornin', ain't it, boys?"

"What?" Luther whipped his head up from where he lay curled in front of the armchair.

"Did you forget we're not home, Johnny?" Rex yawned, then licked his muzzle. "'Cause you don't say 'beautiful morning' unless we're about to go hunting."

"Are we going hunting, Johnny?"

"I'm fixin' to get breakfast. Coffee and somethin' nice for both of us." He moved quickly through the suite, checking his pockets for his phone and his wallet.

"Wait, both of who?" Luther glanced at his brother. "There are three of us."

"Y'all hang tight. I won't be long." Humming a random tune,

the dwarf practically danced toward the front door of the suite and disappeared into the hall.

"Johnny, wait. What about us, huh?"

There was no reply.

With a sigh, Luther stood and trotted toward the bedroom door left wide open. "If he's not gonna let us out, he can't be mad if we use the shower again, right?"

Rex followed his brother into the master bathroom. "It sounds like a fair deal to me. Hurry up. I gotta go."

Johnny passed Lisa's hotel room on his way to the elevators and grinned. *This time, I'll be the one wakin' up early to bring everythin' to her room. She deserves that much. Hot damn, what a day already.*

The film crew was nowhere in sight when he reached the lobby, which only added an extra pep to his step as he strode to the front doors. Johnny smiled and greeted every hotel staff member with a "Mornin'," and took his good mood with him into the street to head for the coffee shop and bakery three blocks down.

He strutted down the sidewalk with a crooked smile, nodded to pedestrians who passed him, and hummed his made-up tune. *Helluva day. It's only gonna get better.*

When he stepped inside the café, he went straight to the order counter and cleared his throat.

"Good morning. Welcome to—"

"Tell me straight, bud, 'cause I ain't fixin' to beat around the bush this mornin'. Can you say y'all got the best coffee in the area?"

The barista chuckled and glanced at the sacks of unground beans lining the counter in the back. "Well, we like to think so, certainly."

"That's good enough for me. I want a large of your best roast —black. Then make one of whatever you think is the best coffee drink you can come up with. Somethin' special, ya hear?"

"Got it." The barista rang up the beverages and glanced at the dwarf. "Anything else?"

"Yeah. Y'all got a fancy pastry plate or somethin'?"

"Not exactly. But feel free to choose from our pastry selection over here—"

"Naw, get me one of everythin'." Johnny sniffed and nodded at the man. "I ain't playin'."

"You got it." The man added the cost to the register, then paused. "You're Johnny Walker, right? The bounty hunter with that—"

"With the damn show startin' again in Baltimore? You bet. That's me. I tell you what, bud, it's a helluva day to be me."

"I can tell." Chuckling, the barista nodded. "I'll go make your drinks. Then give me a few minutes to bag up the pastry order."

"That's fine. Take your time." Johnny stuck his thumbs through his belt loops and glanced around the café, whistling and bouncing on the toes of his boots. *Helluva day.*

Lisa rolled out of bed at 6:30 am and smiled. *Something tells me it'll be a good day.*

She spent a few minutes in the bathroom brushing her teeth and washing her face, then pulled her hair back into a loose ponytail and grinned. Remembering the night before made her laugh at her reflection. *Well, it could've gone worse. Not bad for a first move, Breyer.*

As soon as she'd finished getting dressed and strapped her shoulder holster on beneath a light jacket, a low buzz came from her nightstand. She turned a lazy smile toward it but it disappeared when she saw the burner phone turning slowly on the table with the incoming call. "Shit."

She leapt toward the table, snatched the phone up, and answered. "Hello?"

"He wants to meet you tonight," Kellen said, his voice low and scratchy. "And he's got someone on the way to the Sagamore Pendry right now with a package. It has all the instructions you'll need to get the job done."

"Okay." She took a deep breath. "Where do I pick this package up?"

"Right outside. The runner should be there in the next five minutes if he isn't already. In a red baseball cap."

"Sure. I'll go down and look for him."

"Good. I want verbal confirmation from you and the runner that you received the package alone."

"So I'll call you back at this number when I have it—"

"No," the shifter practically barked at her. "Stay on the phone the whole time. And get your ass downstairs right now."

"Yeah, okay. Let me get my shoes on at least."

She pulled up her Stephanie illusion and stepped into her sneakers. *Shit. I can't tell Johnny or they'll know. I'll go down and get the package, bring it back, and we can go through it together. No big deal.*

She slipped out of her hotel room, grateful for the fact that Phil and his incessant badgering hadn't yet started for the day. "I'm walking down the hall."

"Keep talking," Kellen grumbled.

She narrated her ride down the elevator to the first floor, her walk across the lobby not yet busy with the usual breakfast rush in the restaurant or at the continental breakfast bar, and her exit through the hotel's front doors. "Okay, I'm standing out on the sidewalk."

"Do you see him yet?"

"No."

"He shouldn't be hard to miss, Stephanie—red baseball cap and gray shirt and carrying a large cardboard box."

Lisa squinted against the brisk morning breeze and scanned

the few pedestrians on the sidewalk. "Nothing yet. Are you sure you gave him the right hotel?"

"Don't be smart with me, Light Elf. Stay where you are and keep talking. He'll be there."

The short whoop of a police siren down the street caught her attention, and the Baltimore PD vehicle moved slowly toward the hotel with intermittent flashes of red and blue lights. She turned away from the car and searched the other side of the street. *Worst timing. We need to get this over with.*

The car pulled to the curb in front of the Sagamore Pendry and Lisa. Both officers opened their doors and got out. "Ma'am? Is everything okay? You look a little lost."

"I'm fine officer, thank you. Just waiting for a friend."

"That's a very early meetup in front of a hotel."

"Well, we were supposed to go out for breakfast." *What the hell is going on?* She tried to smile at the officers and scan the sidewalk at the same time.

"Uh-huh. What's your name?"

Shit. The damn shifter can hear everything I say. She kept the phone pressed to her ear.

"What's happening?" Kellen asked.

"A few officers passing by," she replied with a tight smile. "I'm still waiting for you, by the way."

"Who are you talking to?" the bearded Officer Brently asked.

"My friend."

"Okay, well you'll have to hang up and answer our question, ma'am. What's your name?"

"Stephanie Wyndom."

"Hang up the phone, Stephanie."

"Don't even think about it," Kellen growled in her ear.

"I'm sorry, officers. I can't." Lisa glanced up and down the street as the officers approached her on the sidewalk. "My friend's bad with directions. I have to—"

"Do you have any ID on you?" the bald officer asked. His name badge read *McCormick* in faded print.

Shit. "Um...no. I stepped out of my hotel room to meet my friend here, so I don't have anything on me."

His partner glanced down at the open front of her light jacket. "But you had time to strap on a firearm first. Do you have a permit for concealed carry?"

She met his gaze head-on. "Listen, this isn't what you think—"

"This is exactly what we think," McCormick interrupted. "Drop the phone and put your hands behind your head."

"Officers..."

"You have an open warrant in Maryland state, Ms. Wyndom. Hands up. Now."

Lisa glanced at the officers' hands resting on the grips of their holstered service weapons. *I can't show them who I am. Kellen's still listening to every goddamn word.* "Okay. *Okay.* Dropping the phone."

She did that, and the burner phone clacked against the sidewalk, still open with the call still connected to the Red Boar's shifter mouthpiece.

"And I'm putting my hand behind my head." Lisa raised her hands slowly. The minute her fingertips brushed her redheaded curls, Officer Brently stepped forward briskly and grabbed her wrists, a pair of handcuffs at the ready.

"Stephanie Wyndom, you are under arrest for grand larceny. Anything you say can and will be used against you in the court of law..."

She exhaled a heavy sigh and continued to scan the street for the damn messenger with the red baseball cap. There was no trace of him as the bearded officer led her toward the back of the police car and opened the door. *There is no messenger with a stupid package, is there? Stephanie Wyndom doesn't have any outstanding offenses or warrants either.*

The other officer approached and drew her service pistol from its holster. "Get in."

"You're making a big mistake—"

"No mistake." He shoved her roughly into the plastic back seat of the cop car. "This is our job. You made it very easy for us, honestly."

He shut the door and both officers walked around the front of the squad car and got inside. In the passenger seat, the bald man studied her service weapon and typed the serial number into the small computer mounted on the dashboard.

"Really, Officers. I'm not who you think I am."

"You're exactly who we're looking for. Most of the time, anonymous tips don't exactly pan out. But I guess this is our lucky day."

They got a tip? The fucking Red Boar bastard set me up!

"No, I'm serious. Look." Lisa removed her Stephanie illusion and looked at each of the officers with a calm she certainly didn't feel.

"Nice try, lady. We've got plenty of magicals in the precinct. You're a Light Elf. You can make yourself look like anyone—"

"Half-Light Elf, actually. And I need you both to listen to me. There's about to be an attack inside that hotel. Room 434—"

"Save your breath, Stephanie."

"My name's Lisa Breyer. I'm a federal agent with the FBI's Bounty Hunter Division. I'm working a federal case right now, and I need you both to—"

"You said you were on the phone with a friend," the bearded man said blandly.

"I was on the phone with the asshole who's going to attack that hotel room! Because I'm undercover!"

His partner tapped the computer screen. "Well, we can add impersonating a federal agent to your rap sheet too."

"What?"

"The firearm's registered to Agent Lisa Breyer—"

"That's because I am Lisa Breyer!"

"Ma'am, if you can't calm down, we'll have to take more severe measures to do it for you, understand?"

Brently shifted into drive and pulled onto the street.

"Jesus Christ. Listen to me. My badge number is 9740203. I'm in constant contact with Agent Tommy Nelson. He works for the Department of Monsters and Magicals. If you get in contact with him, he'll tell you everything you need to know."

"Including why your alias has an open arrest warrant?" the other officer scoffed. "Now I've heard everything."

"No, that was manufactured—recently. And not by our team. Stephanie Wyndom is an undercover alias. I know she checks out in the system, but that didn't include any recent crimes or an open warrant. I'm on a federal case with Johnny Walker—"

"That bounty hunter dwarf?" He turned to look at her through the wire mesh separating the front of the vehicle from the back seat. "Yeah, I've watched some of those clips. You two look real tight on camera."

"Because I'm his partner." She grimaced at the bite of the cold steel handcuffs pressing against her wrists between her back and the hard plastic seat of the squad car. "You need to look into this right now. Call your precinct captain. Ask them to look into the bounty assigned for a Kilomea named Yarren Brork. That's the federal case that brought us here, file number 834627B concerning Senator Richard Hugh. We were at his house only a few days ago. Run my badge number, huh? 9740203. With my ID number, 288843. How would a dumbass criminal with an open warrant for grand larceny know that off the top of her head?"

"Do I need to get out the taser?" he warned.

"Hold on." The driver pulled over in the mostly empty parking lot of a convenience store on the corner and shifted into park, although he left the engine running.

"What are you doing?"

"I think we should look into this."

"Marco, she's a crazy-ass Light Elf trying to get out of an arrest."

"Run the badge number."

"Officers, I *truly* need you to let me out of these cuffs so I can get back to that hotel. There will be an attack, and I don't think either of you wants this on your heads when it happens."

"You sit tight, ma'am. If all this pans out, we'll drive you to the hotel ourselves. But we can't simply let you go on hearsay."

"It's not hearsay. It's the truth!"

"Yeah, we'll see."

McCormick twisted in the passenger seat and jerked his chin up at her. "You can either wait quietly with your wits about you, or I can come back there and tighten those cuffs. Your choice."

"Fuck." Lisa leaned back against the plastic seat and winced at the sharp pinch in her wrists within the handcuffs. *Hurry the hell up. I was just played by the asshole even the FBI couldn't bring down, and Johnny has no idea.*

CHAPTER TWENTY-FOUR

With a coffee caddy in one hand and a massive bag of assorted pastries tucked under the other arm, Johnny stepped out of the elevators on the fourth floor and grinned. *It only took half an hour. She's probably only now startin' to roll over and wake up with no idea this dwarf brought a damn feast.*

His whistle echoed around him as he hurried down the hall, and he chuckled when he stopped in front of Lisa's hotel room. After switching the bag of pastries to under his other arm, he knocked briskly on the door. "It's me. Johnny."

There was no reply.

"Come on, darlin'. I know you're an early riser. Open up, huh? I brought you somethin'."

He waited for ten seconds and when he didn't hear a sound on the other side of the door, he retrieved his phone from his back pocket and pulled up Lisa's number. The line rang six times, then went straight to voicemail.

"Huh." The dwarf turned and scanned the empty hallway. *Maybe she had the same idea as I did. We must have missed each other on the way.*

He crossed the hall and had to set everything down to pull his wallet out and flash his key card at the door to his suite. The green light blinked and he opened the door and propped it open with one boot while he gathered the drink caddy and the bag of pastries again. When he held them securely, he slipped inside and let the door click shut behind him.

"I'm back, boys. Hey, did y'all hear Lisa steppin' out while I was gone?" Johnny placed the pastries on the half-wall of the kitchen beside his tranquilizer gun. "Boys? I swear, if I find y'all drinkin' outta the toilet again, you're fixin' for a real talkin' to after this."

He set the drink caddy down too, peeled the lid off his black coffee, and took the to-go cup with him down the hall.

"Rex. Luther. What are you up to?"

When he received no reply, he felt a faint prickle of alarm.

Taking a tentative sip of his piping-hot coffee, Johnny walked down the hall with a frown and peered around the corner of the wall blocking the huge living area from view. "Whatever game you're playin', it's time to cut it out. I need to—"

He froze in the entrance to the living area and took in the scene in a split second.

Both hounds lay sprawled on the floor in front of the massive armchair with its back to the wide windows. Neither of them moved but for the barest rise and fall of their bellies, and in the armchair sat the one magical Johnny would've recognized anywhere.

"Welcome back." The Red Boar grinned and his gray, burn-marred skin drew tight around the corners of his mouth on his squashed face. He glanced at the pistol in his hand, which was already pointed casually at Johnny's chest.

"What the fuck did you do to my hounds?"

"I didn't want them to raise the alarm." The intruder shrugged. "It was fairly easy to disable them when their master wasn't around to shout commands."

Johnny gritted his teeth and took inventory of the room. *All I have on hand is a fuckin' cup of coffee. He's likely to blow my brains out before I can put a hand on my knife. Shit.*

He cleared his throat and scowled at the huge, scarred magical in the armchair, which looked like it had been built specifically for an asshole of that size. "What do you want?"

"The first part's very simple." The Red Boar cocked his head, that twisted grin unwavering. "I want to know why you're working again."

"Huh. If you're waitin' to hear me say I came outta retirement to bag your ass, you're gonna be disappointed."

"No. You had no idea who I was until we met face to face in New York." The gray magical chuckled. "So what got you back in the game?"

"That job in New York. You merely happened to be the motherfucker who wanted a shifter girl badly enough to fight me for her. I happened to be better and faster."

"I'll give you that one, Johnny. Sure." The armchair groaned beneath the Red Boar's weight as he shifted and crossed one leg over the other. "That shifter girl doesn't matter anymore. But why don't you tell me why you're hunting me, now."

"Who said I was?"

"The look on your face. Which I wasn't sure I'd see but now you've given me everything I need. The Level-Six Bounty Hunter, Johnny Walker the pissed-off dwarf, has some kind of personal vendetta, isn't that right?"

Johnny studied the magical, then slowly took a sip of his coffee. *He came here for a fuckin' heart-to-heart. Sure. We can play all cards out on the table.*

"All right. I want your head on a fuckin' silver platter. Is that good enough for ya?"

"Because I tried to outbid everyone at that auction?" The Red Boar cocked his head and clicked his tongue. "It took me a while to get out from under that chandelier, but I hardly think one night at a Monsters Ball is enough of a reason for you to hate me so much."

"No. That simply started the ball rollin'." He glared at the huge magical's oddly shaped face and glowing eyes. "You killed my little girl."

"Oh…" The Red Boar clicked his tongue again and inclined his head slightly as if in thought. "There have been so many, Johnny. You'll have to be a little more specific."

"Dawn Walker. Twelve years old. In RedHero Comics on October 27th, 2005. Creed Vilguard and Prentiss Avalon. Your fuckin' goons shot my daughter in the back of the head. Does that ring enough bells?"

"Sure." The gray bastard chuckled. "But Vilguard and Avalon were caught, weren't they? The shifter's finger pulled the trigger, and he's spent the last fifteen years behind bars—"

"It ain't the shifter I give a shit about. It's the motherfucker who told him to pull the trigger."

The Red Boar grinned. "You sound so sure."

"I am."

"Good. Yes, dwarf. I was in the shop that night. Your daughter had some serious guts on her. I'll give her that. Trying to pull that sniveling human out of the clutches of his own mistakes."

"And you had the shifter gun down a little girl!"

"Can you blame me?"

"I can and I do."

With the pistol still aimed unwaveringly at Johnny's chest, the Red Boar gazed around the hotel suite as he stretched his neck. "I had to take certain precautions, Johnny. A little dwarf girl barging into that comic book store and demanding the release of an idiotic man playing drug dealer? She dropped your name, more or less, and I wasn't about to give you an open invitation to make good on her naïve promise."

"You did anyway."

"Because I'm the one who gave the order to shoot the little

girl who said her daddy's a bounty hunter? I suppose that gives you a certain right to want to see me hang."

Johnny's fist clenched at his side and the coffee sloshed in the cup in his other hand as it trembled. "I want far more than that, you bastard."

"Oh, I'm sure. So do I. You have to know by now how many of us truly hate you, Johnny."

"It don't mean—"

A knock came at the front door. "Johnny? It's Phil. I'm trying to start over, man. Come on. We're ready to keep rolling."

Johnny didn't move.

"Howie's out here with me," Phil added dryly. "I thought he knows best how to get you out of your shell."

"Johnny?" Howie said as if to verify his presence.

Every time that damn director shows up is the wrong fuckin' time.

"Tell them to get lost," the Red Boar growled.

The dwarf's lip curled into a smirk. "And disappoint all my avid fans?"

"We saw Stephanie stepping out front earlier," Phil continued, "so we thought this might be a good time to get some one-on-one Johnny time. Come on. Open up."

The Red Boar swung the barrel of his pistol toward the front door before he returned it to Johnny's chest. "Go answer the door. Tell them you'll give them what they want later and that they're not to disturb you. Then you and I can finish this conversation in peace."

Not fuckin' likely.

With a grimace, Johnny turned slowly and walked stiffly toward the hallway.

"Johnny, is everything okay?" Howie called. "You're very quiet in there."

"I'm comin'," he grumbled. "Hold your goddamn horses."

In the blink of an eye, he dropped the coffee cup, whipped his utility knife from his belt, and flicked it open. He spun and tossed the blade toward the bastard seated in his armchair. The pistol in the Red Boar's hand fired and he roared as the blade buried itself in the meaty muscle of his shoulder.

Johnny smirked but it faded when he moved his hand to his belly just beneath his ribs and he felt warm, sticky wetness there. "Fuck."

The pain came, and his entire gut clenched in agony.

"Johnny!" It sounded like Lisa, but that didn't make sense.

He fumbled for an explosive disk at his belt and tried to step toward the door, but his legs gave out. The dwarf fell with a grunt, and the door to his hotel suite burst open.

CHAPTER TWENTY-FIVE

"FBI! Hands in the air, asshole!" Lisa stormed down the hall with her firearm raised in both hands. She glanced briefly at Johnny as he scooted backward across the floor and propped himself up against the exterior wall of the kitchen.

"He's…in there—"

The Red Boar fired again and the bullet crashed into the back wall of the kitchen. Lisa darted around the corner and fired two shots.

Close behind her were two Kilomeas and a half-wizard and all three of them summoned attack spells to help cover her against the Red Boar.

"Drop the weapon!" she shouted. Two more shots were fired and spewed plaster and wood chips in every direction.

The scarred gray magical roared and fired more shots before he finally switched to flinging spells.

"Get him!"

"Shit, duck!"

"Lady, watch out!"

Johnny grimaced as he clapped his hand against the bullet

wound in his belly. The hallway was slick with his blood. *That sounds like Yarren and Percy. How'd they get here?*

The glass coffee table shattered under someone's weight.

"Fuck! Ev!"

"I said hands up!" Lisa shouted again. She launched another fireball at the Red Boar and he bellowed when it struck him in the opposite shoulder. "Don't make me—ah!"

She catapulted toward the hallway and skidded across the floor, clutching her left shoulder.

"Lisa." Johnny tried to shout it, but it wouldn't come out any louder than a low mumble.

Without noticing the dwarf bleeding out on the floor, she raised her service weapon from where she had landed and fired again.

The Red Boar roared and flung aside the Kilomeas storming toward him. Evan summoned a dark spell of crackling, electric-blue light that glanced off their adversary's massive chest and sent him reeling into the armchair. The intruder launched a red bolt of sizzling light into the half-wizard's gut. Evan hurtled into the white leather couch and almost knocked it over.

"What the hell?" Luther raised his head off the floor, blinked, then struggled to his feet. "Rex. Rex! Wake up! There's—" The smaller hound leapt away from the Red Boar's flailing legs as the magical pushed himself out of the armchair. "Shit. Johnny! Johnny, where are you?"

The hound's wild barking snapped Rex out of his groggy sleep. "Holy shit. Kilomeas, bro. Those ungrateful hairy bastards!" He launched himself at Yarren and tackled him as the Kilomea unleashed a shot of strobing copper light. It went wild and crashed into the ceiling instead of the gray magical stampeding through the suite.

"The gray guy!" Lisa shouted as she flung another fireball. "The big guy, Rex!"

"What? Oh, shit." The larger hound leapt off Yarren's chest and spun to snarl at the Red Boar. "Damn, he is big."

Barking madly, Luther darted beneath launched spells and their adversary's huge feet to snap at the guy's heels. Percy's next magical attack cracked against the side of the gray magical's face and thrust him back. He crashed into the armchair again and landed halfway in the seat with one leg dangling over the armrest.

"Johnny! He has your knife!" Luther leapt onto the Red Boar's thigh and clamped his jaws down around the blade's handle. With a vicious jerk of his head, he ripped the blade free and blood sprayed all over the armchair and the living area.

The large magical roared and slapped at the hound, but Luther had already leapt away. "Johnny! Johnny, where are you? I have your knife!"

"Get him, bro!" Rex shouted, snarling and barking.

"Who?" Luther whipped his head back toward the Red Boar, and the blade pierced the inside of the magical's thigh.

"Fucking dog!" He swatted at Luther and barely missed the hound's head, and Lisa fired another fireball at the intruder.

"Who you calling a fucking dog, bozo?" The hound whipped his head back again and stabbed their adversary in the calf before he darted away, his jaws fixed firmly around the blade's handle. "Did anyone teach you manners?"

The gray magical rose from the armchair and stumbled forward, trying to walk on his injured legs. Luther ducked and spun in a circle. "Seriously, has anyone seen Johnny? This is his."

Yarren launched a fireball at the Red Boar, who ducked wildly and fell to his hands and knees on the floor.

"Luther, watch out!" Rex shouted.

"Huh?" The smaller hound whirled with wide eyes, and the blade sliced across the enemy magical's already scarred face. He bellowed, clapped one hand to his cheek, and swiped at Luther with the other. "Hey, back up, two-legs. What the hell?"

In the hallway, Johnny had managed to pull himself to his feet and supported himself on the half-wall into the kitchen. Grunting with the effort, he slapped his hand down on the tranquilizer gun. The bag of pastries toppled and spilled all over the counter and kitchen floor when he whipped his modified weapon off the granite. He turned and struggled to step down the hall to get a clear shot into the living area.

"Luther!" Lisa shouted. "Get out of there!"

"Why is everyone yelling at me, huh?" Luther trotted around the Red Boar and skittered sideways when the huge magical swiped at him again. "Hey, hands off, bud. Johnny! Johnny, where the hell are you?" When he turned, the blade in his mouth buried itself in the Red Boar's pectoral muscle and was ripped out again. "This guy's lost his mind!"

With a roar, the wounded magical reared back on his knees and lunged at Luther and the knife.

Johnny squeezed off all four remaining rounds in the tranquilizer gun in quick succession. The loud pop wasn't nearly as satisfying as the echo of a regular pistol, but the shots found their marks in the Red Boar's neck and chest.

"Fucking dwarf!" The intruder snarled and pushed shakily to his feet. "I'll rip your—"

His wide glowing eyes rolled back in his head. One massive foot came down on the area rug with a thump before he fell like a giant sack of bricks. His chest landed first and the shattered glass of the broken coffee table crunched beneath him and his scarred face followed with a muffled thud. A snort escaped him before he sagged completely.

"Whoa." Luther stepped away from the unconscious magical, his tail straight up in the air. "Holy shit, guys. He's bleeding." The hound sat, and Johnny's blood-stained utility knife clattered to the floor when he licked his muzzle. "Was that me?"

"Good work, boy." The dwarf grunted and staggered against the far wall of the living area. His back thumped against it and he slid to the floor with a groan, leaving a thick streak of blood behind him.

"Johnny." Lisa hurried toward him, limping and clutching her left shoulder. "Oh, jeez. He shot you."

"Thanks, darlin' although that's a given at this point."

"I tried to get here as fast as I could. I'm so sorry."

"I ain't—"

"Those fucking assholes set me up too." She batted his hand aside and pulled up his shirt to get a better look at the wound. "They told me they were delivering a package this morning and instead, Kellen had me standing out front with a huge damn target on my back. I have never in my entire career spent so much time convincing state police officers I'm exactly who I say I am."

"Police?" Johnny grimaced when the soft, tingling warmth of Lisa's Light Elf healing magic did what it could for the bullet wound. The pain and a searing heat quickly followed.

"Yeah. Someone hacked into Stephanie Wyndom's fake records and gave her an open arrest warrant on top of it. I doubt they picked up that it was all fake, but it held me back almost half an hour—"

"Darlin', I appreciate the healin' attention. And the recap." He removed her hand from where it hovered over his wound. "But I ain't sure either of them's gonna do the trick here."

"Shit, Johnny. The bleeding's still bad. I thought I could do more."

"Naw, this should do until we get some bandages or somethin.'"

"This might help." Yarren stepped toward them down the hall and slid his hand into the breast pocket of his uniform work shirt, which was dotted with a few flecks of the Red Boar's blood and had one sleeve ripped off at the shoulder and dangling by a thread in the armpit. The Kilomea pulled out a small, nondescript packet and hunkered down to offer it to the dwarf.

"What's this?"

"Somethin' we like to keep on us in the yard," Percy grumbled as he dusted glass shards and plaster off his shirt. "A lotta guys get hurt on the job, and it doesn't exactly go over well with the higher-ups when they get so many reports. Rocky gives 'em out like candy. It's a Kilomea family secret or some shit."

"I ain't takin' drugs, fellas."

"Neither do we." Yarren ripped the top of the packet open and nodded at Johnny's bleeding gut. "You gotta pour it on."

"Shit." The dwarf took the packet and upended it over the wound. Silver-white powder poured out and instantly sizzled and sparked occasionally as it mixed with his blood and soaked deeper into the bullet hole. "Aw, shit!"

"Yeah, it packs a punch, huh?" Evan joined them, holding the wadded end of his shirtsleeve against his bleeding nose. One of the half-wizard's eyes was blue and purple and almost swollen shut. "But it gets the job done."

"If there's still a bullet in there, you should go to the hospital," Percy suggested.

"No." Johnny grunted and forced himself to watch the rest of the Kilomea healing powder penetrate his gut and spark all over his insides. When it finally stopped, so did the bleeding. He glanced behind him at the smear of blood on the wall and shook his head. "The bullet went through."

"Still, that's a lot of—"

"No hospitals. I ain't fixin' to lay up in a damn bed with a bunch of docs for humans tellin' me what I can and can't do with my own damn self. How long does this stuff hold?"

Percy and Yarren glanced at each other. "Long enough to stop the bleeding so you can get to a hospital. Probably longer if you take it easy for a few days."

"Sure. Right after I finish what I started." Johnny braced a hand against the blood-smeared wall behind him and pushed to his feet.

Lisa reached toward him. "Johnny, I don't think—"

"I know you don't think it's a good idea, darlin'. That don't mean I ain't doin' it." A wave of dizziness washed over him to join the dull throb in his gut, and he swayed before he steadied himself against the wall again. "I suppose I oughtta get a bigger suitcase and start carryin' my damn first-aid kid with me."

"Ooh, yeah, Johnny." Rex padded toward his master, stepping delicately between chunks of plaster and the shattered glass. "Like the one you have at home, right?"

"That's a good one." Luther hopped onto the Red Boar's back to cross the living area, then trotted toward Johnny and the others. "There's some real good stuff in there. We love it. Thanks for leaving it open and—what?"

Johnny raised an eyebrow and glanced back and forth between his hounds. "You've been sniffin' around in my med kit?"

"Well, when it's there..." Luther sniffed dutifully at the streak of Johnny's blood running down the wall.

"Yeah, we thought you wouldn't mind. Otherwise, you would have put that stuff away all the time. Hey, Luther. What were those treats in there we liked so much?"

"I don't know, man. I can't read. The white ones. Long white ones."

"Yeah, they taste like shit when you chew 'em but you feel real nice afterward."

"Jesus." Johnny shook his head. "How long have y'all been helpin' yourselves to my painkillers?"

"What?" Lisa asked having missed half the conversation.

"Oh, that's what they are?" Luther turned in a tight circle and tried to nip his own tail. "They're good, Johnny. Nice and mellow."

"You left them out after the pup got sliced by that hog, remember?"

The dwarf closed his eyes and sighed. "And regular folk with half a brain don't stop to think whether a couple of coonhounds have a tolerance built up."

Lisa set a hand on Johnny's shoulder and frowned in concern. "I'm completely lost here, Johnny."

"Yep." He nodded toward the Red Boar who lay face-down and bleeding in front of the armchair. "The sonofabitch drugged my hounds. He assumed it'd keep 'em down for the count long enough for him to take me out. The damn hounds will eat everything."

"He gave us a big handful, Johnny," Rex muttered.

"It was awesome for like five minutes." Luther sat and licked his muzzle. "Then not so much. I think I threw up somewhere but can't remember if I cleaned it up, though."

"Yeah, well now, y'all learned your lesson about takin' pills from a stranger." With a grunt, Johnny staggered across the living area, his boots crunching across broken glass and plaster.

Staring after the dwarf with wide eyes, Yarren leaned toward Percy and muttered, "Who's he talking to?"

"His dogs. I think."

"I wouldn't have pegged him for a crazy."

Percy shrugged. "Yeah, me neither. But he took a bullet to the gut. The dwarf's as tough as shit."

Johnny stooped to snatch his utility knife up and grimaced at the flare of pain in his belly. He ignored it and approached the Red Boar sprawled on the floor. The blade's handle was still sticky with the gray-skinned magical's blood, but it didn't slip in the bounty hunter's clenched fist. He stooped over the Red Boar's scarred face and growled, his breath quickening. "You picked the wrong dwarf, motherfucker. Now, you're payin' for it."

"Johnny?" Lisa stepped toward him. "What are you doing?"

"Makin' sure this piece of shit don't squirm his way out of gettin' what's comin' to him again."

"Okay, I don't think that's such a good idea right now. Especially with our...company."

He looked up as Cody inched down the hallway with his camera, David close on his heels with the boom mic lifted and outstretched toward the living area. Phil peered around the corner, his eyes wide as he took in the destruction and the blood spatters. Todd panned a second camera around the hotel suite littered with bullet holes, chunks of plaster, glass, and the over-turned couch.

Johnny pointed at Cody and snarled. "Turn that shit off."

"Keep rolling, Cody." Phil slipped around the confused Kilo-meas and the half-wizard. "We're keeping this going, Johnny. This is great. Seriously good stuff. A raw look into the way Dwarf the Bounty Hunter fights and defeats his targets. We have the whole scene."

"I said turn it off!" Yelling triggered another flare of pain through Johnny's gut. "What I'm fixin' to do next ain't somethin' anyone's gonna get on camera."

"Johnny, don't." Lisa shook her head.

"Oh, you mean like evidence?" Phil ruffled his unruly hair and nodded sagely as he gazed around the room. "We already have plenty of that."

"What are you goin' on about?"

The director gestured toward Cody and Dave. "We've been filming since you walked into the suite with breakfast. It looked like a big bag, too."

"Sure is," Luther said from the kitchen. "Johnny, did you bring all this for us?"

"Don't ask, bro. Just eat." Rex licked the spilled crumbs on the kitchen floor.

"Yeah, good thinking. Ooh. Is this jelly?"

Johnny turned stiffly to face Phil and the rest of the crew still filming for their damn show. "You listened in on the whole thing?"

"Sure." The man smirked and spread his arms expansively. "We may be a small indie crew, but we don't skimp on quality equipment. That mic could pick up sound in the bedroom from out in the hall if we wanted it to."

Lisa shrugged. "They were crowded around the door when I got here with our…backup. And thanks for that, by the way."

Yarren nodded. "I have to admit it was a little weird to get your call. But I'm glad I answered."

"Yeah, so are we."

The dwarf glowered at the unconscious Red Boar. "All right. This ain't the day for killin' this bastard. Maybe his cellmate in max can find a reason to do it instead."

Lisa exhaled a small, relieved sigh. "I'll call it in."

"Uh-huh." Johnny delivered a swift kick into the side of the gray magical's head and elicited only a guttural wheeze from the Red Boar's hulking form.

"Johnny."

"That's the least he deserves, darlin'. Go ahead and call. Does anyone have a spare weapon on 'em?"

Yarren and his work buddies glanced at each other with vacant expressions. Lisa rolled her eyes and headed to the open door into the hall. "I'll be right back."

Johnny nodded at the Kilomeas and pulled his wallet from his back pocket. "If I hand you fellas a few bills, can one of y'all run out and grab somethin' to tie this bastard up with? Rope's fine. Heavy chains are better."

"Sure, man. Yeah." Evan stepped across the mess to take the few hundred dollars the dwarf held toward him. "Anything else?"

"Whatever looks like it'll be fun to keep this big fucker down with while we wait for the FBI's cleanup crew. I think you'll know it when you see it."

"Sure."

"I wouldn't mind one of y'all stickin' around in case this shit-head wakes up before we're ready."

"I'll hang out." Yarren crunched across the living area and

grasped the overturned leather couch to haul it upright again. "It's the least we can do."

"I appreciate it."

Lisa returned to the room, slipping between the film crew still rolling Johnny Walker's latest catch. She slid a new magazine into her pistol and handed it to the dwarf. "Here you go."

"Thanks, darlin'."

"I hope all those rounds stay right where they are."

"Don't you worry yourself about it. I ain't usin' this unless it's the last option. But I'm lookin' forward to when this bastard opens his eyes and sees the wrong of end of this barrel first."

"Right." She watched him stagger toward the righted couch, and a fresh wave of blood seeped from the bullet wound in his gut. "Johnny, you're still bleeding."

"It ain't nothin' I can't handle, darlin'. It's fine."

"Evan," Yarren called over his shoulder as he sat beside the dwarf.

"Yeah?"

"Grab some gauze rolls while you're out."

"Sure thing. Call me if you need anything else."

The half-wizard took another wide-eyed glance at the destroyed living area, then snuck past the film crew to slip into the hallway.

Percy stood on the far side of the living area with his huge, hairy arms folded. "Sorry about the mess in here. That's gonna be one hell of a cleanup bill."

"It ain't on my dime." Johnny snorted. "The FBI's frontin' the whole bill."

"Well, that's helpful."

"Sometimes, yeah."

CHAPTER TWENTY-SIX

Lisa called Agent Nelson three different times in the next fifteen minutes, but the man didn't answer. "What is he doing?"

"What's goin' on, darlin'?" Johnny turned his head toward her but kept his gaze firmly fixed on the unconscious Red Boar.

"Tommy won't answer his phone. I have no idea why. He knows we're out here on a case."

"Sure. He knows about both of 'em too. Do you think the Department got wind of what we were doin' out here with the show?"

"I have no idea."

"Johnny, how about a little Q&A now," Phil said. "While the fight's still fresh in your mind?"

"I let y'all stick around to catch whatever you want of this, pal. But I ain't takin' my attention off this scarred lump of meat until I've got him bagged up and shipped out in a SWAT van. Understand?"

"Sure." The man inched toward Johnny with a hesitant smile. "But you can watch him and talk at the same time, can't you?"

"Not gonna happen."

The elevator doors opened at the end of the hall, and Howie demanded, "What the hell is going on here?"

"He got ambushed," Evan said and hurried past the old man with the cane. Yards of rope and a few thick, looped feet of chains dangled around the half-wizard's arm. "And then we...ambushed the ambusher, I guess."

"That's the most ridiculous thing I've ever heard, son. And what are you doing here in the first place? You were at that senator's house, weren't you? With the Kilomeas?"

"Yeah..."

Howie stopped in front of Johnny's suite and blinked at the damaged front door and what little wreckage he could see down the hall. "Johnny?"

"We're in here, Howie. All's good."

Evan moved clear of the old man and hurried into the living area. "I got as much as I could. Rope. Chains. Zip-ties. Duct tape."

The plastic bag and coils of rope and chains thumped to the floor at Johnny's feet.

"Thanks, Evan."

"Sure. Here's your change too."

Johnny looked up at him and shook his head. "Naw, you can keep that."

"What? It's like...two hundred dollars."

"Don't make no difference to me."

"But—"

"Hell, Ev. If you won't take it, I will." Percy reached toward the bill's in his friend's hand with a low chuckle.

"Well, hold on. I didn't say *that*." Evan pocketed the cash and darted his friend a warning glance.

Howie's cane thumped down the hallway. "This wasn't part of the plan, Johnny."

"Plans change." The dwarf turned slowly to look at his old friend hobbling through the destroyed living area. "You know that."

"Yeah, and I know you look like shit too. What happened?"

"I got shot."

"Jesus Christ. And who the hell's the big guy?"

Johnny scowled at the Red Boar again and only had to say, "This is for Dawn."

"Oh, shit."

Luther walked sluggishly out of the kitchen and paused to sniff at the old man's cane. "Oof. You got some kinda stink on you, two-legs."

"I think that's just what old smells like, bro." Rex licked his muzzle and sat in the kitchen. "I don't know. All I smell is doughnuts."

"Boys!" Johnny snapped his fingers, and both hounds waddled toward him. The dwarf shook his head when he saw the powdered sugar coating Rex's muzzle and paws and the jelly filling that somehow made its way up the side of Luther's face. "Y'all had your breakfast, I see."

"And it was delicious."

"Best breakfast you've ever brought us, Johnny."

Luther uttered a low whine and sat. "It doesn't sit well for very long, though. My belly hurts."

"'Cause you ate the whole damn bag, didn't you?"

Neither hound said a word.

A loud knock came at the destroyed open door. "Baltimore PD. Anyone inside?"

"Great." Lisa rolled her eyes and hurried toward the front of the suite. "I'll take care of this. And then Tommy better answer his damn phone."

When she reached the front door, she couldn't hide a wry chuckle at the sight of Officers Brently and McCormick standing there with their hands on their holstered service weapons. "Officers."

Brently pressed his lips together and tried to peer into the suite. "Agent Breyer. We got a disturbance call—"

"Yeah, I bet you did, although I already knew there would be an attack here in this room."

"Yeah." McCormick scratched the back of his bald head. "We had to take our due diligence with that. You understand."

"I understand. It almost cost a few lives, but I get it. You were doing your jobs."

"Is everything all right in there?"

"It's taken care of, Officers. Thank you. Now I need you both to let me do my job and take care of this situation. Federal jurisdiction. You understand."

The officers exchanged a dubious glance. "Sure. But...take my card in case you need anything. And sorry about the trouble," Brently said.

"Well, I appreciate it." Lisa took his card and nodded. "Thanks for the concern."

McCormick tried to peer past her into the suite. "You know, it wouldn't hurt for the FBI to reach out to the precinct when your people have an ongoing federal case in the city. It saves us all considerable time trying to run you through the system in a situation like before."

"Sure. I'll bring it to my superiors' attention. Have a good day." Lisa took hold of the outside of the broken door and tried to swing it shut, but the hinges were bent and broken and it only moved an inch before it wobbled in its frame. Brently sniggered until his partner elbowed him in the side. Lisa gritted her teeth. "Now if you don't mind, I need to get back to handling my case."

"Yeah, okay." The officers tried one more time to peer inside. Brently pointed past Agent Breyer. "You turning this into another one of those YouTube videos?"

"What?" She turned and saw Todd with his smaller camera capturing the entire exchange. "Todd, get back in the living room. Now."

He peered around his camera at her with wide eyes, then nodded and did as he was told.

"It's part of the case," Lisa added grudgingly. "Feel free to see yourselves out."

The officers frowned at the inside of the suite but eventually turned and headed back down the hall, casting her suspicious glances over their shoulders. Lisa stayed in the doorway and watched them to make sure they got on the elevators.

That's the first and last time I take a two-day-old alias. I never thought I'd be in the back seat of a cop car in cuffs. Again.

When she stepped into the living area again, Percy and Yarren were on the floor on either side of the Red Boar, shifting the hulking magical's massive weight between them to get the guy tied up with the rope and the chains. "Don't you think that might be a little excessive?"

Johnny leaned forward over his lap, her service weapon still clenched in his hand. "Not for this piece of shit. I ain't fixin' to let him slip away again."

"Okay. Well, you do have him unconscious…"

"I don't know for how much longer, darlin', so we're workin' with what we got. It should hold until cleanup gets here."

"Yeah, as soon as I can get hold of Tommy." Right on cue, her phone buzzed in her back pocket. She yanked it out and immediately answered the call as she negotiated the wreckage-strewn room gingerly toward the bedroom. "Why the hell haven't you answered my calls, Tommy?"

"I was in a meeting, okay? Why did you have to blow up my phone so many times?"

Lisa stepped into the bedroom and closed the door with a bang when she saw Cody turning to catch her on film. Fortunately, the door handle had a lock, so she used it. "We got him."

"The Kilomea? Great."

"No, not Brork. Okay, we did find him, but that's a whole different story we'll have to go over when there's more time. I'm talking about the Red Boar." There was a long pause on the other end of the line. "Tommy?"

"No shit." Nelson sighed into the phone. "How'd you get that done?"

"Well, the 'filming a new season' part of the plan worked out the way we wanted." She sat on the bed, frowned, and pulled Johnny's stupid voice-recording pedal out from under her thigh. "And he came for Johnny too, although sooner than we expected."

"But you have him now."

"Yeah. Johnny's tying him up in the living room right now."

"Who's living room?"

She took a deep breath. "He showed up in Johnny's hotel suite. Drugged the dogs—"

Tommy snorted.

"That's not funny."

"No, I know. Sorry. You're right. Are they…are they okay?"

"The dogs are fine. Johnny got shot."

"And you let him tie up the bastard on his own with a bullet wound?"

"No, we have…help. Everything's under control right now, Tommy, okay? What we need from you is a cleanup crew to collect this asshole and take him in."

"Huh…" Nelson sighed heavily and cleared his throat. "I'm not sure I can make that happen for you this time."

"What?"

"Sorry."

Lisa leapt from the bed, hurried into the bathroom, and shut the door behind her. "We have the Red Boar tied up in a hotel suite, Tommy. That's part of the job you agreed to help us with when we started this whole thing, and now we need you to come through. The same as every other case."

"Yeah, but this isn't like every other case."

"Why the hell isn't it?"

Nelson cleared his throat again. "Because you and Johnny aren't officially on a case for the Red Boar. You're there for Yarren Brork. And by the way, I've heard some very strange things about a few calls Senator Hugh made to his contact in the Bureau."

"Yeah, we can go over that later. Right now, we need a way to get this asshole out of Baltimore and behind bars."

"Lisa, I'm sorry. I can't send anyone out right now. There's no record of going after the Red Boar. We all agreed to not make one. I can send something up the line that says otherwise, but it'll take me a few days."

"We don't have a few days." She slapped a hand on the counter at the sink and stared at her reflection in the mirror. "Honestly, I don't think Johnny will be able to hold back for much longer. I barely managed to keep him from slitting the guy's throat in front of me."

"Don't you have a rental out there?"

Lisa scoffed. "Oh, sure. Throw a five-hundred-pound magical into the bed of a rental truck and drive him to DC. What could possibly go wrong in that scenario?"

"You'll think of something, Lisa. Sorry."

"How did you not think far enough ahead so we had this covered?"

Nelson paused for another long moment, then sighed. "Honestly, I wasn't sure this *Dwarf the Bounty Hunter* scheme would work."

"You funded the entire thing on the Department's dime assuming it was a dud operation?"

"Yeah. Basically. Look, I can try to put something together in twenty-four hours, but that's the best I can—"

"Forget it." She hung up on him and thunked her phone on the counter. *He was pandering to Johnny's revenge quest. I can't believe he let us think he was all the way on board.*

Staring into her own eyes in the mirror, Lisa took a deep breath. *Pull it together. If the Department doesn't have our backs, at least we have each other's. We'll think of something.*

CHAPTER TWENTY-SEVEN

Johnny's tranquilizer darts were starting to wear off by the time Lisa unlocked the bedroom door and stepped into the living area. The Red Boar grunted and tried to push himself up. He took a few groggy seconds to try to determine why he couldn't move his arms from where they'd been bound tightly against his heaving sides.

"What the...fuck is this?" He growled in annoyance.

"This is what happens when assholes like you try to fuck with me." Johnny lifted Lisa's pistol toward the Red Boar. His hand didn't shake, but he didn't look like he could keep a firm hold on it for much longer, either.

"You tied me up?" The gray-skinned magical bucked against the chains and rope and grimaced as the knife wounds in his thick flesh cracked open again. A low chuckle escaped him, accompanied by a long wheeze. "You're pathetic."

"Yeah, say it again from behind bars, fuckface."

"Johnny." Lisa walked behind the leather couch and leaned down to whisper in the dwarf's ear. "We have a problem."

"I ain't lettin' this one outta my sight darlin'. Whatever it is, go on and say it now."

She glanced at Yarren on the couch beside Johnny. The Kilomea's gaze was fixed firmly on the sneering Red Boar and the thick line of saliva dribbling from the corner of their prisoner's mouth. "We don't have a cleanup crew," she whispered.

"What?" Johnny kept the pistol trained on their prisoner and twisted to look over his shoulder to look at Agent Breyer with a grimace. "Did you talk to Nelson?"

"Yeah, he's the one who told me."

"Well, did you tell him to get his head out of his ass and do his fuckin' job?"

"Of course I did but this wasn't an official case so he doesn't have a crew to send out." She shook her head. "I knew there was way too much bureaucratic bullshit to sift through, but I had no idea it went this far."

Johnny turned slowly toward the Red Boar and growled through clenched teeth. "He didn't think we'd get this far."

"It would appear so, yes."

"Dammit, Nelson." The dwarf turned toward Yarren. "Any idea where we can get a bigass van? Preferably reinforced, but at this point, I ain't gonna be too picky."

The Kilomea's eyes widened. "For what?"

"Transport."

Percy gestured toward the front of the suite. "We have a van."

"Yeah." Evan folded his arms. "The one that was supposed to get us to work on time this morning. Rocky's gonna flip his shit."

"Well, how about I make y'all a deal, fellas?" Johnny sniffed and handed the pistol to Lisa. "You let us borrow that van, and I'll make a personal call to your foreman and give y'all some recognition for helpin' with a federal case backed by the FBI and everythin'."

Yarren rubbed the side of his hairy head. "We might as well. We're probably out of work already anyway."

"And I'll make sure we get that fixed up for ya." Johnny stood from the couch and grunted at the pain in his gut.

"What are you doing?" Lisa asked.

"Gettin' a few more things for the road. If the goddamn Department won't come to us, we'll bring this fucker to them. It's only…what? An hour and a half to DC?"

"Johnny…"

"Just keep that gun trained on this prick's ugly face, will ya? I'll be right back."

Lisa stared at the Red Boar and held her pistol with both hands. The bound magical grinned at her through a mouth stained with blood, the side of his face swelling horribly where Johnny had kicked him. "Trouble in paradise?"

She ignored him.

Rex and Luther kept their distance, although they grew bolder by the second in order to sniff the guy's wounds. "Hey, Rex. You know what this two-legs smells like?"

"Like a pile of shit?"

"Eh, I'm getting more of a fresh-grass kinda vibe."

Rex sniggered. "I can see that."

"You know, plenty of other critters runnin' through. Maybe a big ol' Great Dane came by and tried to draw a line all to himself."

"Better show him who's here to stay, Luther."

"Yeah, that's what I'm thinking." The smaller hound sniffed at the Red Boar's shoes and jerked his head away when the prisoner flailed uselessly in his bonds.

"Get this fucking dog away from me."

"Relax, man. I don't even have a knife with me this time." Luther stared at the back of the Red Boar's scarred, misshapen gray head as he lifted a leg and relieved himself on the drug lord's back.

"What the—hey! Hey!" The Red Boar jerked but couldn't avoid the stream soaking through his shirt.

"That's right, asshole!" Rex barked. "You're not calling the shots anymore, are ya?"

Luther lowered his leg and snorted. "You know what that means, don'tcha? It means Johnny's got your ass in the bag now."

Lisa grimaced at the display but couldn't bring herself to intervene.

After backing up a few paces, Luther sat and licked his muzzle. "Don't worry, Johnny. I taught him a lesson he'll never forget."

The dwarf staggered through the living area as he slipped six more tranquilizer rounds into his modified pistol.

"Guess what the lesson is, Johnny," Rex said and his tail thumped on the floor and scattered shards of broken glass.

Johnny stopped in front of the Red Boar, his jaw set in a tight grimace and his face alarmingly pale beneath his wiry red beard. "Don't fuck with me."

All six tranquilizer rounds buried themselves in the thick skin of the Red Boar's neck. The magical's face thumped against the floor at round number four.

With a grunt, Johnny turned and handed the pistol to Yarren. "I think I outta sit down for a spell. Do you mind stowin' that in the black bag in the bedroom for me?"

"Uh…sure." The Kilomea took the pistol cautiously and stood to comply.

"Whoever's got the keys to that work van best pull the thing on around back." Johnny didn't so much sit on the couch again as fall back into it. "Then we're takin' a drive."

"I'll get our things." Lisa placed a hand on his shoulder and leaned over the back of the couch to look at him. "Johnny, you don't look good."

"This ain't the worst I've taken, darlin'. Not by a long shot. As soon as we drop this fucker off at the Bureau's front door, I'll be as right as rain."

"Where are we heading, exactly?" Phil asked.

Johnny shook his head. "Ain't no we about it, Phil. If you and your damn crew don't get the hell outta my way, I still have enough rounds left for you. So y'all can leave now on your own, or you can get dragged out with a full dose of sleep-juice. It's up to you."

Howie shuffled toward the director. "He's fucking serious this time, Phil."

"But—"

"Now is not the time." The old man cracked his cane against the side of Cody's camera. "Out. Everyone out right now!"

"We're not done filming!"

"Leave the camera," Johnny muttered. "We're takin' that with us."

"What? This is high-tech equipment," Phil blustered. "You can't—"

"Anyone who feels like showin' these folks out, I'd appreciate that gettin' done right fuckin' now."

Yarren came out of the bedroom and stalked toward Cody. "Hand it over."

"Yeah, yeah. Jesus. Okay."

"Everyone out!" Howie whacked here and there with his cane to usher the film crew out of the suite so Johnny and his makeshift team could finish the job on their own. "You call me if you need anything, Johnny."

"You bet."

Evan pulled their work van around to the back of the hotel and left the back double doors open. Twenty minutes later, Lisa burst through the rear exit of the hotel and held the door open while Percy and Yarren struggled to carry the unconscious Red Boar between them.

"The fucker weighs a ton," Yarren grunted.

Percy scowled at the bundle of magical drug lord wrapped up in nine-hundred-thread-count king-sized sheets. "He smells like piss too."

"Did you expect anything else?" Luther called after them as he trotted through the door. "It's like everyone's lost their mind or something."

"Come on, Johnny. Hurry up." Rex turned to watch his master step through the back door. "Shit. You don't look so good."

"I'm fine, boys. Keep movin'." Johnny steadied himself on the doorframe.

Lisa tried to offer him a hand, but he waved her away. "Are you sure you can handle this?"

"Who else is gonna?" He chuckled wryly. "No, I know you're perfectly capable, darlin'. But I ain't lettin' you truck that shithead down to DC on your own. No way."

"Then promise me that as soon as we get him off our hands, you'll lay down in a bed and not get up for a few days. That bullet hole won't magically heal if you don't rest."

"Yeah, you have my word."

Evan leapt out of the van's driver seat and shrugged. "It's all yours. You want us to help with anything else?"

Percy and Yarren heaved the Red Boar into the back of the van and deposited him carelessly. A few boxes toppled on top of the unconscious magical before they shut the door with a bang.

"Like what?" Johnny asked.

"I don't know, man. Make some calls or...hell, if anyone has another car, we can come with you."

"Don't worry about it." He nodded at the half-wizard. "Y'all have done enough to help us out for one day. I think we'll be fine on our own from here. Thanks, fellas."

"It's the least we can do." Yarren reached out to shake the bounty hunter's hand. "We kinda owe you for what you did at the senator's house."

"Yeah, we'll get that cleared up too. You can take my word on it." Johnny whistled and waved for the hounds to join him. "Come on, boys. Time to move—" He stumbled and caught himself on the side of the van.

"Okay, Johnny." Lisa headed to the passenger door and pulled it swiftly open. "I think it's time for us to break at least one of your rules."

"Which one, huh?"

"The one where you always drive because I don't think we'll make it to DC with you behind the wheel."

He sniffed and waited for the dizziness to clear. "I think you're right, darlin'."

The hounds bounded into the passenger seat, then dove into the back to accompany the unconscious Red Boar for their drive. "We got him, Johnny."

"Yeah, right where we want him. If he wakes up, I'll piss on him again."

"The van ain't ours, boys," Johnny muttered as he hoisted himself up into the passenger seat with a grimace of pain. "Save it for when we dump this sack of shit outside Nelson's office, huh?"

"Oh, yeah. I can piss on him too."

Lisa nodded at the Kilomeas and half-wizard standing around the van. "Thanks for your help. We'll make sure the van gets back to you, and we'll do whatever we can to make sure you guys aren't out of a job because you didn't have to help us."

"Weird times, right?" Yarren shrugged. "Good luck."

"Yeah. Thanks." Lisa opened the driver's door and tossed Johnny's duffel bag and her roller suitcase into the back. She buckled up and stared at the dwarf until he did the same. "I need you to stay awake while we're on the road, got it?"

"I ain't got a problem stayin' awake, darlin'. It's this damn hole in my gut."

"Yeah. I won't take you to a hospital, but you'll get better medical attention as soon as we're in DC and that asshole in the back is *out* of the back."

"Fine. Just go."

She shifted into drive and gritted her teeth. *If he didn't have a hole in his belly, I'd give him a dose of his own crazy driving medicine right now.*

CHAPTER TWENTY-EIGHT

As soon as they were on the highway headed toward DC, Lisa picked up speed more than she would have for any other normal drive across state lines. She glanced from Johnny breathing shallowly beside her and the rearview mirror through which she could see a white truck that had been following them since she'd first paid attention.

"Johnny, I think we might have a tail."

"Huh?" He raised his head from where he'd rested it against the window and frowned. "What is it?"

"A white truck. It kind of looks like our rental, but they haven't gotten close enough for me to see much more."

"Don't worry about it, darlin'. Just keep movin'."

"Well, I'm not about to stop and make whoever it is get out and ID themselves." She glanced in the rearview mirror again. "But that doesn't mean I can simply ignore it."

"Go ahead. Say what's on your mind."

"That shifter called me this morning and set me up to get arrested. Whether he had any idea who I am or not, he had to know the Red Boar was moving in on your hotel room. And if he hasn't worked out by now that his boss isn't walking out of there with your blood on his hands, he soon will."

Johnny grunted. "It don't matter. None of these assholes expected us to rent a work van from a couple of new pals. The shifter won't know where to look for us."

"That's not what I'm worried about." Lisa glanced in the rearview mirror again at the sheet-wrapped mass of the Red Boar's unconscious form sandwiched between Rex and Luther. "I gave Kellen the wrong room number on purpose when he asked. And they still found your suite without ever even checking in on the wrong room."

"Shit. So the burner phone was bugged?"

"I think so, yes. And I had it on me in your room last night." She brushed her hair away from her eyes and glanced in the side mirror at the white truck behind them. "And now I'm starting to regret the fact that neither one of us thought to check our cargo back there for—"

A large gray SUV rammed into the side of the van and they spun sideways toward the right-hand shoulder of the highway. Lisa jerked her hands away from the wheel to steady herself against the doorframe. Johnny's head thunked against the window with a crack. The hounds yelped and barked in the back of the van and scrambled over the Red Boar's unconscious body as they were tossed around with the rest of the Kilomea crew's work supplies.

"Johnny!"

"What's going on!"

"Who's driving this?"

When the van finally stopped moving, Lisa blinked heavily and tried to shake off the dizziness. "Johnny. Hey, Johnny. Come on."

With a groan, she unbuckled her seatbelt so she could lean toward him and shake him by the shoulder. "Johnny! We need to—"

"Hey, who the hell's the ponytail?" Rex asked with a snarl.

Lisa gazed out through the windshield to where Kellen stalked toward them from across the other lane of traffic. The shifter's eyes flashed silver above a wicked snarl.

"Shit. Johnny!" She jostled him again, and the dwarf only groaned before his head slumped over his chest. When she turned his face toward her, his temple was sticky with blood. Worse, the bullet hole in his gut had started to bleed again.

She drew her firearm and turned back to the highway. Kellen was gone, although the pile of his clothes left in the middle of the lane meant he'd already shifted.

Pull it together, Breyer. Get rid of him. He must not get the Red Boar out of this van.

Steeling herself, she shoved the door open and slid out to scan the highway with her weapon held in both hands. Rex and Luther leapt up from the back and followed her through the open door.

"I smell shifter, lady."

"Yeah. Close. Aren't we supposed to be driving right now?"

Lisa stepped slowly down the side of the van and turned every few seconds to glance behind her.

"Hey, Rex. You hear something weird?"

"Movement. Yeah."

When she finally reached the back of the van, Lisa spun around the corner and prepared to fire but there was no one there. *Where the hell did he go?*

Rex barked madly. "Up there!"

"Watch out, lady!"

Instinct warned Lisa and she spun in time to see the huge brown wolf bound at her from the roof of the van. She couldn't bring her weapon up in time and was knocked onto her back by his massive weight. The gun flew from her hands and clattered across the asphalt.

"Not cool, asshole!" Luther lunged at the wolf, snarling and snapping his jaws.

Kellen turned and bashed Rex aside when he leapt toward him. The larger hound careened into the metal barrier along the side of the highway and yelped when he landed.

"You asked for it now!" Luther lunged at the shifter, and Kellen clamped his jaws around the hound's hind leg before he flung him aside too.

Lisa regained her wits and tried to scramble along the shoulder toward her weapon. Kellen leapt in front of her with a snarl, then shifted right there and picked her pistol up.

"It's not your lucky day, is it?"

She glared up at him, breathing heavily and fully aware of the naked man standing like a lunatic off the side of the highway. "You won't get away with this."

"No, I'm very sure I already have."

The passenger-side door opened slowly with a creak, and Johnny slid out. His knees almost buckled when his boots touched the asphalt, but he steadied himself with a hand along the side of the van and shuffled toward the back. He drew his utility knife from his belt and flicked it out and a crust of dried blood fluttered to the ground.

"It ain't the best look for ya, pal," he muttered when he reached the back of the van. "Naked shifters out in the swamp is one thing, but this is broad fuckin' daylight."

"Oh, look." Kellen grinned and lifted Lisa's gun toward Johnny. "I think I hit a lucky streak."

"Johnny, get down!" she shouted and lunged toward the shifter's arm.

A shot cracked deafeningly across the highway, and Kellen slumped forward. Lisa scrambled out of the way to avoid being pinned to the road shoulder beneath a huge, naked man with a long ponytail. When he landed face-first on the asphalt, that ponytail was a matted mess of blood, barely covering the bullet hole.

"What?"

"Johnny!" Howie hobbled toward them from the front of their white rental truck parked fifteen yards down the shoulder.

"All good, Howie." The dwarf waved his friend aside. "You still have your good aim. I'm glad to see it."

"I have a bum leg," the old man grumbled. "There's nothin' wrong with my arm. Are you all right?" He bent down to offer Lisa a hand.

She took it but couldn't stop staring at Kellen and the pool of blood that spread quickly around his head. "Yeah. I only...you were following us the whole time."

"There's more than one reason Johnny called me in for this trip. Isn't that right, Johnny?"

"You bet." The dwarf grunted and stumbled sideways against the van. "We should move, darlin'."

"Go on." Howie nodded at her and slid his firearm into the waistband of his pants. "I'll get this cleaned up. You two have somewhere to be before that dwarf bleeds out all over the seats."

"Right. Thank you." She retrieved her gun from beside Kellen's naked body and turned toward her partner. "Johnny, get back in the van."

"I'm workin' on it." He slipped his knife onto his belt and whistled weakly. "Boys, get in or get left behind. We're rollin' out."

The hounds shook themselves and staggered toward the van. "We sure taught that shifter a lesson, Johnny."

Rex snorted. "Yeah. He threw us a little farther than I thought, but the bastard got what he deserved."

"Y'all doin' all right?"

"Only a few puncture holes in my leg, Johnny," Luther said as he hopped up onto the seat and almost didn't make it. "I'm very sure I'm doing better than you are right now."

"We're good, Johnny. Let's go." Rex leapt up after his brother, and they took their places on either side of the still unconscious drug lord lying in the back.

Johnny barely managed to climb in himself before he slumped in the passenger seat and closed the door behind him. "Let's get goin'. I think I'll be ready to see some kinda healer when this shit-bag's off our hands."

Lisa strapped herself in and took a long, slow breath before she steered the beat-up van back onto the highway. "We were almost done back there, Johnny."

"Yeah, but we weren't." With a thick swallow, he dropped his head back against the headrest and chuckled painfully. "I told you Howie wore a bunch of hats, didn't I?"

Despite the close call, she couldn't help but join him with a wry laugh of her own. "And that was Howie the bodyguard. Yeah, I get it."

CHAPTER TWENTY-NINE

One week later...

Johnny burst through the front doors of FBI Headquarters in DC and grimaced at the dull ache in his belly every time he made even a sharp move. The hounds trotted along at his sides, sniffing at the floors and occasionally looking up at a passing agent or federal employee staring at them.

"Can I help you, sir?" The receptionist stood from her chair with a smile, but it faded when she saw the scowl on the bounty hunter's face.

"Probably not, darlin'. Don't you worry." He nodded at her and continued to walk down the hall.

"Sir. Sir?" she called hesitantly after him. "I can't let you go back there."

"You can't stop me either."

The farther he moved through HQ, the more people stopped and stared at the dwarf who stormed through the various department levels. When Johnny and the hounds stepped out of the elevator to head toward the director's office, more than a few familiar faces turned toward him in surprise.

"Johnny." Tommy turned away from the cubicle he'd been

leaning on in conversation with another agent and headed toward the dwarf with a frown. "What are you doing here?"

"Gettin' the damn job done, Nelson." Johnny sniffed disdainfully. "Feel free to stick around and watch how it's done. You could learn a thing or two."

"Hey, my hands were tied, okay? And you brought that bastard in anyway."

"Yeah, no thanks to you."

Nelson sighed and tried to keep up with the dwarf as he lowered his voice and glanced at the other agents who stared at them. "You got your bounty in, Johnny. The Red Boar's off the streets. We're still sorting through the details and filling out the paperwork. I don't blame you for that—"

"Good."

"Because I signed up for the whole thing and helped you make it happen under the Department's radar. But you can't rush the process, Johnny."

"Watch me."

"Come on. Shouldn't you still be in bed, anyway? You know, recovering from a bullet hole?"

The dwarf thumped his fist against the bandage over his gut and grunted. "I'm feelin' fine, Nelson. Now get outta my way."

He stared at the agent and gritted his teeth. *He's tryin' to prove a point but yeah, that shit still hurts.*

"Johnny—"

"Move."

"Fine. But I'm coming with you." Nelson stepped aside and Johnny brushed past him with a snort.

"I just told ya you should." When he reached the director's office, he didn't even give the courtesy of a warning knock and simply shoved the door wide with a bang. "All right, here's the deal. I've been waitin' a whole damn week to have this meetin' and I'm real tired of havin' it pushed back over and over. So now you forced my hand."

The director looked up from what he'd been reading on his desk and darted a wary glance at Tommy. "Agent Nelson?"

"It's harder than you'd think to keep him away from something he wants," the man replied with a shrug.

"Johnny, I've had to move back these meetings because we still haven't resolved certain outstanding factors of the Hugh case—"

"I ain't here for Senator Hugh. As far as I'm concerned, that was over and done with before I left Baltimore." Johnny pounded a fist down on the director's desk, then pointed at the man's face. "Y'all have simply been tryin' to avoid this conversation, 'cause now the whole damn FBI knows what I dug up and how I managed to fix all your fuckin' mistakes without so much as a thank you."

Tommy stepped toward him. "Johnny—"

"Naw, I ain't finished. And boys, if he tries anythin', you know what to do."

"Yeah, we do, Johnny." Luther turned and snarled at Tommy. "You stay right there, you salty two-legs."

"We're all over it, Johnny." Rex sat where he could keep an eye on both Agent Nelson and the FBI director behind his desk.

"Now." Johnny spread his arms. "We're havin' this talk, whether you like it or not, and I don't give a shit if the paperwork's not even halfway done. Y'all lied to me—straight to my face. For fifteen fuckin' years you covered all your shit up so I wouldn't find it and come down on the whole damn Bureau. Well, look what I'm doin' right now, huh? Did anyone ever plan to tell me Dawn's murderer was arrested and convicted? Or to tell me the fucker who gave the order to kill her was still out there and Operation Deadroot was supposed to bring him down?"

The director lowered his head, his lips pressed together in a thin line as he hesitated. "Johnny, I don't know—"

"Bullshit. You know exactly what I'm talkin' about. Now I'm here to even the score, understand? You lost the Red Boar the first time and made it real damn hard for me to feel like there was any justice in sight for my daughter. *My daughter!*"

"Yes, I understand—"

"No, you don't! How the hell am I supposed to trust anyone in this damn agency if y'all keep the lie goin' for fifteen years and won't even agree to a fuckin' meetin' to tell me I was right and y'all were wrong?" Johnny leaned over the director's desk and lowered his voice into a dark, warning growl. "You told me you'd always have my back. I trusted that. What happened to your personal stake in her case, huh? I never bought into your whole talk about this agency bein' family, but it looks a hell of a lot like you never believed a word of your bullshit either."

The director leaned back in his chair, stared at him, and cleared his throat. "Johnny, I have no idea what you're talking about."

"Don't tell me the director of the goddamn FBI's lost his memory from fifteen years ago."

The man glanced at Tommy, who closed his eyes and shook his head with a grimace. "Well, given that I wasn't the director fifteen years ago, I can't accurately respond to that."

"What?" Johnny stepped back and looked at the nameplate on the director's desk—M. Zimmerman. *FBI Director's a ten-year gig. Rein it in, Johnny.* "Fuck. You look exactly like Fitzgerald sittin' behind that desk."

"Well, thanks, I suppose."

"After he lost all his hair." Johnny spun away from the desk and pointed at Tommy. "Where the hell is Fitzgerald?"

"Retired, Johnny." Agent Nelson gestured vaguely. "Eight years ago."

"Yeah, I bet. Should we go pull him out of his retirement too for fun?" The dwarf scowled, glanced around the director's office, and shrugged. "It don't matter, anyhow. There are many agents here in Magicals and Monsters who were around fifteen years ago. Nelson's one of 'em. I think I saw at least five others on the way here. And I'm willin' to bet not a single one of 'em's forgotten about what the whole fuckin' Bureau covered up to keep Johnny Walker silent and stewin' in his grief. I'm here to get what's mine."

Director Zimmerman folded his hands on his desk and leaned forward. "And what exactly is that? Given that you don't technically work out of this building or even for the FBI if we're talking logistics."

"Naw, we're talkin' my logistics." He pointed at the man and gave him crooked smile that looked more feral than amused. "I have everythin' I need to expose the giant fuckup this agency made out of Operation Deadroot and my daughter's murder file. I'm sure y'all have copies of the records somewhere, but if you don't, I'm happy to bring your private stack of proof against yourself."

Zimmerman glanced at Tommy again with a grimace. "So what do you want, Johnny?"

"It ain't about what I want. It's about what the whole damn FBI owes me. Ya hear?"

"Yes." The director pursed his lips. "You've been yelling since you stepped into my office."

"Good." Johnny stepped away from the man's desk and hooked his thumbs through the belt loops of his jeans. "But since you asked, I'll tell you exactly what I want. And if I don't get it as soon as I step out of this damn room, I'm out. Forever."

"Maybe that's a little premature," Tommy started.

"Yeah. So was your lack of faith in my ability to bring the Red Boar in on my own fifteen years after y'all failed."

"I'm sorry," Zimmerman cut in. "When you say 'Red Boar,' you're referring to..."

"Chiron Fort," Tommy muttered.

Luther sniggered. "I call him pissface."

"Ha-ha. Good one, bro."

"We're still working on identifying exactly what he is," Tommy continued.

"He's an asshole who's gonna spend his unusually long Oriceran life rottin' behind bars," Johnny growled. "And shut up, Nelson. I ain't talkin' to you." He turned to Zimmerman. "Do you hear what I say over all this pissant's naggin'?"

"I heard you preface your unstated demands with a threat to remove yourself from a partnership with the FBI if I understand you correctly."

"Naw, that ain't a threat." Johnny shook his head and glared at the man. "That's a promise. If I don't get a handshake and contract written up with both our John Hancocks on it before I leave this buildin' today, I'm done. No more Johnny Walker. No more monster hunter. Y'all are on your own, and there ain't no comin' outta retirement a second time."

"Fine." Zimmerman opened his desk drawer and pulled out an expensive fountain pen, which he laid neatly on the center of his desk. "State your terms, Johnny. Then I'll call in my assistant and we can draw that contract up. I was only starting my career when you came to work with the Bureau for the first time. It doesn't take being Director to know how valuable you are."

"Damn straight."

"So go ahead." Zimmerman cocked his head and stared at the dwarf. "What is it you want?"

A slow grin spread across Johnny Walker's face. "You wanna write this down."

Johnny stepped out of the kitchen with a bowl of freshly popped popcorn in his arms. "I tell you what, darlin'. You had the right idea about bringin' snacks to a show, but there ain't nothin' like the do-it-yourself kind."

"Snacks?" Luther whipped his head up and sniffed the air.

Lisa turned on the couch and smiled at the dwarf. "Well, I didn't exactly have a kitchen to pop my own in last time."

"Sure. And I'd say this is an upgrade even from the last suite. Before we ruined it."

"Johnny, are you gonna share those snacks or what?" Luther padded after his master with wide, hopeful eyes.

"Boy, get on outta here." He pointed toward the other side of the large living space he and Lisa shared between their adjoining bedrooms. "Y'all had your supper already, and it wasn't tiny either. Plus, I aim to keep y'all off the human food for a while. Whatever those pastries did ain't somethin' I'm fixin' to repeat."

"But it smells so good—"

"Git."

Luther stalked away with a sigh and cast hopeful glances over his shoulder at the bowl of popcorn.

Johnny joined Lisa on the couch facing the large entertainment center in the living room the Department had set them up in for the next week. She turned toward him and took a handful of popcorn. "So how did it go?"

"Aw, we're gonna talk about that now? I thought it was movie time."

"Sure. After you tell me about your surprise meeting."

He snorted, set the bowl in his lap, and wrapped an arm around her shoulders. "Let's say I got what I wanted. For now."

She put a couple of pieces of popcorn in her mouth, chewed thoughtfully, and snuggled into him. "And what's that?"

"Well, to start, you get to stay in the Glades as long as you want to. If you want to, that is."

"Why wouldn't I want to?" She took another handful of popcorn and grinned at him. "We're...partners."

Her slight hesitation didn't go unnoticed by the bounty hunter, and Johnny turned his head slowly to look at her. He didn't remove his arm from around her shoulders, and she didn't give any indication that she wanted him to. "Partners, huh?"

Lisa gave him a coy shrug. "There's more than one definition, right?"

"Huh. Reckon there might be." *It took me this long to say she's my partner. If she wants me to start sayin' she's my girlfriend, she can leave that at the fuckin' door.*

"So you're still working with the Department, then. Right?"

Johnny sniffed and studied the blank big-screen TV across the living room. "We'll see. And you can decide exactly what you wanna do once I have everythin' in motion. The Department's workin' on it now."

"Okay…"

"And I'll need your help with it, darlin'. If you're willin' to pitch in. It might be a little slow goin' at first, but I ain't too worried. It gives me time for me to enjoy myself on my property, and the rest can roll on in as it comes."

Lisa laughed. "Okay, now you have to tell me what's going on."

"Nope."

"Johnny, come on." She slapped his lower chest playfully and he grunted.

"You sure don't hit like a fed with good aim."

"Oh, my God. I'm sorry. Sorry." She patted the top of the bandage strapped to his healing bullet wound gently and grimaced. "I wasn't thinkin'."

"That's fine."

"Seriously, though. What are you planning?"

He cast her a sidelong glance and grinned. "You'll see when it's ready. Then we'll go from there."

Lisa rolled her eyes and leaned forward to take the remote from the coffee table. "Fine. It's time to zone out now, right?"

"Go for it."

She turned the TV on and the first thing that came up was Johnny's face.

"What the fuck?" He sounded horrified.

"Oh, my God." She laughed. "The first episode aired today. I completely forgot!"

"Dammit. Come on. I ain't fixin' to sit here and watch this—"

"Wait, wait. I think it's the end. Let's see, okay? I want to know how they managed to salvage everything into a coherent episode." Without waiting for his approval, Lisa turned the volume up and crammed another handful of popcorn into her mouth.

Heavy metal blared in the background as clip after clip of the fight in the Baltimore hotel suite faded into the next. The last one was a shot from inside the suite's front door of Johnny scooting back across the hallway floor with a hand pressed to his belly and blood pooling around his fingers.

The image faded and a still frame of Johnny Walker and Stephanie Wyndom filled the screen, and the music now became a slow, dark metal ballad instead of a fight song.

"Johnny Walker got his magical like he always does." Phil's voice blared through the speakers. *"But he lost something else as he pursued vengeance for his daughter and sought to apprehend her killer. A chance at love."*

"Jesus Christ." Johnny turned away from the TV and snorted.

The show rolled through a montage covered with some sappy violin music—Johnny and Stephanie at dinner together, laughing in the park, and walking up to Senator Hugh's front door.

"At the time of airing Season Eight's first episode, no one knows what happened to Stephanie Wyndom, Johnny's beautiful Light-Elf assistant. She was nowhere to be found when he fought his largest bounty yet and prevailed. Maybe it's too late for second chances if the woman who could have been Johnny Walker's whole world only served to fuel a romance gone wrong instead."

Lisa sniggered. "This is hilarious."

Johnny grunted.

"If love's out there waiting for Johnny Walker, he still hasn't found

it. But if we know anything about Dwarf the Bounty Hunter, it's that he never gives up."

"Fuck, turn that shit off." Johnny reached for the remote in Lisa's hand. "This is terrible."

She pulled the remote out of his reach and laughed. "Oh, come on. I'm sure there's someone out there for you."

"Uh-huh." He shook his head and grunted. "It don't matter, anyhow."

"Why's that?"

Johnny turned his head to meet her gaze, their faces inches apart. "Well, if I was lookin' before, I sure ain't lookin' now, darlin'."

Lisa grinned and changed the channel without moving her gaze from his.

THE STORY CONTINUES

The story continues in Dwarf Bounty Hunter book five , coming early February to Amazon and Kindle Unlimited.

Get sneak peeks, exclusive giveaways, behind the scenes content, and more. PLUS you'll be notified of special **one day only fan pricing** on new releases.

Sign up today to get free stories.

Visit: https://marthacarr.com/read-free-stories/

AUTHOR NOTES - MARTHA CARR
DECEMBER 8, 2020

Happy New Year! Congratulations on making it to 2021. No small feat. I'm writing this in mid-December and still have a few weeks to go. But when you read this, picture me raising a glass and letting out a sigh of relief.

Right at the moment, the sweet pittie Leela is staring at me hoping for a treat. I'm doing my best not to look in her direction. The good dog Lois Lane is at the front window hoping for a dog or a car to go by so she has a reason to start barking again. The usual routine.

Best I can do right now is try and imagine what I hope the new year looks like, which is pretty fitting for the end of 2020 and the beginning of a whole new world. So much this year was put on hold or closed forever or split apart or even came together. New ideas turned out better than they should have while others that should have lasted years just couldn't make it.

What I envision for myself is getting rid of all the 'shoulds.' Stick with me on this one. It's a great plan.

First one is finally knowing what kind of things I like to do that I see as fun as opposed to the dreaded 'exercise'. I've been working on this one for a good part of the year and weirdly, I'm making progress. With the help of my trainer, Laura we've been coming up with a list of things I find fun to do. Kayaking, yoga, walking in nature, boxing, swimming. And getting rid of anything I see as one more thing to check off that I'm supposed to be doing. Pilates, running, weightlifting. My goal is to get back to that kid who ran through the backyards of all my neighbors to get to my best friend, Paula's house at the end of the block. Decades later I still remember how much I loved running toward an adventure. Or rode my very heavy bike with no speeds, up and down the hills of my neighborhood. It never occurred to me to think about how much good it was doing me. It was just fun.

When did it stop being fun and becoming something I *should* be doing?

I suppose it doesn't matter when it happened and it's more important to just fix it.

Other should are that I should be able to wear everything in my closet. I've wrestled with this bad boy for a while and won some of the internal arguments and lost others. Each time, though I get rid of more and recognize that whoever I am today will do just fine, thank you.

Or should be meditating more, or should be working less.

Enough with the shoulds. This new year will be about the possibilities of things I really want to be doing. Game nights at my place, hanging out in that new garden, hearing live music again in a sweaty crowd, hiking and swimming, and sitting in small restaurants laughing with friends. Reading good books out in that garden (A lot of these will end with 'out in that garden') That's it. Maybe some of my new dreams will take time to build, but I'm setting out on that road and seeing where it takes me. More adventures to follow.

2020 was like being captured in Jello. The year seemed to be moving but really it was just a lot of jiggling.

Thank you for reading through this book and to our author notes in the back.

TRAEGER.

What is it you ask? Is it a new badass good guy, maybe a new enemy to sharpen the neighborhood (if you live in the Florida Everglades) bounty hunter?

No, it's a BBQ pit.

Specifically, it's a wood pellet bbq pit first created (I'm reading) like a bajillion years ago, and I didn't know much about it. In fact, at least two years ago my dad spoke about a cheap one he was using.

All I could think of was 'why would you put chunks of wood in a pit and call it awesome? Much less pellets? Aren't they a PAIN to deal with all of the time?'

In short, I had my head up my a$$.

I want one. In fact, I think I'm fantasizing about amazing bbq I could cook on one and how cool it would be to just cut open the top and pour in twenty amazing pounds of high-quality smoking wood that has been highly pressed together, delivering amazing heat with little ash.

In short, I am a sucker for the advertising on these bbq pits and therein lies the problem with having the mind of an author. I will, given the time and opportunity, create a story wherein I do amazing superhero stuff that no normal American male can accomplish.

Like cooking amazing Texas-style brisket.

Some people imagine scoring a winning touch-down. Some others (in my age bracket) believe shooting a low score at a famous golf course would be the highlight of their later years. I just want to do one brisket that is so melt-in-your-mouth delicious I can call it meat-butter.

I think maybe this pit could do the trick. But there are two problems. First, my wife needs to be onboard and second, I have many different brands to choose from. Because let's face it, if I go TRAEGER, I go for the big bucks.

Is there any other way to go? I don't know... No one I know personally has one of these amazing sounding bbq smokers except my dad.

I'm not sure if I dare ask him. If I do, will I get the answers I'm looking for or another story that I've heard about eight times?

It's a gamble... but I want that amazing brisket sticker.

Damn it... I gotta go call my dad, now.

Ad Aeternitatem,

Michael Anderle

Solve a murder, save her mother, and stop the apocalypse?

What would you do when elves ask you to investigate a prince's murder and you didn't even know elves, or magic, was real?

Meet Leira Berens, Austin homicide detective who's good at what she does – track down the bad guys and lock them away.

Which is why the elves want her to solve this murder – fast. It's not just about tracking down the killer and bringing them to justice. It's about saving the world!

If you're looking for a heroine who prefers fighting to flirting, check out The Leira Chronicles today!

<u>AVAILABLE ON AMAZON AND IN KINDLE UNLIMITED!</u>

If smart phones and GPS rule the world - why am I hunting a magic compass to save the planet?

Austin Detective Maggie Parker has seen some weird things in her day, but finding a surly gnome rooting through her garage beats all.

Her world is about to be turned upside down in a frantic search for 4 Elementals.

Each one has an artifact that can keep the Earth humming along, but they need her to unite them first.

Unless the forces against her get there first.

AVAILABLE ON AMAZON AND IN KINDLE UNLIMITED!

Made in United States
Troutdale, OR
10/06/2023

13459022R00166